# MURIEL'S MANHUNT

I0638352

# DENNIS FORSTER

UK Book Publishing.com

Editing, design, typesetting and publishing by UK Book Publishing

www.ukbookpublishing.com

ISBN: 978-1-917329-21-7

# MURIEL'S MANHUNT

# BY THE SAME AUTHOR:

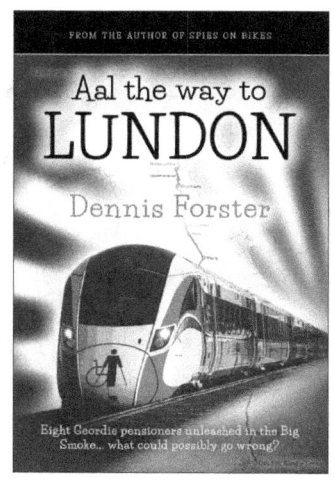

To *Olivia* and *Sam*.

But do they believe in witches and wizards?

# AN E-MAIL SETS THE ALARM BELLS RINGING

**W**hen a Geordie witch falls in love with an American wizard do not be surprised if snow brings traffic to a halt in Newcastle, in August; do not be surprised if hailstones the size of golf balls knock out the away team's goalkeeper at St James' Park.

Let me introduce myself. My name is Muriel Thayne. In my public life I am a primary school teacher. I teach year five. I love my children and they love me.

In my private life, I am a witch. And so is my best friend, Mary. We teach at the Jubilee Primary School. Mary teaches year six.

Mary and I are white witches. We strive to use our supernatural powers to make the world a better place. We care about the vulnerable. We give to food banks. We are in favour of electric cars. The prospect of global warming gives our besoms alopecia.

Mary and I have our differences. Mary is right wing. I am left wing. Mary is not so much in favour of increasing the minimum wage, as I am. We came close to falling out over Brexit. I voted to stay in the EU, Mary voted to opt out; all credit to Mary that she is now close to admitting she voted the wrong way.

In the pecking order of witchery Mary and I are somewhere at the bottom of the Witch's Premier League. We have limited powers. We have flesh and blood bodies. We are not immortal. We wash dishes. We pay utility bills. When it rains we use an umbrella. If we slip on a patch of ice, we bruise. After levitating for ten seconds, I am knackered.

Our human weaknesses have stopped us rising up the ranks. There is little chance of us ever becoming Mother Superior Witches. I have a mischievous sense of humour. Mary is a snob. Both of us are susceptible to falling in love with men who are rich.

We are paid up members of Coven HQ (Whitby branch). We do our best to obey the rules of witchery… keep a low profile… resist the temptation to show off by flying over rooftops when it's a full moon; that sort of thing.

The LGBQT community have a voice; the Scots have a voice; the Welsh have a voice. The Irish are open in their love of leprechauns and fairies; witches would love to be as open but, not wishing to be burnt at the stake, are of the opinion that the time is not right for them to come out.

If the tale I am now going to relate was a brew in a cauldron, I'd say that it began to boil and bubble while yours truly was having her breakfast one Friday morning in October.

My cat, Tilly (black of course) was on the kitchen table. We were having honey and toast. She was purring, I was watching breakfast television.

When the e-mail from Whitby arrived it was like someone banging on your front door in the middle of the night. It was on group chat; it had also been sent to Mary.

Mary and I are SOSAs; that is to say, we are Whitby's official 'Surveyors of Supernatural Activity' over a large area of north-east England. As Lord Lieutenants represent the British monarchy, SOSAs represent witchery. For reasons of security I am not able to give you the latitude and longitude of the area we are responsible for surveying.

The e-mail was marked SOSA WEO (Witches' Eyes Only). Not the highest level of security on the Met-a-Web but, nevertheless, high. The 'Met-a-Web, by the way, is the witches' equivalent of the World Wide Web; META being short for 'metaphysical'. My apologies if you'd already sussed that and I was carrying coals to Newcastle.

The e-mail warned Mary and I to be on the look-out for an American wizard. He might or might not be paying us a visit.

The vagueness of the e-mail worried me. Why did Whitby and New York not know more about him? Had they not been able to break his code? Our American sisters never withheld information. The secrecy surrounding him suggested to me that he was 'supernatural aristocracy'; in temporal terms... at least a duke.

Whitby wanted Mary and I to be on the lookout for unexplained supernatural phenomena. If he did show up in our neck of the woods we'd have to keep an eye on him. We do not take kindly to trespassers.

As I mulled these instructions... doing four things all at the same time – mulling, munching toast, feeding Tilly honey off a finger and watching breakfast television – there appeared on the TV an interview with a Tyne pilot.

While entering the river Tyne yesterday morning the radar screen of the ship the pilot had been bringing into the Tyne had shown the face of a woman. The river's estuary and piers had disappeared… had been replaced by the face of a woman.

The pilot had photographed the mysterious image. He had evidence.

What popped into my mind, stopped me munching… was… could there be a link between the image on the radar screen and the possible arrival on Tyneside of the American wizard Whitby had warned us about?

The appearance on the ship's radar screen of a human face suggested supernatural shrapnel. Let me explain. When a wizard in a bad temper casts a spell he is like a mad man smashing plates in a china shop; bits and pieces fly all over the place; windows get broken; aspidistras get decapitated.

That something was amiss in the supernatural world was brought home to me when Tilly jumped off the breakfast table and began talking to a mouse. What was going on? Cats were supposed to chase mice.

I speak French, German and Feline. When Tilly had finished passing the time of day with the mouse I asked her: 'What's going on, Tilly?'

'What do you mean, mistress?'

'Why were you talking to a mouse? Cats do not talk to mice. Cats chase mice and eat them.'

'But, mistress, I am not a cat… I am a mouse.'

'You think you are a mouse.'

'Am I not a mouse, mistress?'

'No, Tilly, you are not a mouse, you are a cat.'

'I don't feel well.'

'Go and lie down… recovery position. I fear you have been hit by supernatural shrapnel.'

'I don't feel well…'

'Go and lie down… recovery position.'

# THE JUBILEE
# PRIMARY SCHOOL

**S**ometimes I cycle to work. Sometimes I drive. It depends upon the weather. It depends upon how I feel. I am going through the menopause.

It was a Friday, the last day at school before the start of the half-term holiday, called, in my part of the world, 'Blackberry Week'. In five days' time it would be Halloween. Mary and I would celebrate behind locked doors and drawn curtains. Something to look forward to.

In the meantime, what had made silly Tilly think she was a mouse? Had the American Whitby had warned us to look out for already arrived on Tyneside?

Physical exercise I have found helps me answer difficult questions or at least brings me closer to answering them. It helps me think. It helps me ponder the imponderable. And, boy, did I need to ponder.

Cycling is physical exercise. Thus it was, that morning, I cycled to work. While pondering the imponderable I cycled, like a five-year-old, through duvets of red and yellow autumn leaves.

For the last three days I'd been getting 'vibes'. 'Vibes' come to me, willy-nilly. I don't ask for them. I don't light black candles at an altar and pray for them... they, just happen... you know, like when you were little and you put a tooth under your pillow and hey presto in the morning you found the tooth fairy had been.

The 'tooth fairy' was telling me to expect a new man to enter my life. I was between husbands. And, as you do, I was on the look-out for a rich third husband. A ninety-nine-year-old billionaire ticked all the boxes. Just so long as yours truly didn't have to sign a pre-nuptial. Rich old guys don't trust anyone.

People call me the 'Merry Widow'. Not to my face. They wouldn't dare. But, I know they do.

And as for those spreading the rumour I'd something to do with my husbands' deaths, skating close to calling me a murderer... malicious gossip.

I miss my men. When they departed this life I was down in the dumps for days. But you have to get on with things, don't you?

*******

The Jubilee Primary School, at which Mary and I teach, was built during the reign of Queen Victoria. It has gables and turrets. It overlooks the River Tyne. In the setting sun its conical turrets make it look as if it is wearing lots of witches' hats.

It is not in a posh area of town. Its pupils wipe their noses on their sleeves. They call a handkerchief a snot-rag.

I keep my bicycle in an out-building in the school's yard. If I did not lock it away it would be stolen.

'Hello, Miss,' children shouted at me as I walked across the yard. 'Can a carry ya bag?'

I shook my head. Monica, the school's headteacher, was adamant: 'No pupils in school until the bell has been rung.'

I was carrying a bag of apples and a bag of sugar. My class were in for a treat. We were going to make toffee apples.

What stopped me in my tracks, in the middle of the yard, was a cloud that looked like St George and a cloud that looked like a dragon.

Clouds can sometimes look like things... like, chairs or tables or horses' heads but rarely are they videos. When the two clouds, as if they were actors, played out the story of St George, killing the dragon, I went all shivery. I knew at once that I was watching an effect caused by supernatural shrapnel. What the hell was going on?

I walked up the stairs to my classroom deep in thought. To make two clouds perform like actors in a mystery play, took a galactic amount of supernatural energy. What I'd seen was a cumulus video of a good guy, St George, thumping a bad guy, the dragon.

Where was Mary? I had to tell her what I'd seen. I had to tell her about Tilly thinking she was a mouse. What, I wondered, had she made of the e-mail from Whitby. As far as I was concerned, it was not if or when this American wizard might or might not arrive in our neck of the woods... as far as I was concerned he had arrived... and he'd arrived playing a supernatural sousaphone. There was nothing subtle about this wizard. In real life he'd be OTT.

I met Mary in the Ladies'; a room with two cubicles and a frosted glass window loved by spiders. If its wash basin had been a human being it would have been in a wheelchair; its porcelain had more hairline cracks than the Mississippi has tributaries. Its brass taps were of the sort you'd expect to find in a second-class cabin on the Titanic. When you turned them on, before water spurted out, they gargled. Sir John Betjeman would have loved the Jubilee Primary School's ladies' loo. I and my colleagues put up with it.

'SOSA meeting,' I said, '... have you been crying?'

'Yes—' showing me a pair of frilly panties in a plastic bag bearing the name of a well-known supermarket chain. 'I found them in the Tom Cat's car... glove compartment... hidden under a National Trust brochure.'

The 'Tom Cat' was one of our nicknames for Byron Richard Hedgerow, Mary's philandering husband. Face to face I called him Dick; behind his back, to Mary and I, he was sometimes the Arsehole; sometimes, Dick the Prick; sometimes the Bidet: it depended on what the bastard had been up to.

'Try not to be upset. We'll get him.'

'I know... I know how to get rid of him... what I do not know is how to get rid of him while keeping all his money... and I mean, all his money. Muriel, I am used to a certain way of life. I have no intention of driving a Model T Ford when I am used to driving a Jaguar. I am too middle aged to learn to double declutch.'

'We'll discuss... chat... over the holiday... SOSA... the e-mail from Whitby... what did you make of it?'

'We've had warnings like that before.'

I told her about the woman's face that had appeared on the ship's radar screen. Had she seen the local news? I told her about Tilly thinking she was a mouse… about St George killing the dragon… about my vibes.

I knew I wasn't getting through to her when she said, looking at the knickers: 'If I was a witch powerful enough to make his balls shrivel to the size of peas…I would do it… I would.'

A bell rang. The school day had started.

'We'll talk later. I'm making toffee apples.'

'I'm making plasticine people. I can't smash plates but I can stick a pin into the forehead of the plasticine model I will be making. I'll give Dick a migraine that will kill his sex drive.'

A bell rang. We dashed to our classrooms… assembly… hymn singing… sums… chanting the three times table.

The staff were a mixture of the young and the middle aged… all women. The young members of staff talked about sex, gays and lesbian relationships the way the older members of staff talked about Mary Berry's recipes.

To the best of my knowledge no one suspected that Mary and I were witches.

During the morning coffee break the chatter was all about the half-term holiday. A lucky few were going abroad. Monica, our headteacher, popped her head into the staffroom to remind whoever was on yard duty to get themselves out pronto and to remember to blow the whistle at half past ten and not at twenty-to-eleven.

At lunchtime I walked down back lanes full of wheelie bins spewing rubbish to Ma Mason's pie shop. Mary and I were fond of Ma Mason's pasties.

'I need comfort food,' Mary had told me, 'a Ma Mason hot pasty will help me forget the Bidet...'

'The Bastard...'

'The Arsehole...'

'The Tom Cat...'

'Dick the Prick...'

In the privacy of the Ladies, in which the above conversation had taken place, we had allowed ourselves, after having made sure no one was hiding in a cubicle, a muted cackle. Yes, we were witches but we were also human. There were times when we needed to let off steam.

# TED

Mary and I ate our pasties in the staffroom; more of that environment anon.

Ten minutes before the bell rang to signal the end of the lunch break, I was in my classroom checking my toffee apples. I was after a toffee, like Baby Bear's porridge... not too brittle, not too soft... more chewy than runny.

My examination of my children's culinary efforts was interrupted by Ted the school's caretaker. What did he want? Ted always wanted something.

Ted and I had a symbiotic relationship. In exchange for my being first in the queue to have my radiators bled, I gave him pens and pencils. Ted had a 'thing' about stationery. Funny, what turns some men on... but there you go. It takes all sorts.

Ted was a Rottweiler, you had to keep him on a short lead. He was a thief and had a dirty mind. He was my eyes and ears in the school. He told me things I wasn't supposed to know. He was my paid informer.

'I've got something to tell you,' said Ted. 'It'll cost, mind.'

'What do you want?'

'A roll of Sellotape.'

As well as having spent the morning making toffee apples my class had made witch's masks. As you, dear reader, know, I am a witch; you can therefore well imagine my heart and soul had gone into the making of those masks. Halloween was fast approaching.

The masks were glued to lollipop sticks. I now held one up in front of my face. I stared hard at Ted through its eye slits. To provoke him I stuck out my tits. He knew the rules: look... but do not touch.

Ted licked his lips the way a hungry man in a silent movie has been directed to show 'desire' for a plate of mince and dumplings.

'If they hadn't taken out me prostate, Mrs Thayne, I'd be after you, I would. I'm like one of them blokes called "Eunice" what works in a harem.'

I'd heard all this before. Load of bollocks. His 'office' in the boiler room was a picture gallery of female nudes. No landscapes. No Cezanne prints of apples and oranges. If he was impotent then I wasn't a witch. 'Impertinent', yes... but 'impotent', no.

'One roll of used Sellotape,' I said, handing him a used roll. 'Do we have a deal?'

'There's nowt left on that ... howay, man! Ouch!'

'What's wrong?'

'A pain in my side. You in one of your moods?'

'The pain in your side has nothing to do with me.'

He knew I was lying and he also knew that I knew he knew I was lying... if that makes sense.

'What have you got to tell me?'

'You and the rest of the sheep are going to a staff meeting at four o'clock.'

'How'd you know that?'

He tapped the side of his nose; a nose with as many pustules on it as the moon has craters.

'It's about a new teacher... a man teacher. He's coming to replace Miss Jolly. I liked Miss Jolly.'

'Some women have all the luck.'

Two days ago Miss Jolly had stopped playing 'All Things Bright and Beautiful' in morning assembly and walked out.

'I've seen her sick note. She's had a nervous breakdown. For a packet of felt tip pens I'll tell you the name of this bloke who's coming to replace her.'

'Go on then.'

'Howard Star.'

'How'd you know all this?'

'Because I've met him. And I'll tell you this... he's trouble. I wouldn't like to tangle with him. He's big.'

'Fat?'

'Nar! Nar! Tall and lean... not a picking on him.'

'Lean and mean, eh?'

'He came into my boiler room about an hour ago... gave me a fright he did. When I asked him what he thought he was doing he told me he was looking for the headteacher. I told him, "You won't find her in here... teachers divent like getting their hands dirty... especially headteachers." If he hadn't told me who he was and that he'd be starting work at the Jube after the half-term holiday I'd have said he was police. I'm telling yuh, Mrs Thayne, this bloke's trouble. Yuh nar what he did? On his way out he knocked on the boiler room door. "Knock! Knock!" he said. When I asked him what he was doing, he said, bold as brass, "I'm knocking for the "Knockers", Ted." "How'd you nar my name?" I asked him. "I've been talking to Ma Mason," he said. Then, he said, handing me my wallet, "I think this is yours… don't you know." He'd picked me pocket. How he did it, I divent nar. "It's a good job I'm honest, Ted… don't you think?" Then he asked me if I was honest. Why did Ma Mason tell him me name? That's what I want to nar.'

'Who are the "Knockers", Ted? I've heard rumours. Are you one of them?'

'It's alreet for you, Mrs Thayne, you live in a posh part of town… that's all I'm saying… and another thing… this big bloke's an American.'

You will have guessed the question I was asking myself: could Howard Star and the American wizard Whitby had told Mary and myself to keep a look out for, be the same person? The vibes I was getting told me, he was.

# THE STAFF MEETING

I t was towards the end of the afternoon that a monitor came into my classroom and handed me one of Monica's pink paper 'round robins'. Monica's 'round robins' were always on pink paper. It was one of her... 'little ways'.

Ted had been right, the staff would not be dashing off home for an early start to their half-term break; instead, they'd be at a four o'clock staff meeting.

'Miss, you haven't signed it,' said Thomas, the monitor.

'Sorry, Thomas... silly me.'

When I had dismissed my class... sent them off home clutching toffee apples and witches' masks... I trudged through metaphorical glue to the staffroom.

The staff room was a long narrow room with a high ceiling. The staff sat in basket chairs set in rows down its two long sides. One of the room's three Gothic windows was boarded up with plywood. Through the remaining two there filtered the fading light of a Thomas Hardy autumn afternoon.

A lukewarm cast iron radiator the size of a baby elephant and a single bar electric fire stopped the water dripping from a tap having ideas that it might turn into an icicle. The staffroom was a hospital waiting room in a third world country.

When Monica failed to appear on time, I said, in a voice loud enough for everyone to hear: 'It's four o'clock. Where's Monica?'

'It's not good enough,' said Mary. 'I have a chiropodist appointment.'

'We're on time,' I said, 'why can't she be on time?'

'Because,' said Mary, 'there's GMT… BST and MT… "Monica Time". We all know that… or should do if you've worked in this dump for longer than a term.'

'You could set your watch by the old head.'

'He was a real gentleman.'

Monica breezed into the staffroom ten minutes late. As far as she was concerned she was on time. Classroom teachers had no idea of the pressures involved in the day-to-day to running of a school. How dare they look sullen… they should try doing her job.

'Everyone here?'

'I've put your cushion on your seat, Monica,' said Belinda, the school's deputy head.

The bum protector was printed with a Union Jack and a photograph of Her Majesty Queen Elizabeth. I called it 'Queen Monica's cushion'; QMC for short. When that cushion was placed on a chair everyone knew that chair was reserved for Monica. I had often been tempted to replace it with a cushion which farted when you sat on it.

'Coffee?' said Belinda.

'I'm exhausted… quite exhausted,' said Monica, then, 'that was quick…' accepting the mug of coffee Belinda was handing her.

'Preparation, Monica. The Boy Scouts do not have a monopoly on "preparedness". I knew you'd be exhausted.'

'You are wonderful, Belinda… quite, wonderful.'

'While you look after us… someone must look after you. Where would we be if you went off ill like Miss Jolly?'

'I'm sure the school would survive… somehow or other.'

'Monica,' I piped up, 'the Jubilee needs you the way Great Britain needed Winston Churchill in 1940.'

When I said this I kept a straight face.

'Very well put,' said Belinda, 'you have a way with words, Muriel. If you're not careful senior management will rope you in to write the school pantomime.'

'Which is why we are here,' said Monica, 'all this support… dear me… I do hope I'm not going to faint.'

'Do you need air?' said Belinda. 'Would it help if I opened the door?'

'Put her head between her legs,' said Margaret. Before training to become a teacher Margaret had been a nurse.

'Monica is not a contortionist,' said Belinda.

A teacher new to the school suggested opening a window.

'None of the windows open,' said Mary. 'They are sealed with mastic to keep out draughts.'

'And one window is plywood,' said another teacher. 'You can't open a temporary plywood window.'

'Ursula,' said another teacher, 'you've only been here two terms. It was blocked up when I came here two years ago. I fear it is more permanent than temporary. I still don't have a permanent contract but the plywood in that bloody window does.'

Monica brought the meeting to order by tapping a teaspoon on the LOVE and KISSES logo on her coffee mug.

'Milk bottles,' said Monica, 'pupils are leaving straws in their milk bottles. Last year we all agreed... I have the minutes. I quote: "Bottles placed in crates must have their tops removed and not have straws left in them." We started the term well. On my SWs (Surveillance Walkabouts) I'm seeing more and more bottles with straws in them. We are on a slippery slope. We owe it to the children to do better.'

'Here! Here!' said Mary.

'Mary,' said Belinda, 'we are not in the House of Commons.'

'The next item on the agenda,' said Monica, 'is Juniper... Miss Jolly.'

'When will she back?' asked a teacher who wanted Juniper's classroom because it was on the school's sunny side.

'Dear Juniper is very poorly. I am not allowed to say what her problem is.'

'Should we not send her flowers and a get-well card?'

'That, Miss Pearson, has already been seen to. After half-term we will have a replacement for Miss Jolly. Juniper was our music teacher. After half-term we will have a piano player to replace her.'

'Does she have a name?'

'That, Miss Pearson, is the reason I have called this staff meeting. I wish to give you all time to get used to the idea.'

'What idea?'

'Your new colleague is male.'

'A man,' I said, feigning surprise.

'Yes, Muriel… a man.'

'OMG,' said the teacher in charge of netball, 'I keep my netball posts in the men's loo. I suppose they'll have to be moved. I can't barge in there when he's using the facilities, can I?'

'There's no room for them in the shed where I keep my goal posts,' said the teacher in charge of football. 'Bein' a bloke, he'll love football… they all do. I'd be more than happy to let him run the school team… having to run the football team is interfering with my yoga class.'

'He will not be here long enough to take over the running of anything,' snapped Monica. 'He is temporary.'

'Like the plywood in the window?' I asked.

'No, Muriel… not like the plywood in the window. When Juniper returns, hale and hearty, he… goes. His name is Howard Star. He's an American… heaven help us.'

'Who will be his "buddy"?' asked a teacher with a pile of exercise books on her lap.

Ah! The 'Buddy System'. One of Monica's 'enthusiasms'. All the staff had an official 'buddy'. When you were feeling stressed you went to your 'buddy 'for TLC.

'I was Juniper's "buddy",' I said. 'If this American is come to replace her I suppose I'll have to be his "buddy"… looks like I've drawn the short straw.'

'I don't wish to be rude,' said a teacher, standing up to show she was off, 'but I've a plane to catch. I'm off to Corfu.'

'This meeting, Monica,' said another teacher, 'did come rather out of the blue. It is a Friday afternoon. It is the start of our half-term holiday. Men always cause trouble. If we'd been getting a female replacement for Juniper this meeting would not have been called.'

'If you don't mind bein' this man's "Buddy", Muriel,' said Doris, an elderly teacher who while the meeting had been going on had been reading the pamphlet 'Your Pension and Retirement. What it means for you', 'that will stop me worrying that I might have to be his "Buddy". Do you think we should get a lock put on the ladies' loo?'

'Whatever for?' said Monica.

'In case he barges in when one of us is in there doing, you know, whatever one is doing. I know this is just silly old me talking but isn't that what men do?'

'Doris, I assure you, you will be perfectly safe.'

'I wonder if he looks like that actor who played Poldark.'

'I'm off,' said the teacher flying off to Corfu. 'Bye... ee.'

'Monica,' said another teacher, standing, 'I have a train to catch. I am off to London to see my boyfriend.'

'He will be taking you round the museums?' said Doris.

'No, Doris, I am meeting him for sex. Now, if you'll excuse me, I'm off.'

'Young or old?' I asked Monica after Ursula the teacher who was dashing off to have sex had closed the staffroom door behind her.

'What?'

'Howard Star.'

'Oh, him.'

'If I'm to be his "Buddy", Monica, I think I should know as much about him as possible... don't you?'

'He's about your age.'

'Married or single?'

'Muriel,' sounding exasperated, 'I don't know. He was foisted on me by Marilyn.'

'The chair of our school governors?'

'Yes… when she heard about Juniper going on the sick she knew we'd need someone to play the piano. This… Howard Star plays the piano. You know as well as I do… Marilyn is a huge fan of our Christmas pantomime. Fenwick's has its Christmas window… the Jubilee has its panto. She confided to me that as far as she was concerned it wouldn't be Christmas if HER school didn't have its pantomime… and not just any old pantomime but a pantomime full of music. She reminded me, quite forcibly, I might add, that even the silent movies had a piano player. She loves the school's pantomime tradition as much as I detest it. Every year it spoils my Christmas. It turns my school upside down. This man… this, Howard Star will be difficult to control… I know he will.'

Her mobile rang.

'Darling!'

Listens.

'I'm still at school.'

Listens.

'I don't know how long I'll be. Belinda and I have to discuss the English curriculum.'

Listens.

'Why do you need clean underpants?'

Listens.

'You did what? You broke wind and followed through. I know you have colitis, darling, but… well… really… what can I say?'

Listens, this time raising her eyebrows at myself and Mary.

'Try looking in the tumbler dryer. I'm not certain but I think there might be some underpants in there.'

Listens.

'What was that? Where is the tumbler dryer? Now, we are being silly… aren't we? It's in the garage.'

Listens.

'What do you mean the kettle won't boil? Is it plugged in?'

Listens.

'It's working now, is it?'

Listens.

'Thank goodness for that. Go and make yourself a cup of tea. Darling, I must go… I really must.'

Listens.

'And I love you too. Bye… ee … kisses and cuddles.'

Switching off her mobile she mouthed 'Men!' at myself and Mary.

'Men!' I said.

'Men!' said Mary.

# ANOTHER VISIT TO MA MASON'S PIE SHOP

After the staff meeting, instead of breezing off home, I went to Ma Mason's pie shop. I wanted to ask Ma what she knew about Howard Star. I told Mary where I was going and why.

People who do not know me, call me 'nosey'. Utter rubbish! But I am curious. One would never say Alexander Fleming discovered penicillin because he was 'nosey'. Of course they wouldn't. Fleming discovered penicillin because he was 'curious'. He asked the right questions. Folk who are 'curious' do not get watery eyes from looking through keyholes.

Ma Mason's meat and potato were a local legend. Newcastle had its football team. North Shields had Ma Mason's.

Ma and I went back a long way. A few years ago, her grandson, Stanley, had been in my class. Stanley had been what education psychologists call a 'challenging pupil'; in street argot he was an evil bastard. Are we born evil? I don't know. To get him to conform had been like trying to grow pineapples at the North Pole. He now lived with his grandmother above the pie shop. I was of the opinion that he'd turned out a better baker than a pupil.

Opening the pie shop's door, I tinkled a bell.

'It's you, is it,' said Ma, pushing her way through a bead curtain. 'I've nee pies left.'

'What about a nice piece of cod fillet, Ma?'

'Divent be funny. Yuh nar fine well a divent sell fish.'

'Take a joke, Ma.'

'Stanley's been getting at me. I can't take much more of his finger wagging.'

'You haven't been wandering around naked, I hope?'

'Mrs Thayne, I'm a naturist not a show off. When Stanley's around I always have a nice piece of net curtain wrapped round me bits and bobs. I hates bein' constructed. We shouldn't be ashamed of our bodies, Mrs Thayne. Let the air get to your body, that's what I say. I can dee without soap and water but not without air. We aal nar what a room's like when its windows have been closed for a month... bodies is the same. They need circulation. Cold, today, is it? I can tell by the way yuh aal wrapped up. I divent feel the cad, see, cos I have good circulation. Good circulation keeps me warmer than that sheepskin coat yuh are wearing. If yuh had good circulation like what I have yuh could walk out that door with nowt on and yuh wouldn't feel the cold... not even when icicles is hanging from gutters. And another thing... I might be old but I'm still attractive to men. I knows some come in when I'm letting everything hang out for a pie and a peek but... not aal of them ... that new teacher you're going to be working with is a bit of how's your father... I wouldn't mind him turning me upside down and putting a penny in me slot.'

'Is he? I've never met him. I've only just heard he's coming to work at the Jubilee. Ma, you know more about what's going on in my place of work than I do.'

'He knows your name.'

'Does he?'

'He came in to buy a pie... or so he said. He did buy one... I'll give him that... but only after he'd asked a lot of questions. "Where do you get your meat?" "Do you have a baker?" That's when I asked him if he was FBI... yuh nar he's an American, divent yuh?'

'Yes.'

'When he thought I thought he was police he knew he'd gone too far. He knew he was constricting me... yuh nar ... like those corsets me mother... god rest her soul, used to wear. To get back into me good books, he gave me these,' drawing my attention to a posy of pansies in a jam-jar.

The colour of the water in the jam-jar was spirogyra green; the sort of water in which you'd not be surprised to find a frog.

'Lovely, aren't they? I don't know where they came from, Mrs Thayne. He clapped his hands and there they were. "For you, Ma," he said. I didn't nar what to say... course, I took them... what lass wouldn't? They're lovely, aren't they? And do you know what? When he gave me them he kissed me mole. Not many would do that, Mrs Thayne. He said he'd put a magic spell on them... that they'd last for as long as I loved them. "In that case," I told him, "they'll last longer than what them dinosaurs did...

did you see that bloke Attenborough on telly last neet? I fancy him.'

'Ma, you have fallen for the oldest trick in the book. A bloke gives you a bunch of flowers and you give him your heart. It's like giving someone change for a twenty-pound note when they have given you a fiver.'

'You're jealous, Mrs Thayne... wait till you meet him. I'm telling you he's a charmer. What can I get you?'

'I've got what I came for.'

'Have yuh?'

'Yes, I have.'

On my bicycle ride home I thought about nothing else but Howard Star; he just had to be the wizard Whitby had warned me about. How had he known my name? He'd picked Ted's pocket... he'd produced a posy of pansies out of fresh air; all the hallmarks of your typical show-off wizard. He'd made Ma Mason feel like a teenager. He was in cahoots with Marilyn... chair of the school governors; the memsahib who came into your classroom without knocking, full of enthusiasm to show the children a hedgehog wrapped in a tea towel.

At home I rang Mary and brought her up to date.

# MARY'S FOR COFFEE VIA A DETOUR

**T**he next day, a Saturday, I cycled to Mary's for coffee. The morning was one of 'mellow fruitfulness'. Gardeners were burning leaves. The air smelt like smoky bacon.

What was the relationship between Howard and Marilyn? How did they know each other?

It occurred to me that Howard... I was already on first name terms with him... the wizard Whitby had warned me about... I was more or less certain that that was who he was... would need board and lodging; wizards are like everyone else, they need somewhere to sleep. Wizards do not sleep under railway arches. What if he was lodging with Marilyn, chair of the Jubilee's governors and her Conservative councillor husband?

Out of 'curiosity', I made a detour that took me down Marilyn's street and past the front of her three-storey house; a house built for a sea captain in the nineteenth century.

Wouldn't it be funny, I thought, if I should, just by chance, bump into him. I was on the lookout for a tall, dark, handsome man. I was on the lookout for every woman's dream. My vibes would tell me it was HIM;

my vibes would tell me it was HIM the way radioactivity makes a Geiger counter bleep.

I passed the house slowly as if cycling up a hill in third gear.

On one of the properties' gateposts a poster advertised a circus. Did Marilyn know it was there? The only posters I'd ever seen Marilyn display were posters for the Conservative Party.

The circus had been visiting our town at this time of year for as long as I could remember. Its big-top was on a field close to the sea front. The school would be taking pupils to see its show. I looked forward to going. I have a 'thing' about men in leotards.

Sadly, my kerb crawl did not introduce me, by chance, to anyone; not even a seagull. I arrived at Mary's in sore need of a caffeine boost.

Mary and Dick, aka, the 'Tom Cat', the 'Arse Hole', the 'Bidet', lived in a four-bedroomed detached house with a back garden the size of two tennis courts. Its front drive was a horseshoe. You drove in one way and out the other. No need for three point turns when you paid Mary a visit. Mary was proud of this facility. Dick... the Arse Hole etc, owned a scrap metal business. There was brass in scrap.

It was Mary's mission and mine to facilitate the Arse Hole an early death. Notice, I said, 'facilitate', not, 'murder'. Mary and I are not murderers. As I have mentioned and will keep mentioning ad nauseam, Mary and I are white witches. We do not chop up folk into little pieces and boil their bones to make glue.

Mary greeted me with a hug.

'I know why you've come on your bike,' she said. 'You were hoping to bump into him, weren't you? The American... I'll bet you cycled past Marilyn's.'

'What a perceptive witch you are,' I said.

'Did you see him?'

'No... where's the "Arse Hole"?'

'Out playing golf.'

'When are you going to get rid of him?'

'When he makes a will leaving everything to me.'

'If only that was as easy as making him ogle tits. Yesterday I made Ted's eyes pop out of his head with my womanly bumps. I was bored.'

'Muriel, darling, relieving one's boredom by encouraging a man's sexual desires, is never a good idea. It leads to trouble. When you are bored, do a jigsaw... that's what I do. Don't upset Ted, we need him.'

'I'm concerned the spells I put on him are losing their power.'

'We both know spells are like antibiotics. The more they are used the less effective they become. Shall I be mother?'

The coffee Mary poured came out of the cafetiere at right angles. On the surface of my mug there appeared a frothy witch's hat.

'You have poured witches' style,' I said.

'I find it relaxing to sometimes be able to come out... and we are alone.'

After we had sipped our coffee and were feeling its booster effect, Mary said: 'The silly things that pop into my head... now that we women are allowed to become bishops, what about you and me becoming priests?'

'We can't. We are witches.'

'But no one knows that… that's our secret. We'd be undercover. What if I was the first witch to become the Archbishop of Canterbury? I'd make their communion wine as bitter as vinegar. Do help yourself to a biscuit. I made them this morning… gingerbread men… their fondant genitals are edible. Take that one…'

'He's very well endowed.'

'Enjoy.'

'It's not as good as the real thing.'

'I wonder if he's a Roundhead or a Cavalier.'

'Howard?'

'On first name terms with him already, are we? That's jumping the gun.'

'I feel that I have met him before.'

'Déjà vu, dangerous. When we get to know him he will not be a mystery. We will peel him like an onion.'

'In the flesh… he will disappoint?'

'More than likely.'

'There are exceptions to every rule. What if he's as sex mad as the Arse Hole?'

'I have a new name for the "Arse Hole". He may now be referred to as, "If".'

'"If"?'

'The "Insatiable fornicator". If only I could get "If" to write a will in my favour.'

'Deny him his connubial rights.'

'That wouldn't bother him.'

'Where's he spraying his semen now?'

'Like road works… he is everywhere. Did I tell you, last week I found a thong in the pocket of his pinstripe suit? When he is carving the Sunday roast, I eye the carving knife.'

'Mary, you know as well as I do, we are not murderers. We are "facilitators".'

'He has had the use of my body, why shouldn't I have the use of his money... all of it?'

'Try driving him mad... hide his false teeth... run out of loo rolls... put a plastic turd on the front seat of his Mercedes.'

'If I did drive him mad, I'd still be left with the problem of the will.'

'Get him to give you "Power of Attorney"... that would be a step in the right direction. When he "flips" you will be in charge of the cheque book.'

'A kind of half-way house.'

'I wonder if Howard Star is rich.'

'More to the point, is he the wizard Whitby has warned us might be heading our way?'

'What if he is gay?'

'I wish it was as fashionable to be a witch as it is to be gay.'

'If it was, we could "come out" and be our real selves.'

'We could wear our witches' pointy hats the way un-supernatural women wear summer frocks.'

'May I have another gingerbread man?'

'Of course... I took details of their genitals off a poster advertising Durex.'

'Marilyn has a poster advertising the circus on her gatepost.'

'That doesn't fit with the Marilyn I know.'

'Quite agree... this penis is moreish.'

# I MEET HOWARD STAR.

celebrated Halloween behind drawn curtains and a locked front door. In the privacy of my own home, I wore my favourite witch's black hat, a neck to ankle black dress, black boots with silver buckles and a black cape. On the 'Met-a-Web I received and sent greetings to covens all over the world. To a witch, Halloween is as exciting as Christmas Day is to a five-year-old. I levitated over my bed for a full ten seconds. When I fell back to earth, I had a soft landing.

It worried me, that Whitby knew so little about the American wizard who might be paying us a visit. Was Howard Star the American wizard? I thought he was but could not be certain. What if I was on the wrong track?

That Monday morning I drove to work wondering if I was going to meet him. It was a training day. Did he have to attend? I didn't know. No children. A morning of writing lesson plans and in the afternoon a talk from an expert about handling stress.

I'd opted to drive to work because of the weather. It was cold, windy and threatening to rain. Close to school the driver of a Volvo Estate, with a surfboard on a roof rack, overtook me in a way I thought dangerous. I was in a forty zone and he was doing at least sixty.

I met the dangerous driver in the school's off-street car park.

'Mr Star, I presume?' I said, extending a hand.

'Doctor Livingstone,' he said.

'Ah! A man with a sense of humour,' I said, 'it will come in handy if you are coming to work here.'

His handshake was warm and firm as a slice of bread is when it pops out of a toaster. He had long fingers. I like men with long fingers. He had brown eyes. I like men with brown eyes. I judged him to be six foot two. A tall, dark, handsome man. Every woman's dream.

Do you believe in love at first sight? I do. Standing next to him, I felt warm; as if I was standing next to a night watchman's brazier. For the first time that morning I did not feel cold. The air around him shimmered.

If this bloke wasn't the American wizard Whitby had warned us to look out for, I'd eat the third volume of our coven's pamphlet: 'How to kiss an adder and not get bitten'.

Witches fall in love the same way as non-witches fall in love. Believe me, I know. I have buried two husbands. Actually, they were cremated, but you say 'buried', don't you? To a witch, cremation smacks of Icarus flying too close to the sun; it reminds a witch of how her ancestors were burnt at the stake; being buried suggests planting bulbs with a trowel… anyway, whatever, back to falling in love. Sometimes you know it is happening. Sometimes you don't. Sometimes it is like sunbathing; you are shocked when you begin to burn. Sometimes it hits you as suddenly as a bolt of lightning removes a chimney pot; fairies do press-ups in your womb. Your womb becomes the sea and he who has taken your fancy is the moon, making emotional rivers burst their banks.

I could go on, but I won't. If you haven't got the message after those purple passages that I fancied this bloke Howard, I'll give up celebrating Halloween; I'll eat Christmas cake in August; I'll betray my SOSA (Surveyor of Supernatural Activity) oath and blab the latitude and longitude of my area of surveillance.

If I blurted out I could see his shimmer, he'd know I was a witch... to non-witches, a wizard's shimmer is invisible. I did not want him to know I was a witch. I wanted to keep my powder dry.

'Do you knit?' I said.

'As a matter of fact, yes, I do. My mother taught me.'

'In that case you will be a shoe-in here. We are an all-female staff.'

'Wonderful... I won't have to make my own coffee.'

'You're not a bum pincher, are you?'

'Why? Do you want me to be one?'

'I might.'

'You are a fast worker.'

'Not as "fast" as you drive. You might have caused an accident overtaking me.'

'Driving fast is one of my weaknesses.'

'You are not perfect?'

'I'm afraid not.'

'What an interesting man you are, Mr Star. You have a sense of humour and you admit to imperfections.'

'Just the one.'

'Only one?'

Stretching a hand towards me, as if to flick something off my shoulder, he produced from behind my ear, a lime.

'For you,' he said, handing me the lime. 'Anyone's naughty in my class I don't give them "lines"... I give them "limes".'

'The children are going to love you.'

'But will the staff?'

'You've made an excellent start with me.'

'It would be nice if I knew your name.'

'Muriel... Muriel Thayne.'

'Howard Star... back home in the States folk call me "Twinkle".'

'Twinkle, twinkle, big star...how I wonder what you are... nice to meet you.'

'I say that every time I look in the mirror.'

'No you don't.'

'Yes, I do.'

'No, you don't.'

'How'd you know?'

'When you boasted, you were smiling; egoists who believe their propaganda do not giggle when they trumpet. You may not be a bum pincher, Howard, but you are a tease. If you are nice to me, I'll tell you the members of staff who do not have a sense of humour... here comes one now.'

Hilary, the teacher in charge of the school's netball team, tacked towards us like a sailing ship. She was tacking, that is not walking in a straight line, because she was carrying two plastic trays full of exercise books.

'Wow!' she exclaimed, when she saw Howard.

Her exclamation made her forget what she was carrying. Howard stopped the trays slipping off her chest with a reflex action worthy of a slip making the catch of the century.

'A knight in shining armour to my rescue,' boomed Hilary. 'You're the new man teacher, aren't you? Every school should have one.'

'Like a fire extinguisher?' I suggested.

'Thank you, my darling.'

'Don't mention it,' said Howard. 'Here, let me carry them for you.'

'They are very heavy but you, bein' a man, will think them light.'

'Which way?' said Howard.

Instead of carrying the trays, Howard balanced them on his head. Hilary didn't say anything but I knew she was thinking: 'who the hell is this guy?'.

I thought: what a show off.

'Which way?' repeated Howard.

'Through that door and up the stairs. Muriel will hold open the door for us... won't you, darling? Careful my boxes don't fall off your head. Do you play netball?'

'Do you have a school team?'

'Yes, I'm its coach... careful... crouch down... the door was not meant for tall men carrying boxes on their heads... you are safely through.'

'I used to be a limbo dancer.'

'I can see that.'

'I suppose it's like riding a bike,' I butted in, 'you never forget how to do it.'

'I have mentioned the netball,' continued Hilary, 'because I keep my netball posts in the male loo. I hope I don't embarrass you by barging in for them.'

'Before entering you can always knock.'

'Of course... if you fancied taking over the team, there'd be no problem.'

'I'd love to... I'm only temporary... are you winning games?'

'We are close to the top of the league.'

'In that case I'm thinking you are the right person for the job.'

Standing outside her office at the top of the stairs, Monica could not believe what she was seeing. Howard Star, Miss Jolly's replacement... temporary, thank god... was coming up the stairs with two trays full of exercise books balanced on top of his head as if he was a pantomime dame wearing an OTT hat. To add to her confusion, she was talking to her husband on her mobile phone.

'Darling, I know... I do too... you know I do. Your red socks are in the top drawer... of course I'm at work. Why shouldn't I be? You know where I am if you need me... I know you do... I do too... love you... bye, darling. Mr Star, I refuse to be overawed by your entertaining feat of bein' able to balance trays full of books on your head. Hilary, are they yours?'

Hilary nodded that they were.

'Mr Star, please return the boxes. You are a teacher not a Sherpa. Into my office. We need to talk.'

'Am I going to get the cane?'

'I believe a spanking turns men on,' I said.

'Mrs Thayne... please. Mr Star, I think I need to explain a few ground rules. Muriel, Hilary...'

# HOWARD MEETS THE STAFF

**Y**ou are in the Wild West. A stranger walks into a saloon. Everyone stops talking. That's what happened when Monica introduced Howard to the staff.

'I won't introduce you to everyone,' she said, 'there are too many of us. With the best will in the world you will not be able to remember all our names.'

'I never forget a name if it belongs to a pretty face,' said Howard.

'I'm Hilary,' said Hilary, 'we've already met... remember? I love your American accent.'

'You keep your netball posts in the Men's Room?'

'What a memory.'

'You have a pretty face.'

'I'm, Mary,' said Mary.

'Come and sit here, Howard,' I said, standing up and patting the chair I'd vacated. 'I've kept it warm for you.'

'I've explained to Mr Star... to Howard,' said Monica, 'that today is a training day. No children to teach today, Mr Star. Our mission today is to train ourselves to become better teachers. Here is our agenda. Belinda, hand round the agenda... everyone must have a copy. By now we should be in our classrooms. What is the point, I ask myself, of staying up till three in the morning writing an agenda if we don't stick to it. Mr Star, I will show you Miss Jolly's classroom. She is the teacher you are… temporarily… standing in for. I am getting the strong impression you need an escort. Here are your pencils. When a child is in need of a new pencil you will show me a stub. No stub… no new pencil… do I make myself clear?'

Howard accepted the box of pencils the way royalty accepts a signed photograph of a despot.

'Mrs Thayne,' he said, handing me the box of pencils, 'would you be so kind?'

'I'd be honoured,' I said.

I took the pencils off him the way I have seen on television a lady-in-waiting take a bunch of flowers off the late Queen Elizabeth the Second.

He stood, looked around… was he going to walk out? Had we already bored him to tears? When he was certain everyone was looking at him, that he was the centre of attention, he tore his copy of Monica's agenda into shreds… the agenda Monica had worked on as late as three in the morning.

Where all the pieces went I have no idea.

Before Monica had time to scratch out his eyes, he produced from somewhere behind her head a pristine copy of the agenda he'd destroyed. Where it had come from, I had no idea.

Mary and I led the clapping. Hilary shouted, 'Bravo!'

'Lead on, Monica,' he said, 'I can't wait to see my classroom. Never worked in a grade two listed building before. Does it have a ghost?'

'This way,' said Monica.

'Don't forget your pencils,' I said.

'Thank you, Muriel.'

When they'd gone, after a second of silence, everyone began talking at once.

'How'd he do that?'

'That was amazing...'

I whispered to Mary: 'I think it's going to be fun working with Howard.'

'He's dangerous.'

'Do you think so?'

'He's a show-off... all show-offs are dangerous. I should know. I am married to one.'

'He gave me a lime this morning... I've no idea where it came from.'

'A cheap conjuring trick.'

'Or—' keeping my voice down so no one but Mary would hear— 'someone with exceptional gifts.'

Later that morning reading The Guardian in my classroom, instead of writing lesson plans, naughty me, my boredom was relieved by Howard playing Tchaikovsky's number one piano concerto on the school's upright.

The school's classrooms are down the two long sides of a central hall. The hall has a hammer beam roof. It is the sort of hall in which it is easy to imagine King Arthur throwing meat bones to Afghan hounds.

Howard had moved the school's upright into the middle of the hall. He was not a shrinking violet. He wanted to be seen... he wanted to be heard.

Teachers with reams of A4 paper in their hands – to make themselves look busy – stood spellbound at their classroom doors.

When he stood and closed the piano's lid, he bowed left and right. I led the applause. Hilary whistled. Only Mary and I could see his wizard's shimmer.

# I GO TO MA MASON'S
# TO BUY A PIE

**A**t lunch break Mary told me she was popping into town to buy a new bra.

'Michael Sohn's shop has a two for the price of one offer on.'

Mary loved a bargain.

Other members of staff were off to a coffee shop on the seafront.

'Where's Howard?' I asked her.

'He left early… Monica's furious.'

'Do you think he'll come back?'

'If I was him, I wouldn't.'

'I'm off to Ma Mason's to buy a pie… you want one?'

'No thanks. I'm going on a diet. Until the Arse Hole makes a will in my favour I have to look my best.'

On the short walk to Ma's, I was a mother hen sitting on a nest of eggs. My vibes were telling me the chickens inside the eggs I was sitting on, were starting to peck their way out.

'Hello, Ma,' I said as Ma chopped her way through the bead curtain separating the bakery from the shop's customer area.

'One mince and onion.'

'Plate or saucer?'

'Plate... if it's true that falling in love makes a girl hungry then yours truly is famished.'

'You've met him... haven't you? You've met Mr Star. I can tell just by looking at you that you have... just look at the pansies he gave me... weeks old and still as fresh as daisies.'

'He gave me a lime.'

'Better than nowt, I suppose. A "lime"... funny present that. Maybe it means more to an American than it does to us... was it gift wrapped?'

Before I'd time to think up a suitable reply the bell above the shop's door tinkled and a customer we both knew joined us.

'He's dead,' said Una. 'Hello, Mrs Thayne.'

'Hello, Una.'

Una was an admin worker in the Arse Hole's office. Her son, Thomas, was a pupil at the Jube.

'Mr Brown?' said Ma.

'It was expected.'

'It's still a shock.'

'Excuse my French...'

'I didn't know you could speak French, Una,' I piped up.

'Dick... Mr Hedgerow... your pal Mary's hubby is teaching me. It's to impress the customers. I'm front of house, see. Dick... Mr Hedgerow... says I'm like a fairground attraction.'

'The ghost train or the big dipper?' I said.

'I beg your pardon...'

'Never mind...'

Mary and I had our suspicions about Una. Was the thong Mary had found in the Arse Hole's pocket hers? Una had big breasts and a narrow waist. Upstairs she was a 'few pennies short of a shilling'. When Mother Nature had made her body it had left nothing in the kitty to spend on her brain. If a priest told her God had told him to have sex with her, she'd have believed him.

Her overenthusiastic application of lipstick made her mouth look like a clown's mouth.

'Mr Brown...' said Ma.

'The poor bugger lay on the floor for three hours before the ambulance arrived. I don't know what I'd do if my Eddy joined the angels. You've lost two husbands... haven't you, Mrs Thayne?'

'Two lovely men,' I sighed.

'Men!' said Ma. 'They're like those big snakes what squeeze the pips out of you. I shouldn't say this but I was pleased when my George fell doon the stairs and broke his neck... drunken lout. Mind you, he liked me bein' a naturist... couldn't get enough of watching me wobbly bits wobble. He always said if I ever left the pie business I could get a job as a pole dancer. Many a time he'd look up from his mince and dumplings... "Demo," he'd say. I'd always oblige, not to please him but because I enjoyed letting the air get to me bits and bobs. I hate bein' constructed.'

To demonstrate what she meant, Ma flapped open her dustcoat in the manner of a Frenchman selling dirty postcards on the Champs-Élysées. Under the dustcoat Ma was wearing knickers but nothing else.

'There's beauty in ruins,' said Ma.

'You shouldn't do that,' said Una, 'should she, Mrs Thayne? You never know who might see you.'

'Oglers don't bother me,' said Ma. 'I'm proud of my body. Folks go to Rome to see ruins. If Rome had no ruins, tourists wouldn't go… would they, Mrs Thayne?'

'Quite right, Ma,' I said.

'I don't want to be a ruin,' said Una. 'I don't want to grow old.'

'If you want to stay young become a naturist,' said Ma.

'I don't want to become a nudist.'

'Naturist…'

'I don't think my husband would like me showing off my body like that. Eddy doesn't like sharing. What's his is, his… if you see what I mean. Give Eddy a box of chocolates… he won't share… eats the whole box, all by himself. I've told him, "Eddy, that's not good for you. If you're hungry, eat an apple." I read that in a magazine at the vets.'

'Were you poorly?'

'Don't be cheeky, Ma. When I'm poorly I go to the doctors like everybody else. I'm not an animal. Eddy says he wishes I was… if you know what I mean… but I'm not. It's not in my nature. I was at the vet's to get Eddy put down.'

'You went to the vet's to get your husband put down?' I said.

'Don't be silly, Mrs Thayne… not me husband… me hamster. We called the hamster Eddy, because he had small ears like what my husband Eddy has. Eddy… the hamster, I mean, was poorly. He was passing blood. I knew he was poorly when he wouldn't use his wheel. When he was well Eddy loved his wheel. When he wouldn't use it, that's when I knew he wasn't well. Thomas, me son Thomas… you know him, Mrs Thayne?'

I nodded that I did.

'He's looking forward to having a man teacher. He's called Mr Star, isn't he? There's ever so much gossip about him. Anyway, as I was saying, me son Thomas was upset when Eddy went to hamster heaven. I left the vet's with Eddy's corpse in a handkerchief. You know how folk say they'll never wash their hands after they've shaken hands with a pop star… well, I'll never use that handkerchief to blow me nose on… not even if me nose is dripping like a tap what needs a washer. Didn't matter that the vet told me I'd done the right thing sending him to hamster heaven… looking at the poor little thing in his handkerchief shroud made me feel like a murderer. Thomas buried him in the garden. He's ever so good with animals is my Thomas. You know what he did? That woman teacher… Miss Jolly… the one what's always off on the sick… had told him how those Egyptians… the ones what built the pyramids… buried their dead with chairs and beds. So, you know what Thomas did? He buried Eddy with his wheel. I thought that was ever so nice… I did.'

'You miss them when they are gone,' I said.

'You've had pets put down, Mrs Thayne, have you?'

'I was thinking of my husbands.'

'I've heard rumours.'

'What do you mean by that?'

'Nothing, Mrs Thayne… dear me, you sounded sharp when you said that. You sounded like a schoolteacher… if you know what I mean.'

'No,' I said, 'I don't know what you mean.'

I knew what Una was getting at. She was inferring I'd murdered my husbands. It wasn't true. As I have already said and will repeat, no doubt, many more times, I am a 'facilitator' not a 'murderer'.

'You here for your usual, Una?' said Ma.

'Yes, please, Ma… three steak and kidney. Two of them is for my Thomas. Mrs Thayne, I'm sorry for saying what I said before… me and my big mouth. One's for Eddy. Thomas loves his food. I don't tell Eddy Thomas is having two… there's lots of things I don't tell Eddy. If he knew he'd only be jealous. My Thomas loves his meat. Did Stanley bake the pies today, Ma?'

Ma, flapping open and shut her dustcoat to fan air around her bits and bobs, said, after two flaps: 'He's been too busy to help me this week.'

'Thomas will be ever so disappointed. He says your Stanley's pies is best. No offence to you, Ma, but that's what he says.'

'I don't mind you saying that, Una. A few weeks ago I don't know what I'd have done without him. I was down with flu. He baked all the pies. And I'll tell you this… he made more pies with less meat than I'd have used. How he does it, I don't know. I've never seen him work so hard… oops-a-daisy. Better out than in, as they say. I'm as windy as the weather today. Stanley hates it when I fart. He doesn't understand that when you get old you can't help letting rip. This morning he called me a "Windy old fart".'

'I don't think it's nice, him calling you that. He should show you more respect… that's what I think.'

'Sometimes I think he's not well in the attic... you know, up here,' tapping the side of her head.

'That'll be the pylons... Ma, remember he used to live in Grafton Street. All of them flats is under the wires those pylons carry. I read about what the electricity they carry can do to your brain in a magazine.'

'The magazine you read at the vet's when you were sending Eddy to the angels?'

'No, I was at the undertakers because me dad had died... bless his nylon socks. Undertakers have better magazines than vets what put cats and dogs to sleep... that's what I think.'

'Speak as you find.'

'Perhaps,' I suggested, 'the electricity the pylon's cables carry, instead of making his hair stand on end have made him a ten out of ten pie maker.'

'He's a good pie maker,' said Ma, 'because his grandfather and great-grandfather were pie makers. He makes pies with as little meat from the butcher as wouldn't make half of what I make. He's clever when he wants to be. Mrs Fenwick... she lives in Gladstone Street... you know who I mean, Una... liked his pies better than mine. So I knows what your Thomas means, Una... and I don't take offence. Some men have the "touch". Only me Uncle Tom could make pastry like me Uncle Tom... his fingers were meant for pastry.'

'That's why I like a man hairdresser to do my hair,' said Una. 'I like to look my best. Men find me attractive, you know. I think it's my skin. I have smooth skin. I wouldn't tell Eddy but I like to think men find me attractive. I don't mean to boast but, more than once, I've been told I'm a "looker". Don't tell Eddy, will you, but I like a bit on the side. I mean a girl has to have a treat now and again. I mean it's not much to ask, is it? I'm pretty faithful most of the time. I mean it's not as if I'm a member of the royal family and do what they do on their yachts in the Mediterranean.'

'I saw two dogs doing it the other day,' said Ma. 'Animals don't care where they do it, do they?'

'I've read about people doing it at thirty-five thousand feet in a Jumbo jet,' I said.

'What magazine was that in?' said Una.

'The free newspaper.'

'That beats the vet's and the undertakers,' said Ma. 'I've never read anything about folk doing it in Jumbo jets in my naturist magazine... Here's your pies, Una. Where's your money?'

'You're sharp today, Ma. You know I never ask for tick.'

The customer who now entered the shop was Joe. Joe was one of my pupils. He found reading and writing uphill work. He was streetwise to the power ten.

The relationship between a teacher and one of her pupils meeting by chance outside of school is rather like a colonel finding himself having to share a table with one of his private soldiers in a restaurant. Neither are in uniform. Both are aware of the gulf between them. Should the private soldier call the officer 'Sir'? Should the private ask the colonel if he takes milk in his tea?

I had a soft spot for Joe.

'Hello, Joe,' I said, 'you come to Ma's to buy sweets?'

'Miss, this is a pie shop. I've come to buy pies.'

'Silly me.'

'Yee need looking after, yee dee.'

'Will you look after me, Joe?'

'Miss, 'am already looking after me mam and the twins.'

'You have a lot on your plate.'

'Eh?'

'Two plus six?'

'Howay, Miss … 'am not at school.'

'Sorry, Joe… silly me… you are in a sweet shop.'

'In a pie shop, Miss.'

'There I go again… silly me.'

'What kind of sweets do you want, Joe?' said Ma.

'Divent yee start. I want pies. I'm not daft yuh nar. I nar am not in a sweet shop. Auntie Una, tell them to stop taking the mickey.'

The council estate on which Una and Joe lived was tribal… upset Joe and you upset his family… NATO on a small scale.

'Stop picking on me nevvy,' said Una. 'You're ganin at him the way I saw a seagull on the fish quay gan at a chip. Put your order in, Joe. Auntie Una's sticking up for yuh… so there.'

'Two pork,' said Joe, 'and me mother said to tell yuh she doesn't want any hairs in the pastry like last time.'

# HOW TO
# HANDLE STRESS

**T**he Jubilee has a hall upstairs and a hall downstairs. The venue for the afternoon session of the training day was the downstairs hall; the hall used by reception and infants. In its corners there were boxes of Lego, dolls, Teddy bears and a rocking horse with one eye. Staff ambled into the hall as if they were Marie Antoinette on her way to the guillotine.

The hall was bloody freezing; clearly keeping it warm was not one of Ted's priorities; to keep him happy and their hall warm, all the infant teachers had to do was give him pens and pencils. The radiator I touched was lukewarm. Monica and the guest speaker were wearing overcoats, scarves and gloves.

'Excuse, me,' I said, 'I'm off to get my coat.'

'Me, too,' said Mary.

Groups have a herd mentality. When Mary and I left to get our coats so did everyone else. When we reassembled, we were all dressed, not for a lecture but for a picnic on top of Scafell Pike in January.

I eyed the guest speaker… she who was going to tell me how to handle my stress… the way an undertaker's eye measures a corpse. She looked too young to know much about stress. She was a dyed blonde; her shade of lipstick I would not have allowed anywhere near my own lips. And where was Howard?

The plastic chairs we'd to sit on had been arranged in a semi-circle. In the centre of the half circle, there was a TV on a trolley.

I'd no sooner sat down than my bum began to ache. I have read that King Charles has an equerry whose job it is to carry a cushion to take the 'sting' out of such seats. Anyone who thinks this laughable, should try sitting on one for an hour.

Those who'd gone out for a pub meal looked happier than those, who like myself, had not.

'Where is he?' said Monica, in a voice loud enough for everyone to hear.

'Mr Star?' said Mary.

'Of course that's who I mean.'

'Perhaps he's run away,' I said.

'Maybe all of us women have scared him off,' said Mary.

A teacher raised a tentative hand.

'Yes?' said Monica.

'I think he's surfing.'

'Surfing, in this weather... is he mad?'

'He's riding waves on a surfboard.'

'Are you certain? How'd you know?'

'A few of us lunched at the Rendezvous... you know... the coffee shop on the seafront.'

'I know the Rendezvous.'

'We had a window seat.'

'A bay window seat,' chipped in another teacher. 'We could see the sea.'

'He was wearing a wetsuit.'

'Neptune, the sea god…'

'He's a wonderful surfer.'

'I do hope he's not drowned,' I said. 'It would be too awful if, as we speak, sitting here… all warm and cosy…'

'Ha! Ha!' said a teacher wearing one of those fur hats Russian soldiers wear in Siberia.

'… If he was lying, white and cold on a slab of marble in a mortuary.'

'A mortuary would be warmer than where we are,' said another teacher. 'I can see my breath… look!'

'I'm certain Mr Star is quite capable of looking after himself,' said Monica. 'I have formed the opinion that Mr Star is one of those men who, if he fell into a cesspit, would come up smelling of roses. He's that sort of man… I know he is. We will start without him. It gives me great pleasure to welcome Janice to our school… Janice.'

Janice stood. She breathed in deep. She exhaled slowly. The foggy breath she exhaled made her look like a snow making machine. She held up a pencil; not, any old pencil but a brand new school pencil. When she snapped the pencil in half Monica turned white; snapping a brand new school pencil in half was an act of vandalism. It was akin to throwing a pot of paint at a Renoir. Did Janice not know how much a school pencil cost?

'The video I am going to show you is to stop you doing that,' said Janice by way of explaining her vandalism. 'There are times in all our lives when we feel like smashing plates… when we feel like snapping pencils. The video you are going to see is about anger management. To be good teachers we must learn to control our emotions. When a child uses an Anglo Saxon expletive, we must breathe in deeply... deeply... and count to ten. When a five-year-old tells you to F-off, you must not take it personally. To help you handle such confrontations the video will show you various relaxation techniques... deep breathing... touching your toes... having a "buddy". Research by the Cyril Burt Foundation has shown that relaxation techniques reduce the risk of teachers going off with stress. The aim of my talk is to take you on a journey to nirvana; be warned, be prepared for a long journey – reaching nirvana is not as easy as making a cup of tea. You are also guinea pigs. You are the first school to see the video. Monica... be an angel, hand out the booklet explaining the video's aims... would you, please? In the booklet – back page – you will find a questionnaire. One of your tasks this afternoon is to evaluate the video. Oh and another thing... when you tick your boxes, please use a black biro. A computer will be marking... sorry... not marking but recording your evaluations. One of my aims is to build up a database of responses. I advise that you fill in the questionnaire after you have watched the video. If you tick while watching, you will miss key elements of the exposition. If you tick your boxes the way I have recommended, you will not have to remove your gloves until the end of the video. It is my experience that wearing gloves... especially mittens – which I can see a lady over there wearing – makes putting a cross in a box difficult. Any crosses you make outside the box will confuse the computer.'

After the video and we had ticked our boxes, we did deep breathing exercises. We had to hold our breath. We had to exhale slowly. We had to tense our muscles and then relax them.

'Partners,' said Janice, 'for this exercise you will need a partner.'

It was at this point that a six foot two seal... the sea god, Neptune... Howard, in a wetsuit... joined us.

'You are late,' said Monica.

'So good of you to join us,' said Belinda.

Janice eyed Howard the way a store detective eyes a shoplifter. Who the hell was the gate crasher?

'Howard,' I said, 'will you be my partner?'

'Delighted... fox trot or slow waltz?'

'Raindrops!' shouted Janice. 'When you hear the music I want one partner to use her fingers to simulate drops of rain falling on her partner's shoulders. The rain starts as a drizzle... becomes a downpour... returns as a drizzle. When it stops the partner who has been "drummed" will have relaxed shoulders.'

'Drum or drummer?' said Howard.

'Drummer,' I said. 'Turn around.'

I played Howard's shoulders as if I was tapping a tambourine. When the music changed tempo I played his shoulders as if I was knocking hell out of a kettle drum. The funny thing was that standing next to him had warmed me up; or, was it my drumming? As far as I was concerned, the wizard's shimmer I could see coming off him – for WEO (witches' eyes only) – was a hot water bottle.

'Change!' said Janice.

When Howard's drumming fingers emulated rain smacking my shoulders I swooned; an old fashioned word, I know, but… well… I hope you get the picture.

Of course, Belinda and Monica were partners. I observed that they seemed to be enjoying their mutual massages.

When the music stopped, Monica, white breath leaving her mouth, not as snow flies out of a snow making machine but as if she was spraying Howard with white pepper spray, told him: 'Mr Star, I want a word with you… my office, now. Belinda, be an angel and thank Janice for her wonderful presentation.'

Howard's classroom, in the upstairs hall, was opposite mine. When he returned from the – I assumed – dressing down he'd received from Monica, and he saw I was watching him, he did a backward somersault in the middle of the hall… a wizard's equivalent, I suppose, of a fighter pilot doing a victory roll. In his confrontation with Monica, no doubt about it, he had come off best.

'Howard,' I said, dashing out of my classroom, 'are you alright?'

'Why should I not be?'

'Did Monica not give you a dressing down?'

'Of course she did.'

'But you survived?'

'Of course I did. I'm an American. I'm off now.'

'Monica hasn't rung the bell to tell us we are dismissed.'

'You are forgetting, Mrs Thayne, I am temporary. School rules do not apply to me. From what Marilyn has told me, the school needs me more than I need it. Looking forward to meeting the children tomorrow. Now–' looking at his watch– 'I'm off to meet Marilyn for coffee and cake. Your school governor is an excellent host.'

'I do hope you won't find the children too difficult to control… they can be a handful.'

'You know my motto… don't give 'em lines, give 'em limes.'

To talk about Howard in private, Mary and I met in my classroom. We both agreed that Howard just had to be the wizard Whitby had warned us about. But what the hell was he doing in our grotty primary school?

Through the clear glass in my classroom door, we watched Monica go into Belinda's classroom.

'Senior Management is having a meeting,' said Mary.

'Monica's carrying a red rose.'

'Why's she carrying a red rose?'

'I think I know.'

'Howard?'

'He gave Ma Mason a posy of pansies. He woos with flowers. I'm thinking he took the sting out of Monica's dressing him down by giving her a red rose.'

'If the Arsehole gave me a rose, I'd turn its thorns into claws and its petals into fire blankets.'

'He gave me a lime.'

# THE MUSIC MAN

**T**he next day, a Tuesday, I drove to school. I drove because it was threatening to rain. Bicycles are ok in dry weather; a dead loss when it rains. Howard's car was in the school's off-street car park. The surfboard on its roof made me think I was in California.

I collected the keys to my classroom from the key cupboard in the staffroom. Hilary, the only member of staff in the room, was making a cup of coffee.

'It's for Howard,' she explained, 'he's in the hall… playing the piano.'

'I know,' I said, 'I'm not deaf.'

'He has a wonderful touch… listen… that's Beethoven's "Fur Elise"… wonderful.'

'He likes milky café.'

'Are you sure?'

'Absolutely. Do you want me to take it to him?'

'It's no bother… I'll do it. I'm quite capable.'

'Suit yourself.'

'Muriel, believe me, I will.'

I was jealous. Howard was my property.

The pain I sent shooting down Hilary's arm made her spill the coffee.

'Dear me,' I said, 'you'd think you'd wet yourself.'

'Damn!'

The bell rang for the start of the school day... take the register... dinner money. A second bell rang... morning assembly... walk your class, in an orderly file, into the hall.

Howard played us in with 'The Lord's My Shepherd'. He had a wonderful left hand. Nice, soothing music.

To receive her pupils Monica stood on a dais made out of wooden blocks. In the lapel of her jacket she sported a red rose; need I say more?

'Straight line,' Monica told, Howard's class. 'Year six... a straight line.'

Some children marched into the hall like soldiers; some wandered in like zombies; some bumped, on purpose, into the person in front of them.

'Higgins,' said a teacher, 'take your hands out of your pockets.'

When he got home Higgins would tell his mam. He wasn't the only one with his hands in his pockets. The teachers were always picking on him. It wasn't fair. To show he wasn't going to take a reprimand lying down he flicked a snot pellet into the hair of the boy in front of him.

When everyone had settled down... arms folded... sitting cross legged and Howard had stopped playing, Monica said: 'Good morning, boys and girls.'

As they had been trained to do, the children chorused back: 'Good morning, Mrs Thistledown.'

'This morning, school, we have a new teacher. His name is Mr Star. He is the man playing the piano. Mr Star, please say hello to the boys and girls.'

'Good morning, boys and girls,' said Howard, standing up and waving to the children the way royalty waves to plebs.

'Children, say good morning to Mr Star.'

Too many children were not paying attention. They were thinking about bonfire night... about Christmas. One boy was pulling chewing gum off a shoe; two were smelling their armpits; one boy was holding his nose because the boy next to him had farted.

For all of the above and for no doubt many more reasons, the children's 'Good morning, Mr Star' was not choric.

Some said 'Miss' instead of 'Mr'... some started to say 'Mrs Thistle...' some thought Howard was called 'Mr Car'.

'Let's try again, shall we,' said Howard, taking charge.

Howard's taking charge annoyed Monica. I knew she was annoyed because she'd folded her arms the way defenders of a fort pull up a drawbridge.

'My name is Mr Star,' said Howard. 'Good morning, boys and girls.'

'Good morning, Mr Star,' chanted back the children.

'That's better. Hi there everyone. I'm your new music teacher... would you like me to teach you a song?'

'Yes!' I shouted.

'Yes!' shouted the children.

Monica looked shellshocked. What the hell was going on? It was her assembly. She was captain of the good ship the Jubilee Primary School. Howard was a deck hand. Howard was the new boy. New boys were supposed to be shrinking violets not a park full of summer bedding plants.

'Year six… hands up. What's your name?' pointing to a girl at the front of a line of year six children.

'Jane, sir.'

'Jane,' handing her a cardboard trumpet he'd produced out of thin air, 'year six will play the trumpet.'

A boy put up his hand.

'Yes?' said Howard.

'Sir, I can't play the trumpet.'

'Yes, you can,' said Howard, 'you do it like this.'

Playing the piano he sang: 'I am the music man, I come from far away… what can you play? I can play the trumpet…' then playing an imaginary trumpet with fingers dancing up and down on imaginary valves, sang: 'Toot! Toot! Toot! Year six, stand… we'll have a run through. Teachers, please feel free to join in.'

The rehearsal went well. The children loved it. I loved it, Mary loved it; a discreet number of teachers loved it. This was more fun than a homily from Monica about the Good Samaritan.

Howard told each year group the imaginary instruments they were to play. Year five were big bass drums. 'Boom! Boom! Boom!' They hollered.

Year four were bongo drums. 'Bongo! Bongo! Bongo!'

Year three were triangles… 'Tinkle! Tinkle! Tinkle!'

'Teachers, join in with your year group. Mrs Thistledown will play the penny whistle. Mrs Thistledown, you go Peep! Peep! Peep! Now you have the idea we'll play it through year group by year group. A one… a one, two, three.'

I played a big bass drum. Mary played the trumpet. Monica's performance on the penny whistle left much to be desired.

The grand finale involved all the year groups playing together. It was chaotic. It was bedlam. It was fun. A breeze of salty sea air wafted through the hall; no kidding, I could smell it.

After assembly, back in my classroom with my pupils, I saw Monica, through the glass in my classroom's door, remove the red rose from the buttonhole in her jacket and crush it under the heel of her boot.

# WISE ADVICE
# FROM MARY

As I have already mentioned, no doubt to the point of tedium, witches fall in love the same way as non-witches fall in love. When I looked at Howard fairies did press-ups in my womb. No doubt about it I was infected with 'Howard infatuation'.

Sitting at home with Tilly on my knee I found myself thinking about him all the time... bugger, the ironing.

Mary and I had reported his arrival to Whitby. The met-a-web had still failed to confirm, beyond any shadow of doubt, that he was the wizard they had warned us about.

I didn't like members of staff making him coffee. Hilary had taken to dressing like a tart. It was late November. There was cat ice on pools. It was freezing. I couldn't believe it, therefore, when she came into school dressed for summer... short, flowery skirt and a white blouse so transparent I could see a pink bow in the middle of her bra. The bitch insisted on calling Howard 'Darling'.

Mary and I had few, if any secrets, from each other. She was privy to my infatuation. I was privy to her marital problems. Witch sisters hunt in packs; we co-operate. A lone wolf cannot bring down a caribou but a pack can.

One Saturday morning towards the end of November we met in the Rendezvous coffee shop. We liked this coffee shop because we knew Issy, its owner. Issy always insisted we tell her the decoration we wished to be foamed onto the top of our cappuccini. This morning I chose a witch's hat. Mary chose a broomstick.

'You'd think you were witches,' said Issy.

'I wish we were,' I said.

'If we were,' said Mary, 'would you give us free cappuccini?'

'Of course… I do not want to be turned into a frog… Ha! Ha! Cash or card?'

In a window seat, from which we could see the sea, Mary, without a by-your-leave, gave me a piece of her mind. 'You are too obvious,' she told me. 'You have to make a man like Howard think he is doing the chasing.'

'I'm not as obvious as Hilary.'

'True… but all the same I cringed when you asked him to brush dandruff off your collar.'

'It was a test. I have read somewhere that wizards have a love-hate relationship with dandruff.'

'We don't know for certain he's a wizard. Dandruff, Muriel, is not an aphrodisiac. Men are attracted to women who will give them healthy children. A woman with dandruff is an imperfect woman. She is an apple with a blemish. In the Garden of Eden, Adam would never have picked Eve if she'd had dandruff. An imperfect woman will give birth to imperfect children. I know that is not true… you know that is not true… Howard knows that is not true but, you try telling his penis that is not true.'

'His penis thinks otherwise?'

'It's not his fault.'

'What do I do?'

'Get rid of your dandruff and stop dropping things for him to pick up.'

'I get the impression he looks down his nose at us. What's he doing in our school?'

'He's the music teacher… he's here to replace Juniper. Maybe he's doing Marilyn a favour… you scratch my back, I'll scratch yours.'

'You don't think…?'

'No… definitely not. We could try putting a spell on him.'

'Dangerous… if he is who we think he is…'

'A wizard?'

'Yes… the spell will rebound on she who cast it.'

'If he really is a wizard he'll fight back. We must be careful not to overplay our hand. We must keep a low profile.'

'I weary of keeping a low profile. I'm proud of bein' a witch. I sometimes feel an irresistible urge to grab Monica and scream at her… "you're just a headteacher, I'm a witch, First Class".'

'I wonder if he is who we think.'

'Can we not talk about something else?'

'No.'

'Why not?'

'Because I can't stop thinking about him.'

'Oh dear… that's a bad sign. Are you in love with him?'

'Yes.'

'He is wearing a wedding ring.'

'When I asked him if he was married, he gave me his "Labrador look". My god, it was like he'd switched on a sunray lamp in my groin.'

'And is he married?'

'He said he used to be. When I asked him if he was divorced, he said it was more complicated than that.'

'Never mind, married, divorced or single... find out if he has money.'

'The Arsehole has money.'

'When I get my hands on it, he's going through a plate glass window. In the meantime, it's business as usual.'

'Meaning?'

'This morning we had sex in the shower.'

'Poor you.'

'It wasn't that bad. Afterwards I rubbed him down with bleach. "Dick, darling," I said, "if you will demand sex in the shower, it's not my fault if I pick up the wrong bottle".'

'I wonder if Howard would like to have sex in a shower.'

'Get rid of your dandruff and you might find out... did you pick this coffee shop because you thought you might see him surfing?'

'Yes.'

'While we wait to see if he turns up, shall we have another coffee?'

'Why not.'

Needless to say he didn't turn up... but, that's life, isn't it?

# HOWARD'S CLASS ASSEMBLY

**T**he aim of class assemblies is to help pupils get used to standing up and speaking in public; they are about encouraging pupils to be tolerant… to be kind to one another. The Good Samaritan was a favourite subject for a class assembly. Class assemblies were never used to indoctrinate pupils into accepting the dogma of a particular religion.

This Wednesday morning it was the turn of Howard's class to take the assembly. His class had brought in their pets. A placard on the dais upon which the children in his class were sitting, said: *LOVE YOUR PET*

He played the school into assembly wearing a gorilla costume.

'Don't worry,' I told my class, 'it's not a real gorilla. Mr Star is inside the costume… silly Mr Star, dressing up like that and giving us all a fright.'

'Miss, 'am not daft,' said Joe, the pupil we met in Ma Mason's pie shop. 'We aal know it's Mr Star.'

There were dogs on leads… cats in cages… white mice… rats… a rabbit wearing a red velvet collar… a gerbil exercising on a wheel in a cage. Every so often a parrot squawked 'Fuck off'!

What was in the shoe box on the girl's knee... front row, second on the left? It was perforated with air holes; every now and then it shuddered as if whatever was inside wanted out.

Una's son Thomas had brought in his pet python.

'See, Miss,' said Joe, sitting cross legged at my feet, waiting for the assembly to start, 'I told you he had a snake... that's "Percy", Miss.'

The python seemed interested in the rabbit. I don't know when you know a python is hungry, but I think the rabbit did.

'Miss,' said Joe, 'I divent like snakes.'

'Nor do I, Joe.'

Where was Monica? It was her job to introduce the assembly. While we waited for her to deign us with her presence, the gorilla, aka Howard, played 'All things bright and beautiful'.

Monica walked into the hall talking to her husband on her mobile. When she screamed I assumed it was because she'd seen the python.

Under normal circumstances her best pal and soulmate Belinda would have rushed to her aid. This morning, though, Belinda was off. She had a hospital appointment... haemorrhoids... nasty. As I was closest to Monica when she'd let rip, I took it upon myself to escort her, like a policeman arresting a Greenpeace activist, out of the hall. As we left, I heard Howard... the gorilla... tell his class to start the assembly.

'Fuck off! Fuck off!' squawked the parrot.

In the privacy of her headteacher's room, I told Monica, by way of making polite conversation: 'Deep breaths... was it the snake? That wasn't a real gorilla, you know, it was Howard, dressed in a gorilla costume.'

'I'm not stupid... I know who it was.'

'Of course you did.'

'I wouldn't be a headteacher if I was stupid.'

'Of course you wouldn't.'

'Why did Juniper have to go off sick? You were her "Buddy", Muriel. It was your job to look after her. Why didn't you look after her? "Buddies" are supposed to help each other.'

'I did my best.'

'You don't like Juniper... I know you don't. You don't like me. There's something funny about you and Mary I can't put my finger on.'

'I do like you,' I lied.

'Oh no, you don't. You like Howard but you don't like me. Muriel, I can't stop crying... give me a hug.'

'I can give you a handkerchief.'

'You'd give Howard a hug. I know you would.'

'Why do you say that?'

'I've seen you looking at him. You fancy him, don't you? You are lucky you are not married. I'm married. I hate it... hate it. I'm sick of washing his underpants. He's always on the phone to me when I'm at work.'

'That's nice.'

'No, it isn't.'

'Monica, I think it is time you took one of your pills... I really do.'

'Everyone hates me... tell me I'm wrong.'

'I don't hate you, Monica.'

'You don't sound as if you mean that… you are just trying to be kind. I know you are. Everyone hates me… I know they do.'

'Monica, you need a "Buddy". You are the only member of staff who does not have a shoulder to cry on.'

'A headteacher can't have a "Buddy". You are forgetting my position… the loneliness of the commander.'

'Howard could be your "Buddy". He's temporary. He'll soon be gone. Think of him as one of those cowboys who ride into town and kills the bad guys.'

'The Jubilee may be in a deprived area, Muriel, but it is not the Wild West.'

'All I'm saying is… Howard's my "Buddy" but I'm happy for you to appropriate him.'

'He doesn't like me.'

'Try making a fuss of him… give him some coloured pencils.'

'Muriel, I'm a headteacher, not a prostitute.'

'You don't have to go that far. I wasn't suggesting you go to bed with him.'

'I hope he rots in hell… bloody gorilla…'

'Me, Tarzan, you Jane…'

'What?'

'Nothing…'

'You know he's taken over the pantomime? He's told me, without a by-your-leave, that we are doing Hansel and Gretel. I hate… hate, pantomimes. Marilyn says the pantomime's a Jubilee school tradition. If she tells me that once more I will scream.'

'Oh dear... what about going back into the hall and thanking Howard and his class for all the hard work they have put into their assembly.'

'The assembly has started and finished without me?'

I nodded.

'It's a shock to realise I am not indispensable. I will go back into the hall when the rabbit has gone.'

'Not the snake?'

'I like snakes... it's rabbits I'm scared of. I have leporiphobia. When I was thirteen, I wore a brace to stop me looking goofy. Whenever I see a rabbit with big front teeth, I see myself as I might have been if I'd not worn a brace.'

'Poor you.'

'I know.'

My impersonation of a rabbit with big front teeth was involuntary. I found it difficult to empathise with someone who was scared of rabbits... snakes... gorillas, yes... but not bunnies.

My impersonation had made Monica fall into her headteacher's IKEA swivel chair... the only swivel chair in the school. From what might be described as the recovery position she looked at me through splayed fingers, as if she was a nun talking to me through a grille.

'I want Belinda... go and fetch, Belinda,' she said.

'Belinda has a hospital appointment,' I reminded her.

'Get out! You hate me... I know you do.'

# THE START OF
# PANTO MAYHEM

**H**oward had been at the Jubilee since the start of November. It was now December. Christmas was fast approaching. Supermarkets were selling Christmas cards. It was time to start thinking about the school pantomime.

For some members of staff, Howard was a pair of shoes that were too tight a fit; other members of staff loved him; others thought him a big head; others, Mary and myself included, thought him quite wonderful.

Hilary continued to try to turn his head by wearing see-thru blouses. When she squatted to pick up a file her stretched trousers revealed... the way a low tide lets everyone see, the ribs of a ship wrecked long ago... a black thong.

When I asked him, point blank, no messing about, what he was staring at, he said: 'When I was ten years old and living in Wisconsin, I used to have a catapult that looked just like that.'

Doris, the school's matriarch, was knitting him a Christmas jumper.

Monica tolerated him. She had no choice. Marilyn had made it clear to her that he must be kept sweet. The school pantomime needed music. He was the music man.

In the staff room one morning I said to him: 'Howard, the pantomime…'

'What about it?'

'Keep still,' said Doris who was measuring the length of his arm against the length of what she had already knitted, 'if you don't I'll drop a loop.'

'We all know it's Hansel and Gretel… when are we going to start rehearsals?'

'When I've written it.'

'You are writing it yourself?'

'Of course…'

'Keep still, Howard,' said Doris.

'Sorry… I am having trouble writing the witch's song.'

When he said 'witch' I twitched. Did he suspect… did he know that Mary and I were witches? He was smiling. Was the smile 'knowing' or 'innocent'? If he winked, I'd know he knew; but he didn't.

'You are writing your own music?' said Doris.

'Of course.'

'I think you are one of the most talented people I have ever met. Until you came to work here, I was thinking of taking early retirement. I'm not now. You have given the Jubilee a blood transfusion.'

'Doris, you are too kind. When will my jumper be ready?'

'Howard, don't fluster me… Oh dear, I've dropped a loop.'

'I have ideas about the parts I would like each class to play,' said Howard, producing from nowhere a posy of flowers which he gave to Doris, 'all up here at the moment—' tapping his forehead. 'Muriel, I would like your class to do an animal dance… you know the sort of thing… children dressed up to look like hedgehogs, bears, badgers, ladybirds… butterflies. They come to comfort Hansel and Gretel when those unfortunates are lost in the forest… before they meet the witch.'

This time when he said 'witch' he stared at me. It was as if he was telling me… I know your secret. His forthrightness made me twitch.

'I know you are fond of Joe,' he continued, ever so politely ignoring my twitching. 'The other day when I was on yard duty he told me he wanted to be in my class. I was flattered. I told him he was lucky to have your good self, Muriel, as his teacher. In the animal dance your class will be doing I think he should be a bear. Tell him, Mr Star wants him to be a bear.'

The bell rang. Staff trooped back to their classrooms; those who'd witnessed the materialisation of the posy, out of nowhere, were convinced Howard was a member of the Magic Circle.

As far as Mary and I were concerned, it was further evidence that he was the wizard Whitby had warned us about.

# A TRIP TO
# THE CIRCUS

**T**he Jubilee's extra-curricular activities were popular with pupils, less so with teachers.

On the evening we went to the circus, many teachers found they had dental appointments. Hilary had to visit a sick uncle. Doris didn't want to drive home in the dark. Howard said he was busy.

A trip to the circus in November was a school tradition. Mary and I always volunteered. We identified with circus folk; circus folk were quirky; like witches, circus folk were not part of mainstream society.

We, that is, a party of forty children, teachers and parents, travelled to the big-top in a private coach. Monica and Belinda were in charge. When the big chiefs were around, Mary and I were supernumerary.

In the big-top, seated and waiting for the show to start, Joe, who was sitting next to me said: 'Miss, I wish I was in Mr Star's class, Miss. Why can't I be in his class, Miss? Would you like to be in his class, Miss?'

'I'm a teacher, Joe… not a pupil.'

'But if you could, Miss? I bet you would, Miss.'

'What makes you think that, Joe?'

'I've seen you looking at him, Miss.'

'Have you indeed! In the pantomime Mr Star wants you to be a bear.'

'I don't want to be a bear.'

'We'll talk about that tomorrow... look, here come the clowns. The show has started.'

During an interval... there were lots of intervals for the hard sell of raffle tickets... Monica, courtesy of the school's slush fund, bought everyone an ice cream.

To keep things simple no one was given a choice of flavours. It was a tub of vanilla, take it or leave it.

Monica wanted to pay by card. The clown selling them wanted to take the card to his office. 'That card,' I heard Monica exclaim, 'is not leaving my sight.'

'Lay-dees and gen-til-men!' boomed the ring master.

'Your ice-cream, Joe,' I said, handing Joe the tub of vanilla ice-cream.

'I want a lolly,' said Joe.

'I'll have it,' said the pupil sitting behind Joe.

'Do you want your ice-cream, Joe... yes or no?'

Joe wanted his ice-cream.

'That's 'cos yuh didn't want me to have it,' said Billy. 'You're greedy you are, Joe.'

'Fuck off!'

What stopped me reprimanding Joe for using the F-word was a Black knight mounted on a black horse. He was wearing black armour and a black sallet helmet with its visor down. He was holding, under my nose, on the end of his lance, a tiara of flowers. He wanted me to champion him.

I am not an actress but I am used to telling children stories and to addressing the Whitby concave. I placed the tiara on my head in such a way as to suggest the Black Knight was the love of my life; that if he was to die in combat I would swoon.

The flowers were plastic.

'Miss, I want a lolly.'

'He who wants never gets,' said Billy. 'Isn't that reet, Miss?'

The Black Knight's opponent was the Red Knight. On top of the Red Knight's helmet, there swayed, like the bobble on a woolly hat, a plastic bird of prey.

The Red Knight was a dirty fighter. He paid a dwarf dressed as a herald to substitute the Black Knight's lance for a rubber one. When they dismounted and fought with swords, the Red Knight had the Black Knight on the ground.

The Red Knight's champion was a clown on stilts. He encouraged the audience to clap when the Black Knight was fighting for his life.

'Oh dear,' I said, 'I think the Red Knight is going to kill my champion.'

'Divent be daft, Miss,' said Billy. 'It's like the wrestling, Miss. One guy takes a beating so the other guy looks tough. Then, they change, so the other guy gets his own back. You'll see. Me dad loves watching the wrestling.'

The Black Knight's fortune changed when a clown driving a jalopy with an exploding exhaust drove into the ring. The Black Knight's cavalry had arrived. The clown driving the jalopy, threw the Black Knight a flashing sword. The sword flashed on and off like a lighthouse. It was with this stage prop that the Black Knight chopped off the Red Knight's head.

'How'd he dee that?' said Joe. 'Miss, if he'd really chopped off the Red Knight's heed… would there have been blood?'

'Lots… you would have seen a red fountain.'

'Ugh!'

'I divent like blood, Miss,' said Billy. 'I'm like me dad. Miss, me dad fainted at the blood donors.'

The Black Knight vaulted back into the saddle; no mounting blocks for him. On the end of his lance there swung, the way bags of sand swing on the forks of a fork lift truck, a carrier bag.

He showed off his horsemanship. He made his steed walk backwards… made it walk sideways… made it curtsy. After having shown off his horsemanship, he trotted towards me. After the horse had given me an equine curtsy he swung the carrier bag on the end of his lance under my nose.

'I accept,' I said.

The sound of my voice boomed. In the tip of the lance there had to be a microphone.

There was something déjà vu about the Black Knight. I could not see his face but my 'vibes' were telling me that I knew him. I'm a fan of the movie 'Ivanhoe'. I have seen it many times. I knew what to do.

'What is your name?' I asked him.

He shook his head from side to side.

'Take off your helmet… show us who you are.'

Once again, he shook his head; then he was off, cantering round the ring. After two circuits he disappeared through a flap in the side of the tent.

The carrier bag contained two iced lollies. No expensive perfume. No flowers. No gift voucher to buy a dress. Was I disappointed? Of course I was.

It took me a few seconds to realise the significance of the iced lollies. The Black Knight had sent me a message. I shivered.

My supernatural side was hinting at something my rational side found unthinkable.

'Joe,' I said, 'it's your lucky night. I don't know how the Black Knight knew you wanted an iced lolly but, here you are.'

'Miss,' said Billy, 'can I have the other one... please. Thanks, Miss... see, Joe, I've got one the same as you.'

'I've got one as well,' said Joe.

'That's what I said... you're thick, you are, Joe.'

'Mary,' I whispered, 'are you thinking the Black Knight is who I am thinking he is?'

'It crossed my mind.'

'It can't be.'

'No reason why not.'

'Are you getting "vibes"?'

'Throbbing... the big-top is full of supernatural activity.'

'Howard said he couldn't come tonight because he was busy. Hilary told me he'd told her he'd an appointment with a chiropodist.'

'A bloke like Howard cuts his own toenails.'

'Miss?' said Joe.

'Yes, Joe?'

'Miss, Billy says 'am thick and 'am not, Miss, am I?'

'No, Joe, you are not "thick".'

'See, Billy, Miss says 'am not "thick" and Miss knows everything… don't yuh, Miss?'

I smiled. If only teachers were as knowing as their pupils sometimes thought they were I'd know, for certain, that Howard was the Black Knight.

# INTRODUCING BYRON RICHARD HEDGEROW AKA: DICK... THE ARSE HOLE... THE BIDET ETC.

On the Saturday morning, after the visit to the circus, I cycled to Mary's for a coffee.

In her lounge, Mary told me: 'It's your unlucky day... you've just missed him.'

'Who, the milkman?'

'I am glad you can joke about missing he whom you call the "love of your life". It shows you are not completely besotted with...'

'With whom?'

'Stop playing games. You know who I mean... Howard. He's into jogging... did you know that?'

'Howard's a jogger?'

'Yes... a few seconds earlier you'd have pedalled right into him. If that had happened, you'd have had to pretend to fall off your bicycle... you know... pretend to have sprained an ankle. He'd have picked you up... laid you in the recovery position... I know he would. You could have made him think you needed mouth to mouth resuscitation. On the other hand, that cyclist's helmet you are wearing might have put him off. It lacks the allure of one of Hilary's see-through blouses.'

Then, changing the subject, she said: 'Do you like my camellia japonica?' drawing my attention to a twig in a pot. 'It cost an absolute bomb.'

'It looks dead.'

'Wait until the spring... then, you'll see. When it flowers there'll be so many flowers on it, each flower will have cost less than a penny. The Arse Hole loves it.'

'In that case let's kill it... sympathetic magic.'

'I don't want HIM out of the way until he's made a will in my favour.'

'Just trying to help.'

'He's got lovely legs.'

'The Arse Hole?'

'No... Howard. When he was jogging he was wearing shorts. I have a thing about men's legs. You'll find this interesting...'

'That you have a thing about men's legs?'

'No... at my bridge club last night I was playing with a woman who is Marilyn's best friend. She knew all about Howard. She told me Marilyn had told her Howard... our Howard... your Howard was here to right a terrible wrong. Marilyn had hinted to her that he was FBI. He's a widower.'

'A rich widower?'

'You'd be after him, Muriel, even if he was a pauper... I know you would. And that worries me... if I may make so bold as to hint... you are forgetting our modus operandi... chase, capture, marry, inherit... invest. To get your hands on their money you have put up with two husbands. It can't have been easy for you putting up with Reg's flatulence. I'll never forget the night he farted "God Save the King" and shit himself. Muriel... you are infatuated with Howard... I know you are. You are letting your heart rule your head. If Howard is rich, go after him like a heat seeking guided missile. If he's church mouse poor... forget all about him... get real. Like all men he will have as many faults as a colander as holes... take off the rose tinted spectacles... look at him the way Graham Sutherland looked at Sir Winston Churchill. At the moment you are Holbein looking at Henry the eighth. Let's deconstruct him as if he was a sentence... personal traits you have noticed and which you find irritating?'

'He's fussy about his fingernails... forever at them with an emery board. He's a dictator... told us we are doing "Hansel and Gretel"... no discussion.'

'I believe Juniper wanted to do "Little Red Riding Hood".'

'I know... poor Juniper... poor US... have another piece of tea cake.

'I shouldn't... but I will... plum jam... yummy.'

'I wonder if he's a "Roundhead" or a "Cavalier".'

'Howard? A "Roundhead" I hope.'

'The Arse Hole's a "Cavalier".'

'Another reason to get rid of him. Germs love foreskins. Lift up a brick in a garden and watch what scurries out. Men! I sometimes think women who fall for men are like lion tamers. They know lions are dangerous... they just can't resist the challenge of trying to tame them.'

'The Arse Hole's latest is his yoga teacher. I've told him…
"Darling, let's cut a deal. You make a will leaving all your
worldly goods to me and you can have as much skirt as you
want. No questions asked. No more lying about having to
stay late for work… no more saying you have to fly to Belfast.
I know you are clever, darling, but how you can spend a
week in Belfast in January and come back with a Barbados
tan, is beyond me." When I look him in the eye and tell him,
"I'm going to kill you," he thinks I'm joking. Worse… my
threats turn him on… he smacks my bum… throws me on
the marital bed and before making love to me… stands on
his head… the cheeky bugger… reminding me of what his
yoga teacher has taught him. The spells I have put on him to
diminish his libido aren't working the way they used to do.'

'We both know spells are like antibiotics, overuse them
and they lose their power. I tried to make Howard pick his
nose when he was playing 'When a knight won his spurs'
in assembly… didn't work.'

'Another piece of evidence that he's a wizard?'

'Yes… if he's a big shot wizard he'll have a defence
system that makes him immune to the spells of second
division witches.'

'Spells!' cackled Mary.

'Spells!' I cackled.

Our high spirits started a storm. Rain drummed on
the room's bay window. The logs burning on the open
fire hissed and spat; smoky genies with evil grins on their
faces, danced around the room like whirling dervishes.

'Oh dear,' said Mary, 'if the love of my life really is
playing golf and not in bed with his yoga teacher, he'll get
wet… Cackle! Cackle!'

'Drowned,' I said. 'Cackle! Cackle!'

'What a shame…'

'Such a pity…'

To stop the storm our supernatural high spirits had let rip we held our breath. At once the rain stopped. The smoky genies, with evil grins on their faces, flew back up the chimney. The logs burning in the hearth stopped spitting. Instead of smelling like bonfire night, Mary's lounge, once again, smelt of furniture polish.

It was while we were discussing whether or not Whitby would have noticed our lack of discipline in letting our high spirits create a storm out of nowhere that Mary's husband… the Arse Hole… the If… the Tom Cat… the Bidet… he with more pejoratives than an octopus has legs drove into the house's horseshoe drive. He drove in so fast that when he stopped the car's wheels spat gravel at a rhododendron.

'He's early,' said Mary. 'I think he really has been playing golf… sex with his yoga teacher always lasts longer than a round of golf… and he's in a bad mood. I know him the way I know my broomstick. If he'd driven any faster into the drive he'd have put his Mercedes through the bay window.'

'Do you want me to leave?'

'Definitely not. I want you to stay. We'll wind him up… make his fly burst open without him having an erection.'

Before we meet Dick… aren't I nice giving him his day name? I will describe him as he would describe himself: I am tall, slim and extremely good looking. It's not my fault if women throw themselves at my feet. I'm a bloody good businessman. I know how to cut a deal. I don't believe in paying tax. I don't like gays or lesbians. People who use food banks are vermin.

'Dick,' I said, as he came into the lounge as if he was Hitler invading Russia in 1941, 'how lovely to see you.'

'Shut up!'

'That's not nice… telling your wife's best friend to "shut up".'

'You are not my "best friend".'

'Mary, do tell your darling husband to be nice to me.'

'Dick, be "nice" to Muriel.'

'Piss off!'

'Dick,' I said, 'you look like Walt Disney when you are angry… doesn't he, Mary?'

'I'm not stupid, you know… I know your game.'

'Of course you're not stupid, darling,' said Mary, 'you are one of the cleverest men I know.'

'Mary, get me a cup of tea.'

'With or without arsenic?' I said.

'What was that?'

'I said, "Shout if you feel sick".'

'What you on about, woman? I do not feel sick… I am hopping mad.'

Mary walked out of the lounge backwards… bowing.

'Dick,' I said, 'do you dye your hair? A man of your age should have at least one grey hair.'

'I know your game… you won't provoke me.'

'Why are you standing on one leg?'

'Yoga… You can't provoke me when I'm in nirvana.'

'I thought you were impersonating a stork.'

He changed legs.

'Wow!' I exclaimed. 'You can do it on either leg.'

'Out of my way…'

From an armchair he snatched a cushion. After placing the cushion on the floor… the way the referee in a snooker match replaces the black… he did a headstand on it. Very impressive.

When Mary brought him his cup of tea she placed it on the floor, which is how you serve a man tea when he is doing a headstand.

'There you are, darling,' she said, 'don't choke. Excuse me, that's the doorbell.'

A minute later, Mary brought a policeman into the lounge; a very tall policeman.

'Dick,' she said, talking to her husband's feet which were at her eye level because he was standing on his head, 'a policeman wants to talk to you.'

'What's he doing?' said the policeman.

'Meditating,' said Mary.

'Sir,' said the policeman bending his head upside down as you do when you are you talking to someone who is upside down, 'may I have a word?'

'He can't hear you,' said Mary, 'he's in another world. He's in nirvana. His mind has left his body.'

'He's on the planet Jupiter, constable,' I chipped in.

'I'm a sergeant, madam, not a constable,' drawing my attention to the three stripes on his arm.'

'Oops! Sorry.'

'And so you should be,' he said, then, looking at Dick, standing on his head, stiff as a poker, 'I've had meditators before…'

'Would that be for breakfast or lunch?'

'You the house joker?'

'Muriel is my best friend,' said Mary.

'When I said I've had "meditators"... what I meant was, I've had experience of dealing with... "meditators". As a young constable down in... Sum-er-set, I've cleared out many a hippy colony. I don't know if you know this, madam, but hippies are well known in police circles for taking drugs afore they board a jet plane to nirvana... he's not on drugs, is he?'

'Definitely not,' said Mary.

'Down in Sum-er-set...' began the sergeant.

'What a good mimic you are, sergeant,' I said.

'Down in Sum-er-set... bees buzz... my, oh my how they does buzz.'

'Encore!' said Mary.

'Down in Sum-er-set... bees buzz... my, oh my how they does buzz.'

'You have a gift, sergeant,' I said, 'for miming accents.'

'If flattery's a bribe, madam, then I'm guilty of taking bribes. I likes flattery the way villains like robbing banks... anyway, as I was saying, afore your flattery shaved my truncheon to a sliver... as a young constable down in Sum-er-set,' holding up a hand as if he was stopping traffic to let Mary and I know there'd be no more encores, 'I've cleared out many a hippy colony. The head-standers were the easiest to deal with. Be so good as to hold my helmet, madam,' handing Mary his policeman's helmet. 'Thank you, madam. You take them by the ankles, lift and like a bailiff evict them from nirvana by banging their heads on the ground the way my granny used a poss-stick.'

To show he meant business, the sergeant, who as I have already mentioned, was very tall, went through a series of pre-lift exercises worthy of a weightlifter going for gold at an Olympic Games. He squatted. He stood on tiptoe and touched the ceiling. He thumped his chest.

Dick, who was as far away from nirvana as New York is from London, and who had heard every word the sergeant had said, opened an eye.

To prevent his body being used as a poss-stick but at the same time to quit nirvana with dignity, he lowered himself to the floor with the grace of a ballet dancer playing a dying swan. He rose to his feet the way a movie, played backwards, resurrects a demolished mill chimney.

Dick was tall; the policeman was taller. Dick wasn't used to eyeballing Adam's apples.

'Mary,' he said, 'give the constable his helmet… he is leaving.'

'He's not a constable… he's a sergeant.'

'What's the difference? He's a pleb. Do you know who I am, Mr Plod?'

'I know your name, sir.'

'But do you know I know your chief constable?'

'Not, sir, I suspect, as well as I do.'

'Is he worse than the hippies you had to deal with in Sum-er-set?' I said.

'The hippies used to give me flowers. My impersonations of the Sum-er-set accent made them laugh. I've been told I do a very good Elvis.'

'Dick likes Elvis,' said Mary.

'Before you arrest him,' I said, 'do an Elvis impersonation… please.'

'Pearls before swine, Madam... that's my opinion. Now, sir... I will be leaving but not before I've asked you a few questions.'

Being interrogated by a police sergeant didn't bother Dick. He played golf with the chief constable. If this twerp overstepped the mark, he'd have those stripes off his arm faster than sperm leaves a teenager's penis.

'You were, sir, I believe, a witness to an incident on a golf course this morning... is that correct, sir?'

'I play golf with your chief constable,' said Dick.

'Jeff?'

'He's called Arnold... are you so far down the chain of command you don't know the name of your own chief constable?'

'He's called, sir... Arnold Jefferies. Those of us who have known him since he was a constable, calls him "Jeff". You might play golf with him, sir, but you are not as familiar with his funny little ways as what I am.'

'"Funny little ways"... I'll have you know, sergeant, that on the fourth tee, I have shared my hip flask with your chief constable.'

'I have knocked down doors with him, sir. I have saved his life... now, sir, will you answer my question?'

'I'm saying nothing about the incident to which I think you are referring. When the incident to which I think you are referring took place, I was looking for my ball in the long grass... furthermore, I know my rights. I'm saying nothing until I've seen my solicitor.'

'I see, sir...'

'I hope you do...'

'That finger, sir, you are wagging at me… the finger, I'm suspecting, you are close to using on an officer of the law the way in the old days me mother used a poker on a coal fire… if the "wag" becomes a "poke", sir, you'll have assaulted an officer of the law. I'll have to arrest you.'

'Would you like a cup of tea, sergeant?' said Mary.

'No, he wouldn't,' said Dick. 'Goodbye, sergeant, my wife will show you to the door.'

'Before I go, sir, one last question… do you play tiddlywinks?'

'Tiddlywinks?'

'Tiddlywinks!' bellowed the sergeant.

'No,' said Dick, muttering, 'stupid, fucking game.'

'I plays tiddlywinks, sir, with Jeff … him you calls "Arnold". And let me tell you something else, little man, when you've played tiddlywinks on the same team with someone, as me and Jeff has, you become comrades in arms. So, sir, don't you go trying to wriggle out of your civic responsibilities concerning this here incident by telling me you play golf with my boss… hinting you have the power to take away my stripes and have me locked up in one of my own cells. You will have heard the expression, sir… blood is thicker than water… yes or no?'

'Yes,' said Dick.

'In the meaning of that old adage, sir, "blood" is tiddlywinks… you take my meaning, sir? You get my drift? I will see myself out.'

Only when we had heard the front door shut and Mary had checked to make sure the sergeant really had gone did Mary ask Dick: 'What was all that about?'

'It was a mass trespass,' said Dick, 'hundreds of the little bastards.'

'Rabbits?' I asked.

'Kids… brats…'

'Onto the golf course?' said Mary.

'Of course onto the bloody golf course… where'd you think? The bloody Houses of Parliament?'

'How awful for you,' I said.

'Piss off!'

'Dick,' said Mary, 'Muriel was sympathising.'

'No, she wasn't… she was taking the piss. The young idiots were shouting my name… mad, bloody kids of all ages.'

'You knew them?'

'Of course I didn't bloody know them. You and Muriel might… they were the sort of hooligans you teach… bloody schoolteachers… no bloody discipline in schools these days. If I had my way, I'd bring back the birch.'

'But, the children…'

'Hooligans…'

'They knew your name?'

'Yes… they were chanting "Dick the Prick"… they were chanting like football spectators.'

'And golf is not like football, is it, Dick?' I said.

'No, it is not. Golfers are not hooligans… and I know who put them up to it… little bastards. You know what one of them did? He moved Ambrose's ball. You don't mess with Ambrose. He's the club's captain. You know who I mean, Muriel.'

I did indeed. I'd met him socially at one of Mary and Dick's dinner parties. He'd tried to put his hand up my skirt.

'Lovely man,' I said.

'You hate him.'

'Dick,' said Mary, 'your saying that Muriel means the opposite of what she is saying is becoming a trait.'

'Ambrose fancies you, Muriel… for the life of me, I can't think why.'

'He likes my womanly bumps,' I said.

'Your tits… how'd you know that?'

'I can read his mind.'

'Huh! If you could read mine, you'd be terrified. I need a drink.'

'It's on the floor,' said Mary, 'where I left it when you were standing on your head.'

'I meant a proper drink… Ambrose smacked one of the brats with his driver.'

'You saw him do that?'

'Of course I bloody saw him do it. If I'd had a machete I'd have chopped the bugger's head off.'

'That was the "incident" the nice police sergeant came to ask you about?' I said.

'You lied to the policeman?' said Mary.

'My god, woman… grow up. Of course I bloody lied to the copper. Ambrose is the club captain. He has a swimming pool… did you know that, Muriel? Skinny dipping… you and him, Muriel, could have a lot of fun.'

'What's that got to do with committing perjury?' I said.

'Do I have to spell it out? The captain of my golf club can't be taken to court on a charge of GBH. Golfers stick together.'

'If he's done wrong,' said Mary, 'he should be punished.'

'I'm sure it's annoying having your game interrupted,' I said, 'but it seems to me, Ambrose overreacted.'

'Like that duke,' said Mary, 'who put his butler in the stocks for making his bathwater half a degree too hot.'

'You know, Dick,' I said, 'Mary and I could blackmail you. Unless you promise to make a will in which you leave all your worldly goods to your loving wife Mary, I'll tell the nice police sergeant you lied about not seeing... "Ambrosia"... hit the delinquent.'

'Ambrose, if you don't mind... he's not a rice pudding.'

'Perverting the course of justice, Dick, is a serious offence. You could get ten years. Ten years behind bars. Porridge every day. No avocados.'

'Piss off. I'll get my own stiffener... the room service around here is crap. Witches... both of you... bloody witches.'

After he'd driven off to put the world to rights with Ambrose, Mary and I discussed whether or not he knew we really were witches.

'He was letting off steam,' said Mary. 'It was a term of abuse, not of revelation.'

'I wonder how "stiff" he made his "stiffener",' I said.

'You think he might be driving over the limit?'

'Yes... shall we tip of the police?'

'No, I don't want him behind bars until he's made a will leaving everything to me.'

# MARY EGGS ME ON

**H**oward was a jigsaw with lots of missing pieces. Was the gossip Mary had passed on to me about him being on a mission to right a terrible wrong, true or false? Was he FBI? Mary and I were eighty per cent certain he was the wizard Whitby had warned us about; to be one hundred per cent certain we needed more proof.

I found myself, willy-nilly, thinking about him all the time. On the coffee mug I used at school I had a picture of a black cat chasing its tail. On her coffee mug, Mary had pictures of dollars and pounds. On his coffee mug – we all had to bring in our own mugs – Howard had, in large print: LOVE THE AURORA BOREALIS… evidence that he was who we thought he was… perhaps.

It was a Sunday, a few weeks before Christmas that another piece of the jigsaw fell into place; not any old piece but a piece which suggested that there were more pieces missing from the Howard Star jigsaw than I had thought. It happened like this.

I was hand feeding Tilly a pilchard when the phone rang. It was Mary.

'Muriel!' she exclaimed.

'You sound as if you've got your hands on the "Tom Cat's" money,' I said. 'Have you?'

'No... nothing like that.'

'Oh, what then?'

'Howard's out jogging. When he passed my front gate I was in my front garden decapitating a frosted rose bud. When I snipped it off I imagined I was decapitating the Arse Hole. My sympathetic magic worked. Before the two-timing bastard went out to play golf or wherever it was he was really going he had to take an aspirin. Ha! Ha! Howard didn't want to stop... but I made him. I know his route, Muriel. He is going down the wagon way.'

'Why are you telling me this?'

'Come off it... the wagon way is near you... go after him on your bicycle. Pretend to bump into him.'

'Why should I want to do that?'

'Come off it...'

'Is tonight still on?'

That evening, Mary and the Arse Hole were hosting a dinner. To keep her company, Mary had invited my good self.

'Of course, why shouldn't it be? Be at my house, sharp seven. If you want to annoy the Arse Hole, arrive late. You know how he has a thing about punctuality... make the bugger explode. He has a lot on his mind. He keeps telling me that selling scrap is not as easy as teaching. He keeps telling me I have a cushy number. He is an entrepreneur. I am a parasite. He gives the state a blood transfusion; I am sucking it dry. His staff want to join a union. He hates unions. Muriel, he has given these people jobs. He has put money in their pockets. He pays their wages. What more do they want?'

'They want the same as you, Mary, they want his money.'

'I'm entitled… I'm his wife. For a witch, Muriel, you are too left wing. If he gives in to these vultures I'll have nothing to inherit. It will be pointless him making a will. He will have nothing to leave me…'

'Who is coming tonight?'

'Roger and Heather, you've met them before.'

'Roger… the man who bought his wife a chainsaw for her birthday?'

'Heather wanted a bulldozer.'

'Scrapman, isn't he?'

'He recycles metal. Muriel… they are rich. He and Ambrose and Dick do deals together.'

'Ambrose… the rice pudding… is he coming tonight?'

'You don't mind, do you?'

'Just so long as he doesn't try to put his hand up my skirt.'

'It's his job.'

'Groping women?'

'He's an entrepreneur. You know as well as I do that he owns a factory making ladies' underwear. He's used to touching models. He can tell your cup size without using a tape measure. I know you don't like him but, never forget, Ambrose has money. Dick and I have swum in his swimming pool. He is standing for parliament.'

'Labour?'

'You must be off your trolley. He hates socialists. Muriel, if you are serious about getting your claws into

Howard you must be proactive. You must go after him down the wagon way like a heat seeking missile. You didn't become rich by sitting on your bum. You are rich because you facilitated the early demise of your first two husbands. I will be rich when I get my hands on Dick's money. Muriel, on your bike... off you go down the wagon way. What a surprise he'll get when you bump into him by accident... Ha! Ha! Before you go... one more thing. When you come tonight... bring me the packet of frozen sprouts you are keeping for me in your freezer. As you know, the Arse Hole – I must stop calling him that... he is my husband – Dick has a thing about eating veg which has been frozen. His yoga teacher has told him frozen veg is full of germs. It's amazing what someone with a big chest and a narrow waist can make you believe. At the moment I don't want to upset him. I am keeping him sweet.'

'The way a farmer fattens a pig for market?'

'Something like that... give the sprouts to Una.'

'Thomas's mother... she will be there?'

'As a waitress... she needs the money.'

'You don't suspect...?'

'Yes, I do. I don't care. She can have his body but not his money. Muriel, I have told you what to do. I always give you good advice... you know that.'

'You can lead a horse to water...'

'But you can't make it drink... I know. It's up to you... byee.'

# A WITCH SPIES
# ON A WIZARD

**W**hen a witch spies on a wizard expect glaciers to melt. My protestations about not cycling down the Wagon Way in pursuit of Howard had been phoney. No sooner had I put down the phone than I was off.

I cycled down the Wagon Way like a pirate ship flying the Red Ensign; only when I bumped into Howard – by pure chance – Ha! Ha! – would I fly the skull and cross bones; take out the grappling irons and board him.

I always think of the Wagon Way, not as a grotty, cindery disused railway line but as a magic carpet. After a few minutes of pedalling, you leave suburbia and are in the country. In a trice I was cycling, not past the back gardens of detached houses, but between bushes of yellow gorse, entanglements of bramble and ploughed fields, white with frost.

I was not wearing my cyclist's safety helmet. I had taken Mary's criticism to heart. If I did bump into Howard, I did not want to look like something from Mars. I wanted to look red cheeked and rosy, like an eating apple. My desire to look glamorous overrode my fear of falling off my bike and bumping my head.

When you fall in love you do silly things. If your lover likes football, a game in which you have hitherto shown no interest, you are suddenly passionate about Newcastle winning the Premier League.

My shoulder length black hair, streaming out behind me, was a battle pennant.

I passed the back of the Arse Hole's golf course. When was Mary going to facilitate him an early death? Putting arsenic in his cuppa wasn't hers or my way of doing things. We had no wish to end up in the clink. What was the point of inheriting a tidy sum if you couldn't spend it?

We weren't murderers, we were facilitators. We'd no wish to bring Whitby into disrepute. It was important, at least it was to me and Mary, that our coven had a good reputation.

No, to get rid of a husband and get your hands on his worldly goods, you needed luck; you needed to be patient. How many banana skins had I dropped in front of my first husband, Reg, before he took the hint? 'Are you trying to kill me?' he'd ask. 'What do you mean?' I'd say. 'You know I love you.' 'I've noticed you keep dropping banana skins in front of me… do you want me to do this?'

It was his decision to use a banana skin as a slide… not mine. A proper show off was Reg. His penis was not always Blackpool Tower but his ego was always a penthouse. When he fell he hit the back of his head… a fatal blow… a freak accident. I found his pin number on a piece of paper in his wallet. I kept repeating it… 6932… 6932. He had thousands in his current account.

To facilitate a man's death all you have to do is find out what he thinks he's good at. Albert, my second, was proud of his ability to fart on demand. One bowl of my pea soup and he'd give me the first movement of Mozart's Jupiter symphony. Mahler made him shit his pants.

One day we were out in the country. It was a hot day. We were kissing and cuddling... billing and cooing like mating pigeons under a bridge over the North Tyne. I knew what he wanted. 'We've never done it al fresco,' he said. 'I'll bet you've never jumped off a bridge farting Tchaikovsky's 1812,' I said. 'If I do, will you?'

The submerged rock he smacked into was a scalpel. I surmise this because whatever it was he hit underwater, chopped off his head. Looking over the parapet I saw red bubbles. How many times had he made bubbles in the bath? This time I was prepared. I had his pin number written down on a piece of paper in my purse. After the sudden demise of my first, I'd learnt to be prepared.

It was while I was pedalling and reminiscing as per the above that I spotted Howard. He was a long way off. I knew it was him, though. I am blessed with long range witch's vision. From ten yards I can spot a ladybird eating a greenfly. Howard was the greenfly, I was the ladybird.

Why had he stopped? What was he doing? He was looking round as if he was looking around... you know, the way people do when they are looking for a hidey hole in which to take a pee.

To avoid being seen I hid in a tangle of bracken and gorse. This wild vegetation grew on both sides of the Wagon Way the way hair grows on the sides of a bald man's head.

I watched him through a net curtain of bracken. Why was he laying – as if he was laying a wreath – a posy of yellow pansies onto a pile of grass... grass, spiky with frost? It was like watching someone laying a wreath at the Cenotaph.

He looked at the posy, head bowed, for at least five minutes. I know this to be true because I timed him. Five minutes, standing looking at a posy, in the freezing cold, is a long time.

Only when he'd disappeared round a bend... when he was out of sight... did I pedal to the site of his homage. As I came close to it, I began to shake and shiver. Yes, it was a freezing cold day... yes, I should have been wearing gloves... yes, my hands were red with the cold... yes, I should have been wearing a hat... yet, if I had done all of those sensible things... I kid you not... my reaction would have been the same.

My involuntary trembling was due to the fact that I was in the presence of a place of pilgrimage. I was in a holy place. Empathy made me weep. It was through a waterfall of tears that my gaze fell on, not one, but three posies. I was looking at a shrine. Think of the banks of flowers laid outside Kensington Palace in remembrance of Lady Diana.

The two posies of red roses had been there at least overnight; probably longer. I knew this because the silver foil wrapped round their stems was white with frost. But why had the freezing temperature not blighted them? They looked as fresh as if they were roses growing on bushes in June.

The posy of yellow pansies was identical to the one Howard had given Ma Mason. Its tin foil wrapping was frost free; this was the posy I'd watched him lay on the grass; watched him place down on the grass as if he'd been laying flowers on a grave.

Why was he laying flowers at an ad hoc shrine? By every black hair on Tilly's back and by the powdery moss on the twigs of my best besom, I'd find out.

The faster he jogged, the harder I pedalled. I soon caught up with him. To let him know the hounds of spring were barking at winter, as it were, I tinkled my bell. Wouldn't he be surprised when he turned round and saw it was me? Would he be pleased, angry or, worst of all, apathetic?

Ting-a-ling! Ting-a-ling!

Why do men never do what they are supposed to do? Instead of turning round to see who was ringing, he waved me on without looking back.

Ting-a-ling! Ting-a-ling!

Turn around, you idiot, I thought, if you don't I'll make you trip. I was not consciously putting a spell on him to make him trip. Top draw, wizards, as I have already mentioned, are immune to spells cast on them by witches low down in the Premier League. Even to this day, I am not one hundred per cent certain if my 'wish' made the pothole that made him trip or whether he'd have tripped in any case.

I jammed on my brakes. Looking down at him over my bicycle's handlebars, I said, 'Howard, it's me, Muriel. Are you alright? Can you get up?'

'I've broken every bone in my body.'

'Don't be silly.'

'Don't talk to me about being silly. Why didn't you cycle past me?'

'Are you not pleased to see me?'

'Under these circumstances… no.'

When he was on his feet and his eyes were throwing daggers at me, I removed a sliver of frozen mud off his shoulder. I removed it the way proprietorial wives straighten their husband's ties.

'Don't.'

'Sorry.'

'Anyway, what are you doing here?'

'Me?'

'No one else here, is there?'

'I have as much right to use the wagon way as you.'

'Muriel, I came out for a jog, not an argument. Fortunately,' touching his toes and tickling the sky, 'I seem to be all in one piece, no broken bones. On the other hand…' looking me in the eye, 'your coming on me out of the blue while I'm trying to keep fit has put me, as you Brits say, "all to pot".'

'Like the pothole that made you trip?'

I laughed at my double entendre.

'Don't laugh at your own jokes.'

'Sorry.'

'Off you go. You go first. I want you where I can see you.'

'No more surprises?'

'No more surprises.'

'Would it help if I said sorry and baked you a Christmas cake?'

'You accept liability?'

'Howard, it was an accident.'

'When you are in a hole you stop digging.'

'When you said that… you sounded like a primary school teacher. Howard, I am not one of your pupils.'

'What you did was childish.'

'It was an accident.'

Before pedalling off I blew him a kiss. When he caught it I knew we were still friends.

# HOWARD TO THE RESCUE

I pedalled off, feeling like a dirigible with a puncture. I had messed up, big time. If I told Mary what I'd done she'd give me a ticking off. Falling in love did not mean causing your Romeo to fall flat on his face and break every bone in his body.

To take the edge off my blunder, I pedalled fast. I pedalled until my legs ached. I pedalled until I was gasping for breath.

I was round a bend and out of sight of Howard when I saw the three teenagers. They were spread out across the Wagon Way like a road block. If they didn't move I couldn't get past. They were as intimidating as gunfighters walking down a street in a cowboy movie. What took the edge off my fear, that I might be about to be mugged or raped, was that I knew them.

'Hello, boys,' I said.

They were all ex-pupils. When they'd been at the Jubilee, I'd wiped their noses. The biggest and tallest of the trio was Stanley Mason, Ma Mason's grandson.

Over the years I have taught many children. You remembered some because they were gifted; some because they made you laugh; some because they were kind. I remembered Stanley because he was evil.

'We're not "boys",' said Stanley. 'You're living in the past, you are, Mrs Thayne.'

'We're not in your class now, Mrs Thayne,' said David.

David was Stanley's buddy. If Stanley ordered David to eat a dog's turd, David would do it.

'Yeah,' said Michael, 'yuh can't tell us what to do.'

Michael was Joe's older brother. In junior school his behaviour had left much to be desired. He had a temper. In senior school I'd heard that he'd been the cause of a teacher taking early retirement.

'Michael, three times six?'

'Piss off,' said Stanley.

'Yeah,' said Michael, 'piss off.'

'I don't think your mam would like you talking to me like that,' I said. 'I know she wouldn't.'

'Are you going to tell her?'

'Yes, I will, when I see her.'

'Am shitt'n me pants.'

'You scared of us, Mrs Thayne?' said Stanley. 'What would you do if I let your tyres down? Stop our playtime? Give us lines? Tell us, "Write out a hundred times… I must not let the tyres doon on the teacher's bike".'

'I'd report you to the police.'

'The "pigs" divent scare us,' said David.

'Let me pass.'

'Say "please",' said Stanley.

'Let me pass… please. It's cold… what are you all doing on the wagon way?'

'Same as you… out for a cycle ride,' said David.

'Where are your bicycles?'

'Questions, questions,' said Stanley, smirking.

'Let her pass, Stan,' said Michael.

'You telling me what to do, Mickey?'

'We all liked Mrs Thayne,' pleaded Michael. 'Let her go. I liked bein' in her class.'

'Mickey's teacher's pet,' said David.

'You fancy her, Mickey? Shagging a witch is dangerous,' said Stanley, then, looking me in the eye, 'that was what we called you behind your back, at school... the witch.'

I knew of course that they did not know I really was a witch. They were using the name as a term of abuse, not in its literal sense.

'Stanley,' I said, 'has it ever crossed your mind that if I really was a witch I might turn you into a frog?'

'Piss off.'

'Let me pass.'

'Pack it in, Stan,' said Michael.

'Because she knows your mam and you want to shag her?'

'We don't want trouble, Stan... trouble's bad for business.'

'Mrs Witch isn't trouble... you're not trouble, are you, Mrs Witch? I think it would teach you a lesson if you had to walk home. Off your bike. You can pass as a pedestrian. Riding bikes down the wagon way is against the law.'

'And whose law would that be?'

'My law... Mason's law.'

'Take your hands off my bike.'

'And if I don't... what you going to do about it?'

'Stan, leave her alone,' said Michael.

'Shut it, lover boy.'

That I did not have to resort to witchcraft to teach Stanley a lesson was due to Howard. He wasn't jogging to help me… he was sprinting.

'Hands off Mrs Thayne's bike,' he told Stanley.

'What if I don't?' said Stanley.

Howard did not parley. To show he was more than a match for the three of them he did a backward somersault. While they were still looking gobsmacked at what he'd done, he cartwheeled towards them like a wheel fizzing with sticks of lit dynamite tied to its spokes. Aided by the momentum of his cartwheeling he spun Stanley around the way you do to confuse the person wearing the blindfold when you are playing 'Blind Man's Bluff'.

After doing a backward somersault away from Stanley, he held up Stanley's wallet, watch and trouser belt.

Stanley was confused, bewitched and bewildered; for the life of him he couldn't understand how this jogger bloke had his wristwatch, wallet and… bloody hell, his trouser belt.

'How'd you do that?' said Michael.

'You a magician?' said David.

Howard threw the wallet into a holly bush; the watch into the frosted grass; the belt into a gorse bush.

'Now,' he said, 'if you scumbags don't mind, Mrs Thayne and I will be on our way. After you, Muriel.'

# I DO NOT DO AS
# I AM TOLD

**T**his time Howard and I did not go our separate ways. We proceeded down the Wagon Way in tandem. I cycled, he jogged. Our confrontation with Stanley, Michael and David had made us an item. For many seconds we did not speak. I was in awe of him. He had come to my rescue. He was my knight in shining armour. I owed him. I was in his debt.

What was he thinking? I knew what I was thinking. I wanted to know why he'd left a posy of pansies on the Wagon Way… had he been laying a wreath; if so, to whom?

When the Wagon Way crossed a road, he told me, in no uncertain terms – very bossy, he sounded – 'I'm going this way, and you, Mrs Thayne, are going that way.'

'Am I?'

'Yes, you are.'

'Parting is such sweet sorrow,' I said. 'Howard, thank you for coming to my rescue. If you hadn't, I'd have had to deal with those teenagers all by myself.'

'Muriel, with respect I do not think you know how dangerous they are…'

'Howard, I know them… I know their mothers.'

'With respect, Muriel, you are naïve.'

'Silly me,' I said, 'and I thought I was sophisticated.'

'Muriel–' laying a hand on my shoulder and looking me in the eye– 'I want you to promise me something.'

The touch of his hand on my shoulder drove a coach and horses through my reserve. Without thinking, I blurted out: 'Are you the Black Knight? You are, aren't you?'

He took a while to answer. His hesitation told me all that I needed to know.

'All I will say at the moment, Mrs Thayne... Muriel, is that there are some things it is best you know nothing about.'

'You do not wish to take me into your confidence?'

'I do not wish you to be involved in goings-on which might, if my suspicions are correct, give you nightmares. You will be in less danger if you do not know my suspicions.'

'Howard, I think it is your good self who is in danger. You humiliated Stanley in front of his friends. I know him. He is vindictive. He will be out for revenge. Howard, why have you come to work at our grotty primary school?'

Instead of answering my question he said: 'Straight home, Mrs Thayne... any way you like so long as it is not back along the Wagon Way.'

'Yes, Mr Star,' I said.

'Good afternoon, Mrs Thayne.'

After pedalling a few yards down the road, I stopped and turned to see if he was watching me. He wasn't. He was going back along the Wagon Way. Why? If he bumped into Stanley, Michael and David, they might beat him up. What were my ex-pupils doing on the Wagon Way? On a whim, I followed Howard back down the Wagon

Way. Reasons? Lots… one of which was I don't like blokes telling me what I can and cannot do.

The Wagon Way and its surrounding fields had been my childhood playground. I knew it as well as I knew the veins on the backs of my hands. It was here that my mother had showed me how to put an adder's fangs into a pad of moss and milk its venom.

At dusk the Wagon Way was turning into a black tunnel. My un-gloved hands were blue with cold. An icy breeze sandpapered my face; strands of my hair blew into my mouth. The setting sun was a big red ball.

After a few minutes of pedalling I came to the spot where I'd bumped into Stanley, Michael and David. Ahead of me, the Wagon Way stretched, flat and empty.

As I mentioned earlier the Wagon Way had been my childhood playground. A track leading off it looked to have been recently used. There were footprints in its frozen mud. Whose footprints? Stanley's? Michael's? David's? Howard's? The track led to a World War Two pillbox. The relic had attracted me when I was young. If there was no one ahead of me, was that because they were up to no good at the pillbox? As I have mentioned, more than once, I am not nosy. I do not look through keyholes, but I am insatiably curious.

A little further on a culvert took the wagon way over the top of a dene. The dene had steep sides and was heavily wooded. To reach the pillbox, unseen, all I had to do was scramble down to the bottom of the dene, jump across its stream, then scramble up its other side.

To stop myself falling on my way down I clung to branches the way passengers on the Metro cling to hand straps. On my way up, I used the exposed roots of trees as footholds.

Close to the top, I heard panting. My commando crawl to the top of the dene had given me a grand circle seat to watch the Arse Hole and Una who, as she'd hinted to me in Ma Mason's, liked a bit on the side – as if sexual intercourse was a salad for which you paid extra if you wanted it – going hard at it.

They were going hard at it on a sheepskin mat, half in and half out of the pill box. Did they not feel the cold? I was bloody freezing.

I knew it was the Arse Hole because of the tattoo I could see of Margaret Thatcher on his bum. He was pumping sperm into Una the way a Victorian overhead beam engine, in the days when coal was king, pumped water out of a coal mine. Up and down! Up and down! His plunging gave Mrs Thatcher wrinkles... made her look wizened... then, ironed her out and made her look young.

What a lot I'd have to tell Mary I was thinking, when a hand being clamped over my nose and mouth made me fear for my life; made me come close to losing control of my bladder.

Before I'd time to struggle... in truth I was being gripped so hard I could not twitch a muscle... Howard whispered in my ear: 'When I take my hand away do not make a sound... nod if you understand.'

Of course I bloody nodded. What the hell was going on? Only a wizard could have crept up on me from behind without me suspecting.

He signalled I was to follow him down to the bottom of the dene. I did as I was told. This was not the time or place for an argument.

Climbing up and down the sides of the dene with him was fun. He helped me all the way down and hand winched me up all the way to the top of the other side.

On the Wagon Way... he sounded furious... he asked me: 'what the hell were you doing up there?'

'I might ask you the same question,' I told him. 'The man having sex was Dick, Mary's husband. The woman was Una... Thomas's mother. You know... Thomas in your class. He has a python called Percy.'

'I know who they are.'

'Oh, you do, do you?'

'Yes, I do.'

He paused.

'Have you heard of the "knockers"?' he said, at last.

'I've heard rumours.'

'Would it surprise you to know that your friend Mary's husband is involved with them?'

'Yes, it would.'

'Mary's husband is a fence. He sells on what Stanley and his thugs steal. The pillbox is one of their warehouses.'

'Stanley and Dick are partners in crime... I don't believe it.'

'They have had a falling out.'

'My god... the golf course invasion...'

'Just so, Muriel... just so.'

'How do you know all this? Why does it interest you? Are you an undercover detective? Are you FBI? Why have you come to work at the Jubilee primary school? Why, Howard, why?'

'Marilyn wants a pantomime. A pantomime needs music. Your music teacher is off poorly. I can play the piano. I am the music man.'

'I have heard a rumour you are here to right a "terrible wrong". Why did you place a posy of flowers on the Wagon Way?'

'You have been spying on me… dear me, and I thought no one was watching. I am becoming careless. Enjoy your dinner party tonight, Mrs Thayne… Muriel.'

'How'd you know about that?'

My question fell on deaf ears. He told me, 'Here's your bike… this time… straight home.'

His tone of voice was that of an exasperated teaching telling off a child.

# MARY AND THE ARSE HOLE'S DINNER PARTY

**M**ary has an insatiable appetite to be kept informed. Back home, she rang me before I'd time to ring her.

'Hi, Mary,' I said.

'How'd you know it was me?'

'I knew you'd be ringing to see if I'd met Howard.'

'Did you?'

'Yes.'

'And…?'

'I've seen the Arse Hole's Maggie Thatcher tattoo.'

'But it's on his bum… my god, he's not been exposing himself, has he?'

I told her everything. I held nothing back. Sisters do not have secrets; though, I did gloss over the mess I'd made of my encounter with Howard. I omitted telling her I'd caused him to fall.

At the end of my summation I suggested we use what Howard had told me to blackmail the Arse Hole.

'I warm to that,' said Mary. 'It's an egg I'll keep warm until such time as I think it will be ready to hatch; in the meantime, when you come tonight bring the frozen sprouts you are keeping for me in your freezer. The Arse Hole says his yoga teacher has told him eating frozen vegetables is bad for his posture. I'm not sure what she wants to keep vertical… his back or his penis. When he's tucking into his cooked frozen sprouts it will give me great pleasure to know I am putting one over on him. Revenge has to start somewhere. Give the sprouts to Una. Be nice to her. The silly cow doesn't know she is playing with fire. I will only turn her into a toad if I think she's after the Arse Hole's money.'

'She can have Dick's dick but not his wallet.'

'The Arse Hole must be made to pay for his infidelity… don't forget the sprouts.'


The fact that the roads were frosty did not stop me cycling to Mary and the Arse Hole's dinner party. Let me explain. The Arse Hole is a snob. Guests at his dinner parties did not arrive wearing bicycle clips and protective helmets that made them look like something out of Star Wars; his dinner parties were black tie and smart frocks. I would also arrive late. If he said black, I would say white. I was in that sort of mood.

I cycled into Mary's horseshoe drive fifteen minutes late. I was on schedule. The Rolls in the drive had to belong to Ambrose. Parked next to it was a yellow Ford Ranger pick-up truck. Both vehicles had number plates suggesting words of Anglo-Saxon origin.

Una answered the door looking bright eyed and bushy tailed. And I knew why. The curtsy she dropped me showed off her breasts. The Arse Hole knew how to dress a waitress.

She said: 'Mrs Thayne... Madam said, if it was you, you was to give me the greens... and when you gives them to me I'm to take them round the back to the kitchen. I'm not to go through the house with 'em in case Dick... I means, Mr Hedgerow... sees 'em. I means the greens. What's going on? I mean... greens aren't the crown jewels, are they?'

'Dick... Mr Hedgerow,' I explained, 'has a thing about eating frozen vegetables.'

'I don't blame him. You don't want your veg cold, like ice cream, do you? I like my veg hot.'

'They are in my pannier, Una.'

'Plenty of pans in the kitchen, Mrs Thayne.'

'The bag on my bicycle is called a "pannier".'

'That's a new word... "pannier". I'll try and remember that... "pannier". I wonder if my Thomas knows what it means. I shouldn't say this, Mrs Thayne, but, my Thomas thinks you are wonderful. It was through one of your nature lessons I learnt cockerels don't lay eggs... just the hens do the laying. I never knew that. Do you like my outfit? Dick says, it shows off my figure. It was his idea I should wear it. He said, if I was waiting on, I should look the part. He says if I do well tonight he'll take me off "stamp licking".'

'Your clerical job in his office?'

'I don't actually "lick" the stamps, Mrs Thayne... I can tell by the look on your face, that's what you are thinking. When I first started I did. It was when Dick saw how my tongue was blistering that he gave me a sponge. He's ever so kind and considerate. He told me it was his opinion I had the nicest tongue he'd ever seen. That was nice of him, wasn't it? When a man says nice things about me, I come to life like what a desert does when it rains. Dick said he could think of better things for my tongue to do than lick stamps. He's a funny one, is Dick. Tonight I'm waiting on and boiling the veg. Mrs Hedgerow, your pal Mary... is doing the meat. I'm getting paid fifty pence a knife and fork and a pound for every plate I serve. If I don't drop anything I'm getting a bonus. I have to call the gentlemen "sir" and the ladies "ma'am". And I don't have to mind if one of the gentlemen pinches me bum. If I do all of them things Dick says... I shouldn't call him that, should I? I should call him "sir"... anyway... whatever, he says he's going to give me something special... "panniers" you call them... get away... you learn something new every day... give's the sprouts. I'll hide them under me flimsy. Last time I looked like that I was six months pregnant. You know the way... I mean I can't be smuggling in "greens" in the back door and taking your coat and silly hat all at the same time, can I? I only have one pair of hands... not like Dick... dear me, I shouldn't have said that, should I? If Eddy... that's my husband... you know Eddy, don't you?'

'I met him at a parents' evening last year.'

'If Eddy had as many hands as Dick... oops, there I go again... as many hands as Dick, I'd never get a wink of sleep... and a girl needs her sleep, doesn't she, Mrs Thayne. I know I do.'

I prepared myself to meet Mary's guests by clamping over my front teeth a set of joke molars.

'Hi!' I said.

The more gobsmacked everyone looked, the more I grinned. I was proud of my joke dentures. They were fun.

'I am not a fan of women who try to be funny,' said Ambrose.

'Do come and join us,' said Mary.

'You should have been announced,' said Dick. 'Our little party may not be a soiree at Buck House but we... I have standards. I like things done by the book...'

'But not the one the taxman sees,' said Ambrose. 'Ha! Ha! Dick's right... you should have been announced by his maid... the one with the big tits.'

'Where is she?' said Dick.

'Una is parking my bicycle.'

'Parking your what?' said Ambrose. 'Who rides a fucking bicycle to a party? Where'd you get the jeans... Oxfam? What the hell are those bangles on your ankles?'

'They are bicycle clips,' explained Mary.

'Ambrose knows what they are,' said Dick. 'He was taking the piss... don't you know when someone's taking the piss? For Christ's sake... Ambrose, another glass of red?'

'Let me take your anorak,' said Mary.

'And her teeth,' said Dick.

'And the bicycle clips,' said Ambrose. 'I've watched women take off their knickers but never their bicycle clips... Ha! Ha! Get them off, Muriel... get them off. I'd like to see you take them off.'

'I'd like to see you in a mortuary.'

'As long as it's a private mortuary... making money for its shareholders. I'd hate to end up stretched out on a slab next to a tosser who uses a food bank. I don't know if you know this but this time next year, if I play my cards right, I'll be a knight of the realm. Knights of the realm do not end their days in communal mortuaries.'

'Ambrose,' I said, 'you are so right wing. If you were a bird you would fly in circles.'

Leering, he said: 'It's a mystery to me, Muriel, how a left winger like you can have such a beautiful body.'

'Flattery, Marcus, will get you a poke in the eye.'

'You know I fancy you… how much do you want?'

'Swivel on that,' I said, offering him a raised finger.

'I'm sick of left wingers,' said Dick, 'every fucker in my business wants a pay rise.'

'Tell them to sod off,' said Ambrose, 'that's what I'd do. If the divine Margaret was still PM they wouldn't know what had hit them. It's like when I look at Muriel… I don't know what's hit me. I know you fancy me, Muriel. I've seen you looking at me. Your ruse of dressing like a tramp doesn't fool me. Nota bene, you provoke me at your peril. I am a powerful man. Dick, give the left leaning colleen a drink… where's that bloody maid of yours?'

'A G and T would be perfect,' I said.

'Make it a double,' said Ambrose, 'we'll get her drunk. She likes big ones. I can read Muriel the way I read a balance sheet.'

My G and T was strong; sipping it I pulled a face; witches stick together – without being asked, Mary drowned it in tonic.

Dick and Ambrose now ignored me. They were on high doh about Stanley's invasion of their precious bloody golf course. They went into a corner and talked in whispers;

conspirators, I thought, like Guy Fawkes before he was hung, drawn and quartered.

I reminded myself, I was not there to enjoy myself. I was there to support Mary. If Ambrose tried to grope me as he had done once before, well, this time, I'd come prepared.

From the kitchen there came the smell of food; every so often, I heard Una, in the kitchen, shout: 'fuck'; was she reminding herself of what she'd been doing a few hours ago?

So far, I've not mentioned the other two guests... Roger and Heather. I've not mentioned them because, since my meeting them, they had ignored me. They'd ignored me because they were playing games on their mobile phones. Roger was in a tropical rainforest trying to stop a crocodile eating a gorilla. Heather was swerving a truck loaded with dynamite around potholes.

I'd met them before. They were rednecks.

Over dinner, Dick said, taking the last sprout: 'I hate waste... that's another reason I will never vote Labour. Hoy! This sprout is cold.'

'Oh dear,' said Mary. 'To keep them fresh I keep them in the fridge.'

'But not in the freezer, eh?'

'Of course not, darling. I know you have a thing about frozen veg. I would not wish to give you belly ache... would I?'

When he was tipsy Dick asked himself questions he hesitated to ask himself when he was sober. The look he now gave Mary when she claimed not wanting to be the cause of giving him a belly ache, said, if I had read it correctly... 'you fucking liar'.

Whatever his faults, Dick was a good host; at least as far as making sure everyone's glass was kept full.

'Another drink, Roger? Roger! For fuck sake let the fucking crocodile eat the fucking gorilla.'

'The cheapest isn't always the best,' said Roger, without looking up. To stop the crocodile eating the gorilla you had to concentrate.

'What the fuck has that got to do with my asking you if you want another drink? You in a mood? Heather not let you get your leg over last night?'

Without looking up from her mobile – if she didn't concentrate the lorry full of dynamite would hit a pothole and explode – Heather said: 'Roger's never forgotten the Russian bulldozer he bought because it was cheap… it's always on his mind.'

'Is that what you are thinking, Roger, when you are screwing… dodgy Russian bulldozers? Ha! Ha!' said Dick.

'It was shite,' said Roger, looking up from his mobile for the first time since I'd come into his company. 'Its bloody lights came on when you didn't want them on.'

'Sounds like some of the women I employ… all bloody commies… always wanting a pay rise,' said Dick. 'What do you say, Ambrose?'

'Tell them to fuck off,' said Ambrose. 'Bloody good glass of red this…'

'To turn its bloody lights off you had to turn them on and off three times,' said Roger. 'It was a commie machine. The commies are shite… shite. I didn't buy another one… that's what I'm saying, see? Cheapest isn't always the best.'

'What a wise fellow you are, Roger,' I said, 'you learn from your mistakes. You know, if you parted your hair down the middle, you'd look like Oscar Wilde.'

'Who's he?'

'He makes bulldozers.'

'Heather, you heard of Oscar Wilde bulldozers?'

'Oscar Wilde bulldozers...' said Heather, her attention, for the first time, wavering from driving a truck full of dynamite around potholes, 'never heard of them. How come, Muriel, you know something about bulldozers, I don't?'

'In the nineties,' I said, 'Oscar sold his bulldozer designs to the Russians. If the bulldozer you bought was rubbish... blame Oscar.'

'This Oscar Wilde... English, was he?'

'Irish.'

'Pull that,' said the Arse Hole, proffering Heather a finger for her to pull.

When she pulled it he broke wind. To make it easier for its gas to escape, he leaned over to one side like a tacking yacht.

'Better out than in...'

'I had a husband who could fart a tune,' I said.

'Sex makes me fart,' said Ambrose, squeezing the top of my leg under the table. 'I wonder if Muriel... Mu, will ever make me fart... I'd ask for a kiss but I don't think I'd get one.'

'More wine, Ambrose?' said Mary. 'Dick buys it direct from a grower in France.'

'Since Brexit,' said Dick, 'it comes here under a tarpaulin on the back of a lorry. Being illegal makes it taste better... that's what I think. Cheese, Ambrose? Danish Blue... make sure you slice it down the long side... I don't want to be left with all the white stuff.'

Ambrose was ambidextrous. While he was cutting himself a wedge of Danish Blue with his right hand, his left hand was exploring my thigh. I had come prepared for an invasion of my private parts. Ambrose had form. He was a serial offender.

All smiles, as if butter wouldn't melt in my mouth, I removed a primed mousetrap from my bag. I gave him a come-on smile. He smiled back. He thought he was a holidaymaker in an airport's duty free shop.

When, under the table, its spring snapped shut on his fingers, I'll give him this... he didn't scream... but, he winced... Oh boy, did he... wince.

'What's the matter?' said Dick. 'You passing a kidney stone? Ambrose, fart if you want to... better out than in... but, whatever you do, don't follow through. Una's here for washing dishes not for cleaning underpants... for god's sake... Ambrose, where you going?'

'A piss... I need a piss.'

'Prostate trouble,' said Dick, 'everyone has it except me. I'm a trained athlete. One round of golf is the same as a ten-mile walk... what's wrong, old buddy? Never seen anyone go for a slash with a hand stuck up an armpit... hopping, cross legged to the loo... seen that before ...done it myself. Roger, what do you think? Roger, for fuck sake put your bloody phone down... I am beginning to find you irritating.'

A door slammed.

'Una!' shouted Dick.

'Do you want me to serve the coffee now, sir?'

'Who is slamming doors?'

'It's Mr Ambrosia, sir, he's buggered off home... oops! What I mean, sir, is...'

'I know what you mean... why has he buggered off?'

'He's hurt his hand, sir. When he showed me his hand, Dick... sir... it was trapped in a mousetrap.'

'Excuse me,' I said, 'I need the loo.'

It was time to abandon ship.

At the back door, while clipping on my bicycle clips, I explained to Mary what I'd done.

'He was groping me,' I explained. 'He thought he was Caesar and I was Gaul.'

Witches stick together. To slow Dick down if he came after me with a carving knife, Mary placed a bucket of water behind the kitchen door.

Someone – it had to be Ambrose – had let my tyres down. The bastard... I don't like men who can't take a joke.

I knew it was time to scarper when I heard Dick fall over the bucket of water.

Pushing a bike with two flat tyres, two miles on a freezing cold night is not my idea of fun. I'd done about a mile when a lorry passed me... slowed... reversed back.

'It's me,' said Una, sticking her head out of its cab. 'I told you it was Mrs Thayne, Eddy... you remember Mrs Thayne, Eddy... she was Thomas's teacher... have you had a puncture? Eddy always comes to pick me up when I've been a skivvy in a skirt... don't you, Eddy. It's in case I'm attacked by a sex maniac... Eddy protects me like one of those tubes I've seen round trees in the park... you know… to stop rabbits nibbling them… Eddy, put Mrs Thayne's bike in the back. Hop in, Mrs Thayne.'

The cab was warm and cosy.

'I know I'm telling tales, Mrs Thayne, but, Mr Ambrose… he called you a cow. I didn't think a gentleman like him would say things like that.'

'He's not a gentleman, Una… he's a groper.'

'Is that why you put his hand in a mousetrap?'

'It was to teach him a lesson.'

'He thought his fingers was broken… you don't like him, Mr Ambrose, do you?'

'I detest him.'

'Do you like Dick, Mr Hedgerow? I think you like Mrs Dick but I don't think you like Dick. When I was serving the sprouts I seen you looking at him… you don't like him, do you?'

'Not a lot.'

'Why don't you put a spell on him?'

'I'm not a witch.'

'Some people say you are.'

'Idle gossip.'

'Some people say Mrs Hedgerow is one as well. She's your best friend, isn't she? That's what Ma Mason says.'

'Ma's a gossip. Eddy, drop me here. Thank you for the lift. If you were in my class I'd give you a "smiley face".'

'Eddy, don't just sit there, get Mrs Thayne's bike for her.'

# AMBROSE AND STANLEY CROSS A RED LINE

**M**y front door was open... not wide open but ajar. Had I been burgled?

For a good few seconds I did not move... shock made me drop my bike onto the drive's cobbles. I looked at the open door the way my witch ancestors must have looked at jurors at witch trials... acquittal or burning at the stake?

I began twitching, three short twitches, three long twitches, three short twitches. SOS. The twitches were involuntary. If I'd been an American cop I'd have drawn my gun. Panic... alarm made me struggle to remember a self-protection spell. Looking at the moon... begging... pleading for lunar help, I intoned a spell powerful enough to protect me from a bullet fired from a handgun but not from being blown up by an atom bomb, which is what happened to me next.

On my doorstep there was a black boa. Who would chop off a cat's tail? I found the rest of my beloved Tilly in the porch... decapitated and spatchcocked. On one of her paws there was a mousetrap. I was certain it was the mousetrap I had snapped on Ambrose's groping hand. On one of the porch's white floor tiles someone had drawn a pentacle… the sign of the devil… in blood… Tilly's blood.

My heart was racing. I found it difficult to think. I found it difficult to breathe. The relationship between a witch and her cat is as sacred as that between a man and a woman married in church: 'Who God hath joined together, let not man put asunder.' My relationship with Tilly had been as sacred as that.

I have a seat in my porch and it was on that that I now sat. My legs were wobbly. If I hadn't sat down I might have fallen down. I deep breathed. I began to work out a sequence of events to explain what might have happened.

Through Howard, I knew that Stanley and the Arse Hole were business partners. But, did Ambrose know Stanley? Was Ambrose also doing business with the Knockers?

I surmised that, when Ambrose had stormed out of the dinner party, hell bent on revenge, he'd phoned Stanley.

Stanley had form. Many years ago he'd put a decapitated cat in the holdall I used to carry books home for marking. He'd denied it, but I knew it was him. And so did his gran. To stop me blabbing she'd bribed me with a meat and potato pie.

Ambrose was an incurable womaniser, not a sadist. He was quite capable of slapping a woman but not of dismembering a cat; there had to be some kind of working relationship between Dick, Stanley and him.

They had crossed a red line. By every twig in my best besom I would revenge Tilly's murder.

Before I rang Mary to tell her what had happened, I made a cup of tea. The making of the tea and drinking it calmed me down. When practicality had replaced the numbness I was feeling, I put Tilly in a Tupperware box; she deserved nothing less.

To avenge Tilly's murder I was prepared to use my supernatural powers.

'Hello,' said the Arse Hole, when I rang Mary.

'Hi, Dick, it's Muriel.'

'Don't fucking hi me… I know what you did.'

'I'm ringing to apologise.'

'I should bloody well think so.'

'I'm sorry.'

'It's Ambrose you should be saying sorry to.'

'That's why I'm ringing. I want to write him an apology… tell him I overreacted. I will write SWALK on the envelope… remember SWALK, Dick?'

There was a long pause before he said, with a sigh: 'They were the days. What was he doing… I mean for you to snap a mousetrap on his fingers?'

'He was groping me.'

'Is that all… what's wrong with that?'

'He didn't ask permission.'

'Give him what he wants and he'll give you a cheque.'

'I've had a thought… what if you give me his home address and I ring his doorbell to say sorry. I was playing hard to get.'

'You were playing hard to get…'

'The address?'

I wrote it down.

'Ambrose has a soft spot for you… you know that, don't you?'

'I attract him the way a turd attracts flies.'

'I don't like the sound of that… Muriel, what are you up to? Take my advice, forget that bloke Howard Mary tells me you have eyes on… set your sights on Ambrose. I know he takes liberties but… in a few years he could be in the House of Lords… stick with him and you could be Lady Muriel. How does that tickle your fancy?'

I had Ambrose's home address. Dick had served his purpose. I now reminded the Arse Hole of a few home truths.

'My fancy, Dick, is all on you making a will in which you leave all your worldly goods to Mary.'

'Sod off… if you were sitting next to me… I'd… I'd give you a Chinese burn.'

'I'd poke you in the eye.'

'Sod off.'

'May I speak to Mary?'

I had to wait a few seconds before Mary came on the line; at least he hadn't hung up.

'Dick's upset, what have you been saying to him?'

'I told him it was his husbandly duty to make a will in which he leaves everything to you.'

'What did he say?'

'Told me to sod off. Are you free to have a private conversation?'

'Yes, he's in the cellar firing his air rifle at photos of people he dislikes… you are in between Tony Blair and Gordon Brown.'

'I'm flattered.'

I told her everything. She agreed with me that Ambrose and Stanley were responsible.

'Are we going to send them to boot camp?' she said.

'The murder of a witch's cat by a devil cannot go unavenged.'

'I agree. Will you get Whitby's permission to use your supernatural powers carte blanche?'

'It states in the Coven's rule book, Article twenty-seven, that the murder of a witch's cat by a fiend must never be allowed to go unpunished. I don't need permission.'

There was a silence which seemed long but wasn't.

'It's our Pearl Harbor, isn't it?' said Mary. 'Japan's attack woke the sleeping giant of the American war machine; the desecration of Tilly has given the sleeping witch carte blanche to use her supernatural powers.'

'Yes.'

Tilly had been my companion for many years. As a witch's cat she'd been useless. Halloween had made her yawn. But I had loved her... even her fleas.

I buried her under a belladonna in my back garden. In accordance with tradition, I broke a ceremonial besom over her grave. I laid the broken besom on top of the Tupperware box containing her dismembered body.

Digging her grave had not been easy. The frozen earth had not wanted her. To honour her memory, I spent the night in a deck chair at the side of her grave. The night was bitterly cold. A wind was blowing from the North Pole.

To keep warm on my vigil I swaddled myself in a duvet stuffed with owl feathers. I hooted revenge spells on Ambrose and Stanley. Those who had caused my heartache were going to be made to pay a high price. In such ways do witches say adieu to their cats.

# THE START
# OF A BUSY
# WEEK AT WORK

**T**he grief I was feeling at losing my beloved Tilly did not stop the arrival of yet another Monday morning. Life goes on. The everyday world didn't give a toss about my sadness. I had to go to work.

It was going to be a busy week. In the afternoon… a panto dress rehearsal… at the end of the week… two performances in front of mams and dads.

Howard had picked the pupils to play the leading roles, weeks ago. He'd stayed back at night to help them learn their lines. Under Howard's supervision, teachers had been rehearsing their class's contribution to the show. I had rehearsed my class's animal dance with him. My pupils would go on stage dressed as ladybirds, badgers and butterflies. Joe was a bear.

In the Ladies', on that first Monday morning back at school, after I'd buried Tilly and was putting on a brave face, Mary – we were alone in the loo – gave me the good news that Ambrose was poorly. She told me: 'Ambrose rang Dick… Ambrose has nettle rash. He told the Arse

Hole his thighs look as if they'd been horse whipped...
your doing?'

'Yes.'

'Spell number eighty-eight?'

'Yes.'

'What level of severity? Not fatal I hope. Death by
nettle rash is a most painful way to die.'

'I am not a murderer, you know that. I am a facilitator.
If the itch makes Ambrose jump off a cliff, that is up to
him... nothing to do with me.'

'You draw a fine line, Muriel.'

'How the rash affects Ambrose will depend upon
factors beyond my control.'

'His metabolism?'

'Yes. I must admit I laid the spell on pretty thick.'

'Duration?'

'A five-hour incantation over Tilly's grave.'

'OMG... you really have let him have it. What about
Stanley? You are certain he was the executioner?'

'I am.'

'Because of the decapitation?'

Monica, entering the loo, and hearing the word
'decapitation', said: 'Are you two talking about how the
Black Knight chopped off the Red Knight's head? The
children keep telling me about it. I, of course, never saw
it. I was not around to bear witness. I was in a caravan
keeping an eye on the school's credit card. I wish I could
smoke. If I lit up here... you'd tell, wouldn't you? I know
you would. I hate pantomimes... hate them... hate them.
I hate men as well. If I didn't have Belinda's support I'd
be on the sick having electric shock treatment like poor

dear Juniper. Damn! I shouldn't have told you that… that's confidential… that was confidential. What I told you… it goes no further. Do I make myself clear?'

'If Juniper doesn't come back,' I said, 'Howard might become permanent.'

'And pigs might fly…'

'Howard has bedroom eyes,' said Mary.

'I think he's sexy,' I said, 'if you know what I mean.'

'No, I do not know what you mean. He is a member of staff, not a Hollywood sex symbol. You are both besotted with him… quite besotted and you are not the only ones. Neither of you are teenagers, you should know better than to talk like fifteen-year-old tarts. I hate pantomimes… hate them.'

Behind Monica's back Mary and I did rabbit impersonations.

When a school sticks to its timetable it is the SBB… Schweinzerische Bundesbahnen; things run, more or less, smoothly; bells ring; children flow in and out of classrooms. When a school tears up its timetable it becomes British Rail: delays, cancellations.

So far, I'd not had a chance to speak to Howard in private. During the morning coffee break, he'd been in Monica's headteacher's room discussing the need for a 'Pantomime Timetable'. The week ahead would be chaos; tempers would be lost; friends would argue; coffee mugs would go unwashed; straws would be left in milk bottles.

My priority was wanting to get Howard on his own and tell him about Tilly.

When the bell rang announcing the start of the lunch break, a pupil with a snotty nose – I was showing her how to use a paper tissue instead of her sleeve – stopped me dashing across the hall to Howard's classroom and telling him, tout suite, about Tilly.

Through dithering, albeit for a good cause, I missed him. Hilary told me he'd gone surfing. How did she know something about him that I didn't?

On a pet lip scale of one to ten, I was nine. I ached to tell him about Tilly. I wanted to involve him in what had happened. I wanted to tell him to be on his guard. Tilly's murder had been revenge for what I'd done to Ambrose. Stanley would be after revenge for the humiliation he'd suffered at Howard's hands. What might he try and do to Howard? I wanted to protect Howard. I wanted to look after him.

To see if the spell I'd put on Stanley had worked, I took myself off to Ma Mason's pie shop. The spell had worked on Ambrose, but, had it worked on Stanley?

At the shop, I stepped aside to let an old woman with a hairy chin go in first.

'What can I get you, Ethel?' said Ma to the old woman with the hairy chin.

'She's before me,' said Ethel, prodding me in my back with her walking stick. 'If you hadn't opened the door for me, you'd have been before me. I'm not a queue jumper, yuh nar. It's not in me nature to jump me turn. My husband died… you know that, don't yuh, Ma? I'm lost without him. He was aalways fussy about taking his turn in a queue and buying his round when it was his turn at the club… and cutting his toenails. I gan to sleep every night looking at his last resting place. Yuh see,' looking at me, 'my semi overlooks the cemetery. When I sit up in bed sipping my medicinal… whisky… two fingers… I can see his grave. It's a comfort knowing he's close and I can see his cross… not that when he was alive he was cross… he never was… well, maybes once or twice. He'd be cross if he was alive and could see what I've seen going on in the cemetery. When I'm staring out at three in the morning with me medicinal, I've seen lights… that's not right, is it? I means, what would folk want to be doing in the middle of the night in a cemetery?'

'A flat gravestone,' said Ma, flapping open her dustcoat, 'makes a canny mattress when them that's so inclined want to do it under the stars.'

'I wouldn't like to think folk were doing things like that on top of my Fred,' said Ethel. 'I'm glad I didn't have enough money… even with the insurance, to buy him a flat gravestone… not if that's what they are bein' used for. All I could afford for Fred… bless his string vest… he loved wearing his string vest… was a stone cross… sandstone, not marble… I couldn't afford marble. I used to put flowers in a vase… waste of time… they kept getting stolen… folk will steal anything. I know that's a horrible thing to say but that's what I think.'

'Folk would steal my best pies,' said Ma, 'if I let them… that's why I don't give tick. If you want my pies you have to pay for them before you eat them. Purse first, belly second. That's a good motto for a seller of pies.'

'I often see your pie van in the cemetery, Ma,' said Ethel. 'I won't tell any lies… I use binoculars. I'm always seeing Stanley. I expect he's visiting his mother's grave… boys love their mothers… that's what I think.'

'Stanley,' said Ma, 'will be in the cemetery because he's keeping in with the undertakers… getting to know them helps him get orders for funeral teas. I know I'm boasting but I've been told… one of my corn beef pasties makes them what's left behind forget their grieving better than a double gin… there's money in funerals, Ethel.'

'There's comfort in them as well,' said Ethel, 'funerals, I mean. I like watching them… watching them is better than watching the telly. I likes it best when the gonner is in a hearse pulled by black horses with black plumes and it's cold and foggy and the horses' breathe out clouds of white smoke. If I'd had the money, I'd have had Fred carried to his last resting place, snug in a box on a hearse pulled by two black horses. He loved it when cowboys went to their final resting place like that. He had the "Magnificent Seven" on one of them things that sound like one of those diseases you never mentioned when you were young… a "VD" or something like that.'

'A DVD,' I suggested.

'That's it… a "VD". Fred used to get upset when I said I'd give him "VD" for his birthday. He was very prim and proper was my Fred. Wouldn't eat his breakfast until he'd his collar and tie on… and so was his mother. We spent our first night in his mam and dad's house. We had no money for a honeymoon… see. His mum gave me a cow bell. If Fred got too much for me I was to give it a tinkle.'

'Did you?' said Ma.

'Course I didn't… but Fred would have if I hadn't hidden it.'

'Does Stanley have a girlfriend?' I asked.

I asked the question because I wished to draw Ma into talking about her grandson.

'If he has,' said Ma, 'she'll not fancy him at the moment. He's come out all over in red blotches.'

'What's caused that?' I said.

'It's going around,' said Ethel.

'Lack of ventilation,' said Ma, flapping open her dust coat. 'I've told him… tight fitting clothes is a killer. Ethel, I'll serve Mrs Thayne first.'

'One mince and onion,' I said. 'I have a busy afternoon ahead of me. It's the dress rehearsal for the school pantomime. Mr Star's in charge.'

'Mr Star… give him my love. If he pops in tell him I'll let him have an egg and bacon at cost price. Howard… Mr Star, Ethel, is an American. He gave me this posy,' picking up the jam jar containing the posy Howard had given her. 'They're lovely, aren't they?'

'You've never given me a bacon and egg at cost price,' said Ethel.

'Ethel, I like you, but I am not in love with you.'

'You fancy this bloke… is that what you are saying?'

'Yes…' said Ma, flapping her dust coat open and shut as if it was a pair of bellows and she was pumping oxygen into her passion for Howard.

'More fool you… next thing you'll be giving Mrs Small tick.'

'Divent be daft, Ethel, am not that gullible.'

# I GET TOO BIG
# FOR MY BOOTS

**M**ary and I were in the staffroom sharing the mince and onion I'd bought at Ma's when Howard blew into our company the way a force eight gale blows curtains into a room through an open window.

'Howard!' I exclaimed. 'You look wonderful.'

Now was not the time to cry on his shoulder and tell him about Tilly.

He was wearing a white tuxedo and a red bow tie as big as an ocean-going liner's propeller. The lace on his white shirt was a flower bed of white alyssum. An Old Glory bandana drizzled out of his breast pocket. The LED on the tip of the conductor's baton he was holding was flashing three short flashes… three long flashes… SOS. He was reacting the way I'd reacted when I'd arrived home and found Tilly's dismembered body.

'Muriel,' he said, looking at me like a Labrador who is desperate to be let out to take a leak, 'I need a witch. Paul has done a bunk… he has done a runner. He has gone AWOL.'

'You picked him to play the witch.'

'I was trying to help him realise his potential.'

'And now he has let you down…'

'He has let himself down… for the dress rehearsal I need a stand-in witch.'

'Why me?'

'I think you know.'

'Do I?'

'You can spell…'

'I know that "i" comes before "e" except after "c".'

'Muriel, banter is not a sticking plaster for a theatrical emergency. Do I have to go down on my knees?'

'It might help.'

'You would humiliate me in front of Mary? Do I not bleed when I am cut?'

To show me how desperate he was he cut the fleshy part of his thumb with the edge of a piece of card… a tiny cut. It oozed the merest hint of green blood. Every witch knows wizards' blood is green. Howard was letting me know he was a wizard. His trust in me made my heart beat fast. I wouldn't go so far as to say that at that moment I became his slave but, like the Battle of Waterloo, it was a close-run thing.

'I don't know Paul's lines,' I mumbled.

'Make them up as you go along… just for the dress rehearsal. I will sort out Paul later.'

'What's it worth?'

'I'll take you out to dinner.'

'You have a deal,' I said. 'I have a black skirt at home.'

'I know you have.'

Did he know I was a witch? Was that why he'd picked me to be a stand-in witch? Did he know I wouldn't have to act? Did he know that when I cut myself my blood oozed out more purple than red?

'I'll be back in twenty minutes,' I said. 'Lucky I came in my car today.'

I arrived back at school dressed as a witch. Joe wanted to know why.

'Paul has done a runner,' I told him.

'Miss, I don't want to be a bear.'

The dress rehearsal was to take place in front of those children in the school who were not taking part in the show and children from a neighbouring school. The hall was packed.

I will be honest. The chance to be the real me in front of a live audience, I found appealing... at least part of me did.

Before the show started Howard, dressed as if he was a snake-oil salesman on a Mississippi stern wheeler, kept everyone amused by playing Christmas carols. He had a wonderful touch. His improvisations on 'Silent Night' took my mind off the fact that for the first time ever I was wearing my witch costume in public. Peeking at him through a side curtain I thought he looked... wonderful.

Back stage the school's emotional atmosphere was febrile... allow me, dear reader, to throw at you a potpourri of metaphors:

The school was a stick of dynamite with a lit fuse.

The school was a beehive when smoke makes bees think their hive is on fire.

The school was a shipyard on launch day. When the launched ship entered the water would it sink or float?

The school was a war zone. It was every woman for herself.

To tell Howard the show was ready to start, Monica mimed him, through a side curtain, the sort of 'go' mime, flight crew on an aircraft carrier give a pilot to tell them they're clear for take-off.

To tell the audience the show was starting, a pupil banged, with much enthusiasm, on a drum. Monica switched off the hall's lights. The teacher in charge of opening the stage's curtains pulled on a wire as if she were a sailor hoisting a sail. The curtains jerked open.

As soon as they saw the scenery, the adults in the audience clapped. We were off to a good start. Hansel, played by a year six boy, had the audience in the palm of his hand. Hilary's 'Villager's Dance' received a round of applause.

Backstage, dressed as a witch, I was ready to tread the boards. I was no longer Mrs Thayne, I was the real me. I wore green makeup, red eyeshadow, a black traffic cone hat, black boots, a black dress and a black shawl.

It amused me that only Mary knew I was a real witch. I did not know Paul's lines... so what? For the first time I was the real ME in public... the real ME.

Things were going so well that, backstage, Monica even had time to ask me: 'Where'd you get the costume?'

'A few old things of my mother's,' I said. 'I nearly threw them out. I always say if you keep things long enough one day they will come in handy.'

'Are you nervous?'

'Monica, darling,' I said – I'd never before called Monica 'darling' – 'you are forgetting, I'm a witch. If the audience don't like me, I'll turn them into worms.'

On a high… showing off… I flew my besom round Monica.

'How'd you do that?'

'Monica, have you switched on the UV light?'

'Oh my god…'

The curtains opened. Lit by UV light my Gingerbread House was Trafalgar Square on New Year's Eve.

My cue to go on was a piece of music, composed by Howard, called 'Prelude to the Arrival of the Witch'. He'd compared it, I hoped with tongue in cheek, to the storm movement in Beethoven's sixth symphony.

I adjusted my false nose. I lifted up my black skirt. I put my besom between my legs. I breathed deep and slow.

To simulate lightning, Monica switched the stage's lights on and off… on and off. Thunder was made by children shaking thunder boards. To simulate rain, the insides of triangles were tinkled; two violins screeched like cats fighting in a back lane over what was left in a tin of pilchards. Recorders tooted… the school bully beat the living daylights out of a drum on a tripod. A girl clashed together two cymbals bigger than herself… my cue …

I flew onto the stage six inches off the ground. I just couldn't resist showing off, could, I? Another thing – the downside – levitating leaves me feeling exhausted.

'Hello, boys and girls,' I cackled. 'I'm the wicked witch. I'm going to put Hansel and Gretel into my oven and turn them into… gingerbread!'

Lots of boos. That was a good start. A good start but what to say next? Howard's script had been written for a child dressed as a witch. I, on the other hand, was the real thing. As I have already mentioned, for the first time in my life I was the real ME… the real ME, in public. I'd come out. I was centre stage and loving it. To call a spade a spade… I had grown too big for my witch's boots.

I told the audience: 'You think I'm just dressed as a witch… don't you? That I'm not a real witch. Would you believe I was a real witch if I turned Mr Star into a frog?'

'Yes!' shouted a teacher from the visiting school.

Pointing my besom at Howard I chanted, 'Hocus pocus, Christmas crocus.'

No way did I have the power to turn Howard into a frog. Out of the corner of my eye I saw Mary, in the wings, adopt the position airline passengers are told to adopt for a crash landing.

I had gone too far. I had threatened a wizard. I had crossed a supernatural red line. A gust of warm wind whipped off my hat and wig. It blew off my false nose. A child in the audience shouted: 'It's Mrs Thayne!'

My long black skirt flew over my head. Thank goodness I was wearing tights. The more my skirt went up the more I brought the house down.

When the wind had abated and Howard had stopped staring at me I raised my besom for quiet.

'I've just remembered,' I croaked, 'I can't turn Mr Star into a frog. This is a dress rehearsal. If it was the real show I could but not when it's a dress rehearsal. Look… here come Hansel and Gretel.'

For the rest of the show I stuck as close as possible to what I could remember of the script. I did not take a bow in the finale. I ignored the shouts: 'We want Mrs Thayne! 'I wanted to go home and cry. If Whitby got to hear I'd threatened a wizard I could be stripped of my supernatural powers for six months or even a year. I had broken a cardinal rule of witchcraft. I had threatened a wizard.

After school Mary and I met at my house. I needed a shoulder to cry on.

'What he did to you when you were on stage confirms our suspicions,' said Mary. 'He's a wizard, isn't he?'

'Yes, he is,' I said. 'He is someone with more power than we have. I told you I saw he had green blood.'

'He was teaching you a lesson.'

'I did provoke him. I was showing off, wasn't I?'

'You were completely OTT. You were one of those silly people who jump off the end of piers with balsa wood wings strapped to their arms.'

'They think they can fly but they can't.'

'Yes.'

'You won't tell Whitby, will you?'

'Of course I won't… you know that.'

'It worries me that Whitby's due diligence on Howard has drawn a blank. He must have friends in high places. He must be a very high-ranking wizard indeed. If he was a football team he'd be top of the Premier League.'

Before Mary left she and I said the 'Prayer of the Martyrs' over Tilly's grave.

# TUESDAY: AN APOLOGY AND A PLEA FOR HELP

The next day, back at school, I put on a brave face. Some members of staff treated me as if I'd come back after a long illness… 'you alright, Muriel?' Others were brutal: 'Good job you were wearing tights, Muriel. Primark, were they?'

'Pride before a fall, Muriel.'

'Muriel, you brought the house down, well done you.'

'How'd you do those tricks with the besom?'

Monica said: 'I'm surprised you dare show your face. If it was me I'd be off on the sick.'

During the morning break, I did not go to the staff room. I could not face breaking bread with my colleagues. I was tired of putting on a brave face. I was ready to snap.

As if he had read my mind – which he quite possibly had – and knew I was feeling vulnerable, Howard came to see me in my classroom. He came to see me, I thought, the way, a long time ago, doctors used to do home visits.

He breezed in carrying two mugs of coffee. He had spelled the steam coming off the coffees into looking like white flags. An invisible hand closed my classroom door.

'Sorry about yesterday,' he said, handing me a mug of coffee.

In my coffee's milky froth, I saw a witch on a broomstick.

'You accept liability?'

'Of course.'

'You are more than what you seem, aren't you?'

'As you and Mary are more than you seem.'

I told him about, Tilly… about, Ambrose and Stanley … about how I'd given them nettle rash.

'I know,' he said.

'You, know… how?'

'When I have accomplished my mission I will be more than happy to take you into my confidence. In the meantime the pantomime needs Paul. Can you help him overcome his stage fright?'

'Leave it to me,' I said. 'Howard…'

'Yes?'

'We are still friends?'

The kiss he blew me made the fairies in my womb do backward somersaults; it puckered my cheeks… you know… the way a plunger unblocks a sink.

Paul lived with his father and grandmother. Years ago, his mother had run off with a clog dancer from Barnsley. His father was a fisherman. Paul's grandmother was the boss. In her youth she'd saved a man from drowning. She'd turned down the George Medal on the grounds: 'a divent want to make a fuss ower what anybody could have done'.

I rang Paul's emergency contact number on Margo the secretary's phone. The school secretary and I were allies. A long time ago I'd used my supernatural powers to give her car a push start. Margo did not suffer fools. She was eccentric. When she typed, she wore a hat. Monica's headteacher's room was the size of a tennis court; Margo's admin room was the size of a broom cupboard.

Paul's grandmother said: 'He's got the trots… that's why he's not at school.'

I explained about stage fright.

'His dad was the same when he fell owerboard. I had to help him gan back to sea.'

An hour later Paul's grandmother, Jenny, brought Paul back into school on a, metaphorical, dog lead.

'Am not deeing sums,' he said, looking at the box of chocolates I was holding. 'A can't dee sums and learn lines…'

'You rest your heed, my darling, on the camp bed Mrs Thayne has put up for you… just for you… in her classroom,' said Jenny.

As soon as Jenny had told me she was bringing the truant back into school, I'd had monitors carry the medical room's emergency camp bed – and this was an emergency – a mental health emergency – into my classroom.

'You are important, you are, Paul,' said Jenny. 'You're like one of them movie stars what has their own dressing room… have a lie down.'

'Chocolate, Paul?' I said.

'Which one would you like, my darling?' said his grandmother.

'A divent like nuts, Gran.'

'I know you don't, my darling.'

'This one has a cream centre,' I said.

'Nice and soft,' said his grandmother.

'Gran?'

'Yes, my darling?'

'What if I forget me lines?'

'That's what the chocolates are for... to help you remember them... have another one.'

'I divent like nuts.'

'I know you don't, my darling.'

'I think we are going to need another box of chocolates,' I told Jenny.

'And mayo... Paul loves mayonnaise.'

In the afternoon, my class and Howard's watched Howard help Paul rehearse his part.

'Bang the drum, Paul... bang it hard. Now shout, 'I'm a witch... a wicked witch. Burst this balloon, Paul... now shout, "I'm a witch... a wicked witch.'

Paul banged the drum. He burst the balloon and yes he did shout, 'I'm a witch... a wicked witch.'

His fellow pupils clapped.

'Take a bow, Paul.'

And he did.

# WEDNESDAY: A BIT OF A SHOCK... NOT AN EARTHQUAKE BUT A TREMOR

A billy-do, on Monica's signature pink paper, brought to my classroom by a monitor, informed me that today was to be given over to whatever parts of the pantomime Howard wished to rehearse. In preparation for tomorrow's evening performance in front of mams and dads, staff and children were to put up their feet and take a breather. Here, here to that. But there is no rest for the wicked, is there? Before I'd time to put up my feet, Monica was in my classroom telling me: 'When you are finished with the camp bed do not forget to return it to the medical room.'

Although he was in Howard's class, I was keeping Paul and his grandmother in my classroom. The pantomime was on for two nights... Thursday and Friday. Until the last performance was over, Paul was a bird in a gilded cage.

In the classroom Jenny proved to be a whizz with scissors. Snip, snip, snip and she'd made a Christmas tree. She put her dexterity down to the fact that in her youth she'd been a fish-filleter on the Fish Quay.

I kept my class busy... hard at it... making Christmas cards. They were hyper. When they spotted a flake of snow they screamed the way adults scream when they have won the lottery.

My classroom was a mess; it was a recovery room and a theatrical costumier's.

When Paul returned from rehearsing with Howard, he stretched himself out, proprietorially, on the camp bed.

'Hot...' he said, whereupon his grandmother wiped his brow with a wet paper towel.

It was the clothes line, from which there hung... tutus... ladybird costumes... rabbit costumes... butterfly wings and one bear costume, that made the classroom like a theatrical costumier's. The line was strung diagonally across the room. The children could walk under it, but I had to duck.

It was in this Mad Hatter's tea party of an environment, that Joe, not for the first time, told me: 'Miss, a divent want to be a bear.'

'I know you don't, Joe, but you make a wonderful bear.'

'Miss, am sorry about your cat.'

I removed my half spectacles.

'What was that you said?'

''am sorry about your cat, Miss.'

'How do you know about my cat?'

'Mickey told me, Miss. He told me to tell you he's sorry. It had nowt to do with him. Miss, do I have to be a bear? Michelle wants to be a bear... divent yuh, Michelle?'

'Miss, he's a liar... a never said that.'

'Yes, yuh did!'

'No, a didn't!'

I held up my hands for peace.

'Joe,' I said, 'do you like chocolate?'

'Eh?'

'Do you like chocolate?'

'Course a do, Miss… yuh nar that.'

Michelle, do you like chocolate?'

'Everyone likes chocolate, Miss.'

'So do, I,' I said.

Michelle, quicker on the uptake than Joe, said: 'Miss was having us on… weren't yuh, Miss?'

'Ah, Miss… Miss, Michelle did say that.'

'Joe, go and ask Paul's grandmother to cut you out a fir tree.'

'I want a Christmas tree, Miss.'

'A fir tree, Joe, is a Christmas tree.'

'A don't want to be a bear.'

At lunchtime Paul went home with his grandmother on the aforementioned metaphorical dog lead… no way was he going to do a runner.

'We're having mince and dumplings,' she told me. 'It's not out of a packet, either. It's proper food. Paul's a three dumpling man, aren't you, my darling? I've got the script, Mrs Thayne. In between mouthfuls I'll get him to say his lines.'

'I'm the wicked witch,' said Paul, 'I turn…'

'What do you turn, Paul?'

'I turn children into gingerbread men… can I have four dumplings?'

'If you remember your lines, you can have five.'

I watched them walk off down the stairs to what, in the world of business, would be called a working lunch.

Where was Howard? He wasn't in his classroom. Looking out of a window in the staffroom I saw him talking to Paul and his grandmother in the school's car park. I wanted to talk to him. I wanted to tell him that Joe had told me, Michael was sorry about Tilly. To talk to him I took the stairs down two at a time.

'If you were wanting to speak to Mr Star,' said Jenny, tipping me a knowing wink, 'you are too late. He told me he was going surfing. He must be mad. I mean, in this weather. It takes all sorts. He's a lovely man, isn't he? Mr Star, I mean. I shouldn't say this, but I think he's gorgeous. He gave me this posy of flowers. I've no idea where they came from. But you don't look a gift horse in the mouth, do you? The perfume coming off them is out of this world. Has he given you flowers? I bet he has.'

'He gave me a lime.'

'A lime... he must have run out of posies that day. Still, he didn't give you a lemon.'

She sniffed the posy the way someone with sinusitis sniffs Friar's Balsam.

'Come on, Paul, next stop... mince and dumplings. If you want to follow in your Uncle Bob's footsteps, you'll need meat and gravy. His Uncle Bob's a stripper.'

'Wallpaper?'

'He takes his clothes off at hen parties,' said Paul.

'Bob swears there's more money in a cod piece than in filleting haddock,' said Jenny.

So, Howard had gone surfing, had he? I supposed it was his way of relaxing. Some folk do yoga, some go surfing... it takes all sorts. In search of comfort food, I walked to Ma Mason's for a mince and onion pie.

You can imagine my shock – then again, perhaps you can't – when I found the pie shop closed.

'She's gone to the Canaries on a cruise,' said an old man on a mobility scooter, 'that's what I'm hearing.'

He had a Santa hat on his head and a dachshund on a lead.

'If you want pies, the newsagent ower there, he sells them. They are not as tasty as Ma's but they last longer. They are wrapped in plastic, see. The plastic stops them gannin off. It's like putting bodies in a freezer. There was this film on last neet about mortuaries… very interesting it was… kept me up late. I divent sleep very well but a did last neet. If yuh buy a pie from ower there–' pointing at the newsagents– 'check its sell-by date. Howay, Goliath… giddy-up… a nar you've got short legs… just tell yoursel, you're a greyhound.'

The newsagent, a Sikh with red sky at night, sailors delight bloodshot eyes, told me: 'No, no, Mrs Ma has not gone to the Canaries. You are one of the teachers from the school down the road, aren't you? I have seen you around. I hope you are not going to start asking questions like that man teacher… the American. He tried to impress me with his conjuring tricks… me! I told him: "Mister, I come from India. I have seen snake charmers".'

I bought a packet of crisps and a cheese sandwich embalmed in a triangle of see-thru plastic. Before paying I checked its sell-by date.

'It is not out of date, lady,' said the Sikh, 'all my merchandise is of the top quality. You have been talking to the man on the scooter. He hates me because I will not give him tick.'

# DID HE JUMP OR WAS HE PUSHED?

The bell rang for the start of the afternoon break. My class filed out to play. They were excited. The schoolyard was skimmed with snow. They wanted to make slides.

Because Howard was on yard duty I did not hurry to the staffroom; also, I was looking after Jenny.

I was talking to her about how to make Christmas cards... Paul had been allowed to go out to play... when I heard the children playing in the yard, scream. To see why they were screaming I looked out of a window.

'Oh my god,' I exclaimed.

'What's wrong?' said Jenny.

'There's been an accident...'

I took the stairs down to the yard two at a time. On the second landing, Joe and one of his pals – they should not have been there – blocked my way.

'Miss, Joe's in a mood. He doesn't want to be a bear.'

'Leave's alone,' said Joe. 'Miss, he's picking on me. I don't have to be a bear if I don't want to... do a, Miss?'

'Not now, boys... not now! Out of my way... move!'

In the yard a group of girls ran to meet me.

'Mrs Thayne! Mrs Thayne!'

'I know…I know. Calm down. First help Mrs Thayne across this patch of ice.' I put out my hands. 'You don't want me to fall, do you? Helping me will stop you thinking about what has happened. Isn't that right? Let me hear your answer.'

'Yes, Mrs Thayne.'

'Louder, as if you meant it.'

'Yes, Mrs Thayne.'

'That's more like it… now I'm going to help Mr Star.'

The teenager lay on his back. His legs … his arms … his neck … were like doors which had been blown off their hinges. There was a lot of blood. It oozed and seeped out of every natural and unnatural orifice in Michael Rowe's body; for that was who I was looking at.

'He's deed, isn't he, Miss?' said, Thomas. 'I've nivva seen a deed body before … Ughh! 'Am ganna be, sick.'

I told him, in no uncertain terms: 'Thomas, you are not going to be sick. Mrs Thayne says you are not going to be sick… so, you will not be sick. Stop looking at him… look at me. Go and get help. Tell someone to phone for an ambulance. Do you understand? Go! I'm staying here to help Mr Star.'

'He's deed, isn't he, Miss?'

'Thomas, I don't know.'

'But you think he is, don't yuh?'

'He will be if we don't get help… go!'

I had never seen Howard look so helpless.

'What happened?'

'He jumped off the roof.'

At each of its ends the school had a third floor. The classrooms they housed were no longer in use. Both had doors leading out onto a flat roof. Looking up from ground level the flat roof was hidden by a red brick parapet.

I was shivering. It was bitterly cold. I was not wearing a coat.

Howard took off his anorak off.

'Thanks...'

'It's for him.'

'Oh...'

To get as close as possible to the body without standing in blood he stood on one leg. The way he fluffed the anorak before letting it fall made me think he'd be good at making beds.

'Howard, what are you doing?'

Why was he hunkering over the body and standing in blood? Why was he holding Michael's wrist as if he was a doctor taking Michael's pulse? What was he looking at?

At that moment Joe came running across the yard. I knew at once he had heard about his brother. His arrival took priority over what Howard was doing.

'Miss, people are saying Mickey's deed... that's him, isn't it? Is it him, Miss? Why's he an anorak ower his heed?'

'Dear Joe, give me your hand.'

Joe did not want to give me his hand. He wanted to see his brother.

'He's deed, isn't he, Miss?'

'Yes, Joe, I think he is. You are going to have to be very brave... Howard, what's wrong? You look as if you've seen a ghost.'

'I have,' he said, looking at something in the cup of his hand.

Instead of explaining why he'd seen a ghost and what he was looking at, he walked, like a sleepwalker, back into school.

'Mr Star... Howard...'

I found it hard to believe he was leaving me to deal with a corpse and a yard full of traumatised children... talk about rats leaving a sinking ship. It was now that Monica came, slipping and sliding towards me.

She was shouting: 'Everyone... back inside... now! What's wrong with Mr High and Mighty?' meaning Howard. 'Blow your whistle...'

'Maybe he can't stand the sight of blood,' I said.

'Blood?'

I pointed at the corpse.

'Oh my god... what happened?'

'Howard said he jumped off the roof.'

'He was on yard duty, wasn't he? I might have known. It's all his fault. Men... men are Jonahs. Take Joe inside. I'll stay until help comes. Whose anorak is that?'

'Howard's.'

'I hope he doesn't expect to be compensated. School funds aren't for that sort of thing.'

I took Joe to the medical room; sat him in a comfy armchair. I couldn't offer him a bed to lie down on – the medical room's bed was in my classroom.

'Would you like a sucky sweet, Joe?' said my ally, Margo, the school secretary.

Joe shook his head.

'He's deed isn't he, Miss?'

'Yes, Joe, I think he is.'

Leaving Joe in the capable hands of the school secretary I, hurried back to my class. Nobody was in the mood for work; all I could think about was Michael and how Howard had walked off, leaving myself and Monica to deal with everything.

I heard a siren; through a window I watched an ambulance pull up close to Michael's corpse; then a police car drove into the yard.

A little while later, looking across the hall from my classroom, to Howard's classroom, I saw a policeman and a police woman talking to Howard.

When they left him they knocked on my door. They wanted to ask me a few questions. Mr Star had told them I knew the identity of the dead teenager. Who was he? I told them.

'And you are certain?' said the policeman.

'Definitely… I know his mother. His brother, Joe, is in my class.'

'Does he know?'

'Yes.'

'Where is the lad now?'

'In the medical room. The school secretary is looking after him. He is in shock.'

'What do you think, Tracey?'

'You know,' said Tracey, 'it might be a comfort to Mrs Rowe if she hears the bad news from someone she knows. I will understand if you don't want to, Mrs Thayne. I'm Tracey, by the way.'

'You want me to tell Mrs Rowe, her son Michael is dead?'

'Yes.'

'He is dead, I take it?'

'The paramedics left us in no doubt.'

# I AM THE BEARER
# OF SAD NEWS

J oe and I sat in the back of the police car. Tracey, the policewoman, drove.

To let Joe know he was not alone, that he had someone with whom to share his grief, I held his hand. I knew he was in shock when he did not object to my mothering; under any other circumstances he'd have shrugged me off... told me he wasn't a cissy... that he wasn't teacher's pet.

'I've never had a ride in a police car,' I said.

'I have,' said Joe. 'Can we put the siren on?'

'If I did, Joe,' said Tracey, 'I'd be breaking the law. I can only use the siren when I'm responding to an emergency.'

'When Mrs Thayne took us to the fire station the fireman put the siren on when I asked him... didn't he, Miss?'

'He did, Joe, but this is different. This is for real.'

'If it's for "real" then we should put the siren on... that's what I think.'

'It doesn't work like that.'

'I'm getting a Play Station for Christmas... he's deed, isn't he, Miss? What happens when you die?'

'I don't know.'

'Miss, can people be god? Stunna… Stanley Mason thinks he's god.'

'I know who you mean… Ma Mason's grandson. A long time ago he was in my class.'

'Mickey was scared of Stunna, Miss. He said Stunna made him do things he didn't want to do. Mickey said he had to do them because… Stunna said he was god.'

'Do you think Stanley is god, Joe?'

'I dunno, Miss. He might be. He got me mam a television… and the twins is getting electric scooters for Christmas… he's deed isn't he, Miss?'

'Yes, he is.'

'What happens to yuh when yuh die?'

'Joe, you've asked me that before. I don't know… nobody knows.'

'Miss, why was Mr Star crying?'

'Who told you that?'

'Thomas, before he went home he sneaked into the medical room. He told me. He likes Mr Star. He didn't like to see him crying… Miss?'

'Yes, Joe?'

'A divent want to be a bear.'

'We'll talk about that later.'

Howard had been crying, had he? Because of what he'd seen in the yard? It was in all the textbooks that wizards only showed emotion under extreme provocation. What had tipped him over the edge?

Four women were standing at Joe's gate. When they saw the police car they folded their arms. Who were they?

Neighbours? Their congregation and the way they kept looking at Joe's house and the police car told me that Gwen must know that Michael was dead. On the Burgoyne Estate news travelled at the speed of light.

The house's front door was open. On its threshold, waiting to meet us, were Una and Thomas.

'Hello, Miss,' said Thomas. 'I've told Auntie Gwen he's deed.'

'Go straight in,' said Una, 'Gwen's expecting you. Out of the way, Thomas, let Mrs Thayne and the nice policewoman through.'

Gwen sat very upright, on a black leather settee. On its shiny surface, dribbles of baby food had, by pure chance, drawn a map of South America.

Two toddlers, Joe's and Mickey's sisters, sat on either side of their mother. They were sucking dummies. Gwen was clinging to them as if, fearing she had lost Mickey, she might also lose them. She was using them the way builders use flying buttresses to stop walls falling down.

Their attention was all on a cinema-sized TV screen. Its flashing colours made me blink. Its volume hurt my ears. On the screen a cat was chasing a mouse. On a side table cigarette stubs smouldered in an ashtray.

Joe ran to his mother.

'How bad is it?' said Gwen. 'You don't have to tell me... I can tell by your faces. Where is he?'

'Accident and Emergency,' said Tracey.

'He's dead, isn't he?'

'Yes.'

'What happened?'

I explained.

'I want to see him.'

'I'll drive you to the hospital,' said Tracey.

'I'll look after the twins,' I said.

'I'm ganin with me mam,' said Joe.

After Tracey, Joe and Gwen had left for the hospital, Una and Thomas looked at me as if I had no right to be there. They were wary of me.

'I'm Gwen's cousin,' said Una. 'Thomas calls Gwen, Auntie Gwen; but really she's his second cousin. I bet you didn't know that? I'm not here 'cos I'm a busybody… I'm family, see. I'm here to help… don't you worry about the twins, I'll look after them. When my Thomas told me what had happened… well, I didn't believe him.'

'You nivva believe owt I tell yuh, Ma.'

'Thomas, that's not nice saying I don't believe what you tell me… is it, Mrs Thayne? I'm your mother. If I won the lottery I'd give it all to you… every penny… so, don't say I don't believe you when I do. That's not nice, is it, Mrs Thayne, him telling me I don't believe him?'

Una was irritating me. She was the Arse Hole's bit on the side. She was causing my best pal grief. To show her who was boss I turned down the television. The twins, slouched on the settee, sucking their dummies, went on, quite happily, watching the cartoon at a much-reduced volume.

'Do you not like cartoons, Mrs Thayne?'

'I watch them all the time.'

Una knitted her brows. After many seconds of mulling, she said: 'I don't think you mean that, Mrs Thayne.'

In the kitchen I found a food mixer, a bread maker, a deep fat fryer, an ice cream maker, a multipurpose microwave, a slow cooker and an air fryer; all looked brand new; more to the point they all looked as if they'd never been used.

What I did not find were vegetables or bread. In a cupboard I found tins without labels. What might they contain? Dog food? Peaches? Baked beans? A combo fridge and freezer as big as a walk-in wardrobe was empty except for, of all things, a rag doll.

I am a witch with a flesh and blood body. I was peckish.

I gave Thomas three ten-pound notes.

'Una,' I said, 'I'm sending Thomas to the fish and chip shop. Is that alright? Thomas, be a good lad, go and get the twins fish and chips and some for yourself.'

'You're spoiling him,' said Una.

'And get some for your mam as well… and I'll have some.'

'I couldn't let you buy me fish and chips… I couldn't … Oh, go on then but I know I shouldn't. I won't eat the fish but I'll take it home for Eddy. You know, Eddy, don't you? I'll tell him you bought the fish for him to say thank you for the lift home he gave you. One good turn deserves another… that's what I say. You don't mind, do you, Mrs Thayne? Eddy likes a nice bit of fish. Would you like a cup of tea? I'll make you one. I like to be busy. The twins will be alright. As long as they are watching the telly they are as good as gold. Gwen's got lots of kitchen gadgets, hasn't she? I was watching you looking at them. They're on the cheap from the Knockers. Do you have the Knockers around where you live?'

'No,' I said, 'I do hope I'm not looking at stolen goods.'

'Divent ask questions, Mrs Thayne… here's your tea. How many sugars?'

'I don't take sugar.'

'You are the same as me… sweet enough.'

While we waited for Thomas to come back with the fish and chips, I observed the twins watching the near silent cartoon. When Bugs Bunny came on, I thought about Monica's rabbit phobia. I brooded on Joe telling me that Michael was sorry about what had happened to Tilly; now, Michael was dead.

A door slammed. Thomas was back.

'I've got them, Mrs Thayne.'

'Salt and vinegar on them?' said Una.

'Course I put salt and vinegar on them… am not daft, yuh nar.'

'I want a nice bit of fish for your dad. Your dad likes a nice bit of fish. Where's the biggest fish?'

Thomas pointed to one of the packets.

'I knew Thomas would know where the biggest fish was. I hope you don't mind, Mrs Thayne, but I'll take the biggest fish to Eddy. I won't be long… I'm two doors away. I'll be back in a jiffy. I'd send Thomas with it, but he'd eat it.'

'No, I wouldn't.'

'Yes, you would. Divent lie to your mam… that's not nice, is it, Mrs Thayne… lying to your mam? I won't be long.'

I knew Thomas only as a pupil. I'd never seen his caring side. I was impressed by the way he hand fed the twins the choicest bits of fish. He warned them: 'Mind me fucking fingers.'

I asked him why he wasn't eating.

'Had mine, Miss... Hoy! Little tiger... you're a cannibal, you are... had mine on me way back from the chippy, didn't I? The fish a telt me mother was the biggest was a sardine to the bit of cod I had.'

The mice, as the saying goes, had been at my own portion of fish and chips. Thomas – he had to be the culprit – had taken a bite out of my battered haddock. I looked at Thomas and thought of Darwin's theory of the survival of the fittest.

Ten minutes later, Una returned. She had not stayed long with Eddy. I don't know how, but I ended up sharing my fish and chips with her. She had a healthy appetite.

Then, Gwen, Joe and Tracey returned. What they had seen in A & E had taken from them what we with close ties to the spirit world call the 'life force'.

'Don't you worry about Gwen, Mrs Thayne,' said Una. 'I'll look after her... she's family... she's my cousin... cup of tea, Gwen?'

'Don't ask,' I said, 'just do it. Thomas, off you go again, get Tracey, your mam and Joe some fish and chips.'

I handed him a twenty-pound note. Diplomacy made me ignore the fact that I'd received no change from the first purchase.

'I'm not hungry,' said Gwen.

'You might be later,' I said.

'I am,' said Thomas. 'I love fish and chips.'

'Off you go... and take Joe with you.'

'I'm staying with me mam,' said Joe.

'Joe loves his mam... don't you, Joe,' said Una.

'Sit down, Mam,' said Joe. 'Twins... bunk along.'

Cold air blew into the living room. Thomas had left the front door open. Una, muttering that Thomas didn't know how to wash a cup or close a front door, went to close it.

To Joe his mother was a redoubt. She was a duvet. He wanted to use her to shut out the wicked world. He'd never seen a dead body before. When his mother had made him look at Mickey's corpse, he knew it was Mickey… but it was… Mickey with something missing. Mickey was there but he wasn't there. Looking at the corpse had confused him. He didn't know what to think.

Gwen, smoking a cigarette, was looking, not so much at the TV but through it, as if it wasn't there.

'I'll do what you said, Mrs Thayne,' said Una. 'I'll make Gwen a cup of tea.'

Tracey and I followed Una into the kitchen. We felt for Gwen. Our empathy with what she was going through was sincere. But her grief was not our grief. Her grief would not stop us talking about the weather and getting on with our day-to-day lives. Her grief would not stop us getting a good night's sleep. It would not make us break our hearts at three in the morning.

In the kitchen I caught Tracey looking at the cooking gadgets. I could read her mind. How come Mrs Rowe could afford so many top of the range cooking gadgets?

Without thinking I told Una, when she was filling the kettle to make Gwen a cup of tea: 'Don't fill it too full.'

'You sounded sharp when you said that, Mrs Thayne. Thomas said you can be sharp. I haven't upset you, have I? I hope I haven't because I like you. I think you are a good teacher. But, if you don't mind, I'll put in as much water as I want. I've a mind of my own, Mrs Thayne. Eddy – he'll tell you that – and I'll look after Gwen… she's my cousin, you know… she'll need time. I'll wait until you and Tracey have gone before I ask Gwen about Michael's shoes. I'm wondering, see, if they'd fit my Thomas. He's a big lad for his age… takes after his father's side of the family. I know he's a lot younger than Michael was, but Thomas has big feet. He gets his height from his father – I like tall men – and his big feet from me. I bet you wouldn't believe me if I told you I was an eight. You wouldn't know what size shoe Michael was, would you? You think I'm awful, don't you? You do… I can tell. But I won't ask Gwen about the shoes until we are on our own. I'll give her time… she needs time.'

When Thomas came back with more fish and chips I held out my hand for my change.

'Do I not get a tip?' said Thomas.

'No,' I said.

Tracey had a few bites of fish and a chip or two. Thomas had seconds. Joe and Gwen nibbled.

When it was clear to me that Tracey wanted to get back to the police station, I reminded her: 'My car is in the school car park'.

'I'll drive you there… don't worry… all part of the service.'

In the police car I told her: 'I don't feel so much like a suspect when I'm sitting beside you in the front seat. When I was sitting in the back seat with Joe, I thought I should be wearing handcuffs.'

'Guilty conscience… you haven't been stealing pencils, have you?'

'In the Jubilee, pencils are kept under lock and key. Monica, our head, keeps them in the school safe. She keeps the petty cash in the top drawer of her desk. Monica has an inverted sense of priorities. No one has overtaken us… no one is speeding.'

'You are forgetting, Mrs Thayne, you are in a police car. I am a visible presence. My presence makes the public obey the law.'

'Your presence is a deterrent?'

'That's the theory.'

'Just rattling the handcuffs is all you need to do… I mean, to keep law and order?'

'If only that were true.'

'And pigs might fly…'

'Something like that.'

'I thought you were very good with Gwen… Mrs Rowe. Police work isn't all about locking people up, is it? I wonder what made Michael jump? Do you think he was on drugs?'

'More than likely… the autopsy will tell us. Some drugs make people do silly things.'

'Like… they can fly?'

'Yes, or murder or steal or rape.'

'Mrs Rowe had lots of gadgets in her kitchen. I saw you looking.'

'I have a list.'

'I saw you write in your notebook. Do you think they are off the back of a lorry? Sorry, I'm getting carried away. I'm bein' nosy.'

'Everyone likes to play detective. I blame the television… Miss Marple and Poirot, you know.'

'And everyone knows better than the police?'

'Something like that.'

At the school I bid Tracey good night. I thanked her for the lift.

The school was in darkness. There were no other cars in its car park. Everyone had gone home. No one had stopped behind to see how I'd got on at Gwen's; not even Mary.

The windows of my car were frosted over. I had to wait ages for the car's heaters to clear them. It was while I was waiting for them to clear, that I asked myself the following questions: Could a drug have made Michael think he could fly? That he was Superman? He was part of Stanley's gang. Joe had told me that Stanley thought he was god... rubbish... utter rubbish... but... if you were young and on drugs... who was to say what Michael had believed. Had peer pressure made him jump? Joe had told me he'd seen Howard crying. Was that true? It was not the sort of thing Joe would have made up. Howard, leaving me in the yard alone with Michael's corpse, had annoyed me. Why had he left me? He might have stayed with me... damn it, he should have stayed with me. I'd attended seminars about wizards at Whitby. The latest thinking was... they had all the faults of less gifted males multiplied to the power ten.

Una and Gwen were cousins, were they? Family ties were important on the Burgoyne estate. They also led to fallings out... domestic violence. Una was the Arse Hole's latest bit of skirt. I couldn't stop thinking about that. Poor Eddy. What Eddy didn't know was that he'd given a witch a lift home. A witch never forgets a kindness. Gwen's kitchen was chock-a-block full of gadgets… very expensive gadgets. Poor Gwen… to lose a child was an awful thing. And why was Ma Mason's closed? Now that Michael was dead would I ever find out why he was sorry about Tilly?

# HOW I CAME TO
# HOWARD'S RESCUE

**A**s I drove home, I was so busy brooding on what I have described in the last chapter, that I found myself doing twenty-five in a twenty zone. Concentrate, Muriel, I told myself... concentrate.

Three years ago, I'd been on a speed awareness course. It was either that or points on my licence. My coven takes a dim view of witches who break the law. Whitby had given me a yellow card... when you break the law you might become a tabloid headline. A witch, I was reminded, must at all times keep a low profile.

In the thirty mile per hour zone I was now entering, the sight of a parked police car, with its lights flashing, made me reduce my speed from thirty-one miles per hour to twenty-eight.

Parked in front of the police car was Howard's car. The surfboard on its roof made it conspicuous. Had he been stopped for speeding? If he had... serve him right. I'd not forgotten how he'd overtaken me on the first day he'd come to work at the Jubilee.

I have mentioned before, I am not nosy ... Ha! Ha! But I am curious.

To find out what was going on, I turned down a side street and back up another street. I parked so I could see the police car and Howard's car.

Doing surveillance and taking part in a vigil have much in common. In the vigil I'd held over Tilly's grave I was praying for her soul. When I was watching the police car, I was wondering what the hell was going on. A vigil is a spiritual experience… surveillance is cold and boring.

It was a bitterly cold night. The roads were frosted. The bare branches of the trees behind the cemetery's railings looked like besoms belonging to a race of giant witches.

Where was Howard? Was he in his own car or in the police car?

A tall policeman and a short policeman got out of the police car. They stretched their legs. They yawned. They shone torches through the cemetery's railings. What were they looking for?

Presumably because they'd seen nothing suspicious, they drove off.

In the meantime, where was Howard? I'd wait for him until hell froze over which, looking at the frost covering the road, might be quite soon.

A few minutes later I was taken aback when the police car, no warning lights flashing now, crept past me at ten miles an hour. It parked ten yards in front of me. I hoped they hadn't spotted me; not that I'd done anything wrong. This part of the town was not a red-light district. It was posh. I was not a prostitute looking for a client.

The policemen, and myself, were using cars the way naturalists use hides. What a funny old business this was turning out to be; now a 'watcher' was watching 'watchers' watch.

What were the police hoping to see? What were they waiting for? Wouldn't it be funny, I thought, if Howard was having a cup of coffee with a pal in one of the semis in the street. If he was and spotted me, I'd have a lot of explaining to do.

A few minutes later I spotted Howard climbing the cemetery's railings. At this time of night the cemetery's gates were locked.

When the police left their car and ran towards him shouting, 'Police!' I was close on their heels.

Witches and wizards have their differences; they are not natural bedfellows. If one says something is black the other will say it is white. However, when those of us blessed with supernatural powers are in jeopardy we forget our differences; we bond. We do our best to help each other. The bottom line is this: witches and wizards have more in common with each other than they have with those not gifted with supernatural powers.

It was while he was balanced on top of the railings, that Howard asked the policemen: 'What can I do for you?'

'You can start, sir, by jumping down,' said the tall policeman.

Howard jumped down.

'Now, sir,' said the short policeman, 'explain...'

'The gate was locked,' said Howard.

'That's not what I meant... sir.'

'Howard!' I exclaimed.

The two policemen turned.

'Darling!' he exclaimed, giving me one of his Labrador looks, 'I found it. Please say you are still speaking to me... please.'

We exchanged telepathic glances.

'Of course I'm still speaking to you, darling,' I said.

'Let me explain,' said Howard.

'I wish you would, sir,' said the tall policeman. He had a broken nose. He looked tough. 'My handcuffs is itching for an airing.'

'There will be no need for the bracelets, officer.'

'Won't there indeed... you giving me orders?'

'Muriel and I...'

'Muriel?'

'The lady whose hand I am holding.'

Howard's hand was large and warm. I was enjoying holding it.

'Muriel and I had a lover's tiff... didn't we, darling?'

He squeezed my hand. I got the message.

'We had a lover's tiff,' I said.

'Muriel is a passionate woman,' he said.

'My grandmother is Italian,' I said.

'In a fit of passion she... Muriel threw the ring I'd given her as a token of my love... of my eternal love... over the cemetery railings.'

He squeezed my hand.

'I regret doing it,' I chimed in. 'I told Howard, I wanted the ring back.'

'What was your tiff about?' said the little policeman.

'Wheelie bins,' I said.

'I've had words with Gladys about wheelie bins,' said the big policeman with the broken nose. 'Gladys is my

178

wife. It's what day you put them out, isn't it? That's what causes the trouble… Gladys said, "Monday" and I said, "Tuesday".'

'Who was right?'

'Gladys… she's always right. I know my place.'

'Can we go now?'

'Just a few more questions, sir. Did you use a torch in the cemetery?'

'I used the torch on my mobile phone… without it I'd never have found the ring.'

'Someone phoned us, sir, to say they'd seen lights in the cemetery. Would that have been you, sir?'

'I suppose it must have been.'

'The old lady who complained, sir, says she often sees lights in the cemetery.'

'Nothing to do with me, officer,' said Howard.

'You're not local, are you, sir?'

'I'm an American.'

'Get away. I'm from Washington.'

# 'DC?'

**'N**o, County Durham.'
'Can we go now?' I said. 'Howard and I like to be early to bed. I crochet, he does Sudoku.'

'Never heard it called that before,' said the big policeman. 'Where's this ring you said you found?'

'We need evidence,' said the little policeman.

From a pocket, Howard produced a gold wedding ring.

'You found this ring, sir, this tiny ring amongst all those gravestones and grass? If you don't mind my saying, sir, you were lucky. If I were you, sir, I'd buy a lottery ticket… seems to me you are on a winning streak.'

'I did have a torch.'

'You'd need a searchlight and a metal detector and still need the luck of the devil to find it.'

'It was in a box… that helped.'

'Where's the box?'

'I dropped it in the cemetery.'

'Get away…'

I suspected the ring had not been in a box. I suspected that Howard had made that up to give his story credibility.

To create a diversion, I held out my wedding ring finger and said: 'Howard, darling, wed me again.'

For Howard, it was Hobson's choice. If he didn't wed me, he might end up in jail. It was either me or bread and water.

'With this ring I thee wed,' said Howard.

'Go on,' said the little policeman, 'put it on her finger.'

'Thank you, darling,' I said, looking at the ring Howard had slid onto my wedding ring finger. I looked at it and admired it the way brides are supposed to look and admire their wedding rings.

'You may kiss the bride,' said the big policeman.

'On the lips, Howard,' I whispered in his ear, 'on the lips. We have to make this look like the real thing.'

'Gan on... go on, the cell door's open,' said the big policeman, removing his helmet as if he was in church and not standing outside a cemetery on a bitter cold December night.

Howard kissed me on the lips as lightly as a butterfly lands on a Buddleia. I kissed him the way water comes out of a burst water pipe.

His kiss gave me a pain in my crotch.

'Are these yours?' said Howard, dangling a pair of handcuffs under the little policeman's nose. 'I found them on the ground. May we go now?'

'What a night,' said the big policeman, 'wheelie bins and a mate who can't look after his handcuffs. Of course you can go, sir... but don't do it again. I'm giving you a verbal. Folk start to wonder what's going on when they see lights in a graveyard when it's dark and the graveyard's all locked up for the night. Off you go, sir... toddle, before I change my mind. And both of you sort out the day your wheelie bin is emptied… fancy dropping your handcuffs… wait till I tell the lads back at the station.'

I linked Howard back to his car. The policemen must on no account think we were not an item.

At the car he said, 'Give me the ring.'

I had saved his bacon. I had stopped him spending a night behind bars. He owed me.

'No… it's my wedding ring.'

'Utter nonsense… give it me. I want it back. Muriel, I'm not going to beg but it means a lot to me.'

'Financially or emotionally?'

'It is a memento mori… give it to me. I want it back.'

'Why?'

'I've told you.'

'Howard, if we have a stand-up row while the policemen are watching they might think twice about letting you go.'

'The police won't be going anywhere… fast.'

'What do you mean?'

'Their car is locked and I have the key.'

We were under a lamp post. By its light I saw he was grinning. A wizard who grins at his own magic was like a stand-up comedian laughing at his own jokes. His self-satisfaction annoyed me. It provoked me into blurting out: 'You're a wizard, aren't you? Wizards can't resist showing off, can they?'

'And you and Mary are witches…'

'At least our secret is safe with you.'

'But is my secret safe with you and Mary?'

'You know as well as I do, Howard, self-interest makes wizards and witches, willy-nilly, stick together. Our esoteric knowledge sticks us together like the glue dentists use when they cap teeth. I still fear the ducking stool...'

'Or being burnt at the stake...'

'I don't like thinking about that.'

'I had pretty well guessed that you knew my secret.'

'You let me see you had green blood. Only a wizard of high status could have created the thermal which caused the disintegration of my witch's costume.'

'You threatened to turn me into a toad. My response was not personal. It was a failsafe reaction. I regretted it afterwards. I apologise. Am I forgiven?'

I blew him a kiss.

'The ring... please.'

'No, I want to keep it. You were the Black Knight in the circus, weren't you? Why did you pick me to wear your champion's crown?'

'Give me the ring.'

He held out his hand.

'No. Howard, you were naughty locking the policemen out of their car.'

'Not as naughty as you... keeping what does not belong to you. The ring ...'

'I'll give it back tomorrow. It amuses me to think I am your wife. What were you doing in the cemetery?'

'The ring. I want it back, now!'

'Good night, Howard.'

Walking back to my car a hot wind blew my hair over my face. Looking back I saw... for my eyes only... Howard wearing the dress uniform of a high ranking wizard. It was like looking at the aurora borealis. Oh dear, I really had annoyed him.

The policemen were arguing.

'You had the key.'

'You're the driver. You had the key.'

'You've already lost your handcuffs.'

'I didn't lose them.'

'How come that bloke found them, if you didn't lose them?'

My car did not want to start. When it did its lights wouldn't work; then its windscreen wipers went berserk. Howard was a wizard with a temper.

I drove past the policemen without lights; who cares about a motorist driving without lights when you are going to have to phone in and tell the desk sergeant: 'Sarge, we've lost our car keys.'

Back in the safety of my own home I examined the ring. On it I read the inscription HS+PS. Before I rang Mary to tell her what had taken place between myself and Howard, I sent a text to Whitby. It was important I kept them up to date.

When I rang Mary, I told her everything. She told me that to help Howard get over the shock of what he'd seen in the school yard she'd taken him to the Dyer's Hand public house for a restorative drink.

'Muriel, I really felt sorry for him.'

'What about me? I saw the bloody corpse as well you know. It wasn't pleasant. Don't you think I'm upset? What about Gwen? She's lost a son. What about Joe? He's lost a brother. And another thing… Howard left me in the yard. He should have stayed with me… kept me company… held my hand. When I saw him tonight he never told me he'd been drinking with you at the Dyer's Hand. He kept that quiet... bloody men. Some knight in shining armour, he is.'

'Muriel... calm down. After you'd gone to take Joe home in the police car... I'm telling you, Howard was in an awful state.'

'He was full of bounce at the cemetery.'

'I don't wish to sound big headed but I'm thinking the talking I gave him in the Dyer's must have done him good. Remember, a few years ago I took a course in counselling at Whitby. I was top of the class.'

'How long were you in the Dyer's Hand?'

'Half an hour, no more. He bought me a cheese panini. Remember how the leader of our coven looked when she found Christ's stigma on her palm?'

'Of course... I was the one who caught her when she fainted. What's that got to do with Howard? Howard didn't faint in the Dyer's, did he?'

'Not quite... but almost. I think he was in shock. When I was speaking to him his flesh and blood body was in the Dyer's but his mind was... I don't know where.'

'I know this sounds silly but you don't think he's a vampire-wizard, do you?'

'Why?'

'When he came out of the cemetery he seemed, well, full of vim.'

'You mean, as if he'd had a blood transfusion?'

'Yes.'

'Muriel, you know as well as I do, vampires feed off the living. You are forgetting your elementary witch knowledge. Wizards and vampires don't get on.'

'They are not blood brothers.'

'You will have your little joke, won't you?'

'Witches and wizards aren't supposed to get on.'

'That's true.'

'In which case, how come I'm head over heels in love with one?'

'There are exceptions to every rule.'

Before turning in for the night I had a whisky nightcap. Without Tilly prowling around, the house felt empty. I sipped my night cap, looking at her grave.

# THE JUBILEE IS A
# CRIME SCENE

The next morning, I drove to school wondering if Howard and I would still be on speaking terms. Last night we had placed our cards on the table. He now knew I was a witch. I now knew he was a wizard. I'd saved him from a night in the cells. He owed me.

At school I was shocked to find three police vans in the staff carpark. A man, in a white coverall forensic suit, was coming out of the school, carrying a cardboard box.

In the staffroom, Mary told me: 'Ted's gone missing… the police are after him … they've found stolen goods in the boiler room… Ted's more than a caretaker … he's a fence.'

'I always knew he was dodgy.'

I flashed Howard's ring.

'When are you going to give it back?'

I shrugged. 'Where is he?'

'Howard?'

'Yes… is he in school?'

'Yes.'

'Where?'

'His classroom.'

In his classroom I found Howard staring out of a window at back lanes and chimney pots. He was deep in thought. He was a non-responding space probe. Why had he not turned round when I'd entered? Only, when I'd said, 'Howard …' did he turn and look at me.

'We need to talk,' I said.

'Give me the ring.'

'No.'

'I want it back.'

'Last night you made use of me. I played along to help you.'

'When do I get the ring back?'

'When you tell me what you were doing in the cemetery. We meet at lunchtime. I suggest we go for a drive in your car.'

'Why my car?'

'Because, Howard, I've never had a ride in a car with a surfboard on its roof.'

The children streaming into the classroom stopped us exchanging further intimacies.

In my classroom, Joe asked me: 'Miss, why's the police here?'

'I don't know, Joe.'

'I bet you do, Miss. Miss, a don't want to be a bear.'

Before the start of morning assembly, a monitor came into my classroom with one of Monica's round-robin notes on pink paper. It was in bullet points. Monica was fond of bullet points. I read:

- No assembly this morning
- Our school is a crime scene!! OMG

- The police may wish to question you and your class
- The evening performance of the pantomime will NOT be cancelled.
- No children to go to the loo during lesson time.
- Straws must be removed from milk bottles.
- I am three presents short for our secret Santa draw.
- Snowflakes and hugs.

At ten o'clock a detective came into my classroom without knocking. This annoyed me. After my aborted chat with Howard, I was not in the best of moods.

'Joe,' I was saying, 'if I cut a cake into two equal pieces what would each piece be called?'

'Miss, a don't want to be a bear.'

'Mrs Thayne?' said the detective.

He looked too young to be a detective.

'You know my name.'

'It's on your classroom door. Sweaty socks?' he said, sniffing my classroom's rancid air the way Tilly used to sniff old food in her bowl.

'It's off the children's damp clothes.'

'Nice quiet class. Little angels, are they? Not like the folk I have to deal with.'

'How can I help?'

'I want to ask the kids if they know anything about what happened when this teenager...' looking at his notebook, 'Michael Rowe, jumped off the roof up there... a flat roof, I believe.'

'It's called the "leads".'

'Get away...'

'Class,' I said, 'pens and pencils down. Everyone look this way. This gentleman is a policeman. He wants to ask you some questions.'

'Miss, if he's a copper,' said Norman, a boy I kept close to my desk (Norman was "challenging"), 'where's his uniform? Have you asked him for ID? That's what me dad does.'

'I'll ask the questions, son,' said the detective. 'Mrs Thayne, I think it would be best if you went outside… have a cup of tea in the staffroom. It's no good me standing here and the angels ha! ha! thinking you are in charge when I'm asking the questions.'

'Are you sure?'

'Mrs Thayne, I can handle a few snotty nosed kids.'

I did not go to the staffroom for a cuppa. I went to see Mary in her classroom.

'I'll give him ten minutes,' I told her. 'Norman's in a helluva mood.'

The detective left my classroom, backwards, the way a lion retreats from a buffalo.

'Have you finished your interrogation?' I asked him.

'Yes and no,' he said. 'I've had more co-operation from murderers… I'm off.'

In the classroom Norman was jumping from desk top to desk top the way mountaineers in the Alps jump over crevasse.

Ever so slowly, all the time watching the children… never taking my eyes off them… I folded my arms. One by one they folded their arms. I put my arms on my shoulders. One by one, they too – including Norman – put their hands on their shoulders. They knew the routine.

When I was certain I had their attention, I said: 'Back to work.'

'Miss,' said Joe, 'Norman told the detective to "fuck off".'

# HOWARD TAKES ME INTO HIS CONFIDENCE

**A**t lunchtime, after we had dismissed our classes, Howard came into my classroom.

'Let's go,' he said.

'In your car?'

'Yes.'

'You agree that we need to talk?'

'Yes.'

On our way to his car we talked about the pantomime. Because stolen goods had been found in the school's boiler room, Monica had wanted that night's performance of the pantomime cancelled. She'd told him, that a crime scene and a pantomime were not compatible; that a pantomime and a crime scene were oil and water. On the other hand, as far as the police were concerned, it was OK for the show to go ahead.

'I told, her,' he said, 'if the law says it's OK for the pantomime to be performed tonight, then, it should go ahead. Why should a few stolen goods stop a children's pantomime?'

'If it was cancelled the children would be awfully disappointed,' I said.

'How is Paul doing? Will we have a witch tonight? Is his grandmother looking after him?'

'Paul will be a wow for the witch tonight,' I said. 'Thanks to his grandmother he knows his lines better than he knows his times table.'

'Thank goodness for grandmothers.'

'And for a real witch who was prepared to be an understudy for a pantomime witch.'

'But, not tonight?'

'Definitely not tonight.'

By way of making small talk, I said, 'I feel like a teenager sitting in a car with a surfboard on its roof.'

'Hawaii is the place for surfing... blue skies, warm water, big waves.'

'You sound nostalgic.'

'Once I've cleared up this business...'

'And what business would that be?'

'Have you not done due diligence on me? Your coven has a reputation for thoroughness.'

'As far as Whitby is concerned, you are a tabula rasa. You might exist, but, then again you might not. For the little Whitby has been able to find out about you... well, I wouldn't be surprised if I was sitting next to an apparition. You are real, aren't you?'

'When I cut myself I bleed.'

'Green blood, I know. Where are we going?'

'To the cemetery... you want to know what I was doing in the cemetery last night... I'm going to show you... and when I've shown you, I want the ring back... deal?'

'Howard, you can have the ring back, now. I wasn't planning to keep it forever and ever. I should have given it back to you last night. I was teasing.'

'I'll have the ring back when you have seen what I have to show you in the cemetery.'

We drove into the cemetery behind a hearse, pulled by two black horses. The undertaker walking in front of the hearse was dressed as a cowboy.

I wondered… would the old woman I'd spoken to in Ma's pie shop be watching?

Mourners were dressed as cowgirls and cowboys. When the cortege turned right, we turned left, into: Visitors Parking.

The cemetery covered many acres. At its centre, birdsong replaced traffic noise.

'She's over there,' said Howard.

'Who is?'

'My wife.'

I followed him to a freshly dug grave. A headstone told me it was the resting place of: Pamela Star. It told me she was a journalist; it told me her date of birth and the month in which she had passed away. Her death was recent.

For how long do you stay silent when you are watching a widower stare at his wife's grave? What was he thinking? Had he broken into the cemetery last night to be near her? To mourn at the side of her grave? I found it hard to empathise. His wife meant nothing to me.

'Howard,' I said, when he bent over the grave and began pulling up a rose bush, 'what are you doing? You will get your trousers dirty.'

'See,' he said, holding up for me to inspect the rose bush he'd pulled out of the grave's soil, 'it should not have been easy to pull up. The earth is frozen. I should have had to use a spade. It was Pam's favourite rose. I planted it myself. I planted it, not where it is now. I planted it in the middle of her grave. Someone has dug it up. When they replanted it, they put it too close to the headstone. They did not plant it as a gardener would... they stuck it in the soil... that was why it was so easy to pull up. I was in the cemetery last night to find out who had moved it and why. My dear wife did not commit suicide: she was murdered.'

'The posy I spied you laying on the Wagon Way... that marks the spot where she was found, right?'

'Yes.'

'You were laying a wreath.'

'If I hadn't had to go on a training course in the Andaman Islands, I'd have been with her, here on Tyneside.'

'Wizards have to go on courses?'

'All the time... courses and meetings.'

'Last year Whitby brought in a consultant to give us a lecture on levitation. The only thing that levitated was her fee.'

'I know what you mean. Muriel, look at the rose's roots... tell me what you see.'

He held the rose bush at arm's length, as if it was a viper and that if he held it too close to his face it might bite him.

'I see,' I said, 'the face of the devil.'

'It must be exorcised.'

To exorcise the evil in the bush he flung it into the air, where it exploded like a firework.

'The mourners at the cowboy funeral will think the cowboy they are mourning is saying an adieu.'

'Possibly… I have kept my part of the bargain. I have told you why I was in the cemetery last night.'

'You want the ring back?'

'Yes.'

I handed it over.

'Thank you,' he said. 'Muriel, before we return to school, there is something else I wish to tell you. I need your help. I wish to take you into my confidence. I think what I am about to tell you may shock you. You have not asked me how I came to be in possession of the ring.'

'If it was your wife's wedding ring, it would be yours to keep when she died.'

'Pam didn't die, she was murdered. That ring was on her finger when she was interred. I should know, I was there when the coffin was closed.'

'Howard, good god, you weren't in the cemetery last night digging up your wife to get your hands on her wedding ring, were you?'

'Don't be absurd.'

'OK, how did you get it?'

'I took it off Michael Rowe's little finger.'

'What!'

'I believe I was meant to find it.'

'Why?'

'Michael was Stanley's postman. Stanley was sending me a message. He was punishing me for the way I'd humiliated him, on the Wagon Way. As a wizard I can use clouds as mirrors to see round corners and over walls.

I saw what the children could not see. I saw Stanley on the roof.'

'Stanley was on the roof with Michael?'

'Yes.'

'Stanley pushed Michael off the roof?'

'When Michael jumped, more than likely, he thought he could fly. Stanley and his gang take drugs. They think Stanley is a god. They believe what he tells them; they do as he says. The children have been bribed to keep their mouths shut with pencil cases. They are allowed to say they saw a ghost on the roof but, not, Stanley. In the mayhem following Michael jumping off the roof, Stanley made his escape unseen. The people in this town know which side their bread is buttered on. They are scared of the Knockers.'

'The Knockers… I keep hearing about them… how do you know all this?'

'I have a network of informers. Gwen Rowe is one. Does that surprise you? And Joe is a never-ending source of information. Stanley killed Gwen's dog…'

And my cat Tilly…'

'Mary's husband and Ambrose are in business with Stanley. They have had a falling out.'

'Which is why Stanley got his gang to invade the golf course?'

'Just so.'

'If you are right in thinking Michael was Stanley's postman… how did Stanley come to be in possession of your wife's ring?'

'There are many possibilities… some are too awful to contemplate.'

'Howard, tell me, I'm a big girl. On a witch's survival course, I skinned a rabbit.'

'A clue is in the rose I showed you.'

'Good god, you are not suggesting Stanley is a grave robber, are you?'

'It is a possibility. On the other hand, the undertaker may have opened the coffin and taken the ring... on the other hand... until I get more facts I am keeping an open mind.'

'Which is why we need to work together.'

'Yes.'

For many seconds we stared at Pam's grave the way men who don't know a carburettor from a canapé, stare at a car's engine.

'Howard,' I said, 'can you feel what I'm feeling? I know the ground isn't really shaking but when I look at your wife's grave I feel that it is shaking... that the cemetery is the centre of an earth tremor... that, at any moment ghosts will pop out of their coffins and give you and I a bloody good talking to.'

To show he was sympathetic to all I had said, he took my hand.

After a few seconds more of staring at the grave, he said, 'Let's go, we have children to teach.'

'And a pantomime to put on. Joe doesn't want to be a bear.'

'I never wanted to be a wizard. It was part of my inheritance. I was told in no uncertain terms that Mother Nature had vouchsafed me a great honour. That I should stop moaning and get on with learning spells.'

'Me too.'

'Witches and wizards have more in common than they think they have.'

Driving back to school he told me why he thought his wife had been murdered.

'Pam was a journalist. She was on to something… I know she was. She was suspicious about Ma Mason's Pie Shop. When Pam was on to a story, she was a bulldog. She wouldn't let go.'

'You think she was killed because of what she knew?'

'Yes… before I return to the States it is a problem I must solve.'

'You will let me help?'

'Of course. I am not one of those men who think they can do everything by themselves. Albert Einstein was helped by a friend who was better at maths than he was.'

'If it's good enough for Einstein, it's good enough for Howard.'

'Something like that. I would be honoured if you were part of my investigative team.'

'Your friends at the circus, do they help you?'

'Yes… playing the Black Knight gives me a buzz.'

'You lied about having an appointment with a chiropodist.'

'Yes.'

'A wizard who admits to telling porkies… whatever next?'

'A witch who broke the rule that witches and wizards do not put spells on each other.'

'Sorry… I got carried away.'

'Impetuosity is a forgivable weakness.'

# A SEMBLANCE
# OF ROUTINE

**B**ack at school Howard went to his classroom; I went to mine. It would be an understatement to say we both had a lot to think about. Before the bell went for the end of the lunch break and the children were allowed back into school, I went to the staffroom... an empty staffroom, and made myself a coffee.

I thought about making one for Howard, but didn't. I had the feeling he wanted to be alone.

I was feeling peckish. If Ma's had been open I'd have bought one of her pies. But, Ma's was closed... why was she closed?

I took my coffee to Mary's classroom. I found her looking up 'Power of attorney' on her laptop. I told her about my visit to the cemetery with Howard. She was interested but I got the strong impression that she was more interested in 'Power of attorney'. She was itching to get her hands on the Arse Hole's assets. I stopped updating her when the bell rang; lunchtime was over. Outside, the teacher on yard duty would be blowing her whistle... the children would be lining up... class by class they would file into school... routine... at least a semblance of routine.

Routine is the cement of everyday life; it is not climbing Mount Everest or doing a first parachute jump. Sometimes we find it boring, sometimes... as I did now, we find it as comfy as an old pair of shoes.

Joe, dear Joe, who yesterday had lost a brother but still had come into school, had his own routine. He kept telling me: 'Miss, I don't want to be a bear.'

I did not ask him how his mother was coping; not having children of my own I found it impossible to imagine a mother's grief at losing a child.

My routine, to help me stop asking why Ma's was closed... to stop me thinking about Howard's wife, Pamela... to stop me thinking about Michael jumping off the roof... to stop me grieving for my beloved Tilly... was helping my pupils make Christmas cards and calendars. When you are making bows out of red ribbon you have to concentrate.

My pupils were hyper. The elephant in the room was the pantomime's evening performance. Who wants to make Christmas cards and calendars when in a few hours... that very evening, you were going on stage dressed as a ladybird... a tree... a badger... a butterfly... a caterpillar?

In a corner of my classroom, close to his camp bed, Paul, under his grandmother's supervision, was cutting a piece of green felt into the shape of a Christmas stocking.

More routine... the afternoon coffee break... the children, including Paul, filing out to play... Monica telling Hilary who was on yard duty to blow her whistle on time and not five minutes late to give her pals a longer break... routine. Howard, in the hall, during the break, playing Handel's 'Dead March' from 'Saul'. When I took him a coffee he was polite and said, 'Thank you' but, he did not stop playing. As I well knew, he had other things on his mind.

When the bell rang to signal the end of the school day, I reminded 'butterflies', 'fairies', 'caterpillars', 'bears', 'trees'… of the time they were to return to school. They had been issued with different coloured badges. Red badge wearers would be let into school earlier than blue badge wearers.

'Miss, why can't I come into school the same time as the caterpillars?'

'Caterpillars take longer to dress than trees.'

'Miss, what time do I have to come?'

'I've just told you.'

'I've forgotten. Miss, Joe doesn't want to be a bear.'

'Half past six.'

'Miss, me grandma wants to come… she hasn't got a ticket.'

'She can pay at the door. If there's room, "tickets" will squeeze her in.'

Paul did not go home. Until the curtain went up he was a prisoner. His grandmother was his warder. There was no way he was going to do a runner. If he went AWOL there was no way yours truly was going to stand in for him, dressed as a witch, in front of a live audience.

To help him cope during the three hours before the show was due to start his grandmother hand fed him grapes dipped in tomato ketchup.

'Paul loves his tomato sauce, Mrs Thayne. You put on as much sauce as you like, my darling. I have another bottle in my bag.'

'Gran?'

'Yes, my darling?'

'What if I forget me lines?'

'I'll be in the wings to remind you,' I told him.

'What's the wings?'

'It's what we call the sides off stage. The bits the audience can't see. It's where stars like you wait before they go on.'

'I like those chocolates with the cream in the middle.'

'Eat your grapes... grapes is good for you.'

'If I eat all the grapes... then can I have a chocolate with cream in the middle?'

'Of course you can, my darling. You can have two.'


Where was Howard? He wasn't in his classroom. I was worried about him. He was a wizard with a lot on his mind. The pantomime needed him. I needed him. Why had he been playing Handel's Dead March? I knew why but didn't like to think about it.

I had jobs to do. I had to carry the costumes in my classroom to the backstage classroom Monica had allocated as a dressing room. It was after I had carried out this task to my satisfaction and was on my way to the staffroom to make myself and Paul's grandmother a coffee that I passed the relief caretaker. He was putting out chairs for the audience. His disguise of a cloth cap and overalls, smeared with paint, did not fool me. It was the detective who had reversed out of my classroom the way a lion retreats from a buffalo.

What on earth was a detective doing in school dressed as a caretaker?

'Mrs Thayne! Mrs Thayne! Me wing's broken.'

I looked at my watch… bloody hell… the butterflies were in. How time flies when you are busy. If the pantomime was a jet airliner the passengers were now boarding.

'Brenda, stop crying. I will fix it. Have no fear, Mrs Thayne is here.'

Ha! Ha! Did I sound confident? I hoped I did.

In another backstage classroom, Paul, dressed as a witch, was learning his lines.

'What do you say, Paul?' said his grandmother.

'I am a witch… a wicked witch.'

'Well done, my darling.'

'Can I have a chocolate?'

'Course you can, my darling.'

The hall, like a tide coming in, was filling up with mams and dads… grans and grandpas… aunts and uncles. I kept out of their way. I knew from bitter experience that you never stopped a parent from the Burgoyne estate moving a chair a metre closer to the front of the stage.

Thirty minutes before the show was due to start I went to the loo. In the loo I found Monica sitting in a wash basin with her head in her hands.

'I hate fucking pantomimes,' she told me. 'Do you think it would hurt me–' looking at the strip of tablet foil in her hand– 'if I took another one?'

'Monica, I don't know. I'm not a doctor.'

'But you are fond of Howard, aren't you? I know you are. I hate him. Sod him, he's taken my school off me.'

'If the pantomime is a success it may help you get promoted.'

'Do you think so? I never thought of that.'

She swallowed a pill.

'There, I've done it now. I don't know why I let him get to me... I really don't. He'll soon be gone. Jupiter is coming back in January.'

'Oh, there you are, Monica,' said Hilary, 'I've been looking all over for you. Hansel has a nosebleed. A fairy tripped him up with her wand.'

'What do you want me to do about it?'

'You have the keys to the medical room.'

'Do I?'

'Yes. You do.'

'Where's Mr Star? Muriel...'

'I don't know...'

'Men... I hate them. Belinda has the keys to the medical room... fucking pantomimes... I hate them... hate them.'

# THE FIRST PERFORMANCE OF THE PANTOMIME IN FRONT OF A LIVE AUDIENCE

n classrooms behind the stage, children, under supervision, were changing into their costumes.

A ladybird had lost a spot. A fairy had a crumpled wing. How much make-up does Hansel need? Yes, Gretel, you can go to the loo but be quick.

It was into this mayhem that Howard, prior to going front of stage to play soothing music to the audience, as they took their seats, now appeared.

Paul was eating a banana. His grandmother was between him and the classroom door; no way was he going to be allowed to do a runner.

'Mr Star,' said Paul's grandmother, 'you look like a movie star.'

'You look gorgeous,' I said, 'pure Hollywood.'

Howard was wearing a red velvet jacket, white trousers, a frilly white shirt and a blue bowtie that looked as if it might have been borrowed from a clown.

'Will you be leaving us when the teacher who is off sick comes back?' said Paul's grandmother. 'If you leave us… we'll shrivel up like autumn leaves.' She paused. 'Dear me, what have I said? I've never said anything like that before… autumn leaves, indeed. If that's what working in the theatre does to you… I'll have more of it. Mr Star, you naughty man, I do believe you've put a spell on me.'

'Madam,' said Howard, bowing, 'I do not come for praise or adulation. I come to ask after the theatrical health of my star performer. How yuh deeing, Paul?'

He and Paul cemented their bond with a high five. When they smacked hands, it rained chocolate buttons. Howard's bowtie spun like an aeroplane's propeller; putting out his arms he flew out of the classroom pretending to be an aeroplane.

'I like a man with a sense of humour,' said Paul's grandmother, 'they make you laugh when they are doing it. Paul, don't you go eating those chocolate buttons off the floor until your gran has washed them. We don't want you going on stage with a belly ache, do we?'

'Can I put tomato sauce on them?'

'Course you can, my darling. Paul loves tomato sauce, Mrs Thayne.'

Children who'd escaped their minders peeked through the stage curtains.

'There's me mam.'

'Let me see.'

'Me mam's with her boyfriend.'

'There's me Nan.'

'Mr Star's playing the piano.'

'I know that… I'm not deaf.'

'My dad thinks Mr Star is sexy.'

'Is your dad gay?'

'Nar but me Uncle George is.'

Monica signalled Howard to start the show… a roll on the drums and we were off. The curtains jerked open. The audience, when they saw the scenery, clapped.

Peeking through a side curtain I saw looks of total amazement on the faces of the audience. How come their child… the little bugger who this morning had refused to eat his breakfast, was singing like an angel? How come the child dressed as a ladybird… the child, who that morning had called her baby brother a fucking idiot… was smiling at the audience as if butter wouldn't melt in her mouth?

Paul, dressed as the wicked witch, came off stage, exhausted but elated. He hadn't forgotten his lines. Pearls of sweat dripped off the end of his green nose.

'Miss,' he said, 'they're clapping.'

'I know, Paul, they are clapping for you.'

'For me, Miss?'

'Yes, Paul, for you.'

'Paul, my darling,' said his grandmother, 'have a chocolate.'

'Nar, I'm sick of chocolates. I likes claps better than chocolates.'

In the backstage classrooms, children, waiting to go on, under the supervision of teacher and parent 'minders', watched television.

Being a minder was boring. It was hard work. It lacked glamour. You were away from the action. 'Minders' had a reputation for going AWOL. You'd find them backstage, getting in everyone's way. As soon as a parent 'minder' knew her child was on stage she deserted her post to watch the apple of her eye.

Excited children had weak bladders.

'Miss, Miss, I need the toilet. Miss, 'am desperate.'

'Do you really need to go?'

'Yes, Miss… honest, Miss.'

Fairies used their fairy wands as swords. The paper wings of butterflies were handkerchiefs. Spiders used their legs, made out of rolls of newspaper, to poke ladybirds.

'Miss… Miss, Beryl's poked me in the eye with her wand.'

'Didn't.'

'Did… Miss, a can't see.'

'Of course you can see, Dylan.'

'Can't…'

'How many Maltesers do I have in my hand?'

'Two, Miss.'

'Take them…'

'Thank you, Miss.'

Two mice argued about their 'squeak'.

'You sound more like a cat, than a mouse.'

'No, I, divent.'

'Yes, yuh do.'

'Mr Star said I'm a good squeaker… so there.'

'Bet he didn't.'

'Yes, he did.'

'No, he didn't.'

A big boy dressed as a tree – he was inside a tube of corrugated cardboard – was stopping a woodcutter seeing the television.

'Bobby, let the woodcutters see the television.'

'Can't move, Miss,' said the tree, 'I'm a tree... trees divent have legs.'

'Kevin, move... if you don't, I'll tell the woodcutter to cut you down.'

'Miss,' said Joe, 'I don't want to be a bear.'

A 'jug' screamed: 'Miss, me handle's bent... not ganin on with a bent handle... look stupid... fuck off, Kevin. Miss, Kevin's laughing at me 'cos me handle's bent.'

And, what fun it was to pull the cellophane bow tied around the neck of a 'sweet'. If you pulled hard enough you could make its wearer choke... you could make the wearer gan red. When a 'sweet' turned red you shouted 'strawberry'.

It was my job to transfer the children from a 'holding' classroom to the back of the stage. It was Monica's job to tell them when to go on.

I was on my way back to a 'holding' classroom, having just delivered ten mice to 'stage wing/left', when, looking through a window I saw a nearby warehouse was on fire.

'Miss?'

'Yes, Ruby, what is it?'

'Miss, I've lost a wing. Barry pulled it off. He's hid it. He won't tell me where it is.'

'Why'd he do that?'

'Cos a wanted to give him a kiss.'

'Come with me.'

I found the missing wing stuffed behind a radiator.

Strapping it on Ruby, I said, 'There you are… you are once again a fairy with two wings.'

'Miss?'

'Yes?'

'Do boys not like girls kissing them?'

'Some boys do, some boys don't.'

'Barry, didn't…'

'Off you go.'

How might Howard react if I tried to give him a kiss?

That's what I was thinking when the street lights went out; followed a second later, by the lights in the school going out. The nearby warehouse on fire was no longer a warehouse on fire; it was an erupting volcano. Every few seconds something in it exploded.

A parent helper shouted: 'It's the solvent factory.'

Children began to scream.

A parent, holding the hand of a ladybird, was telling Monica: 'If the street lights are off as well as the school lights, it means it's a substation failure… could take hours to fix. I used to work for the electricity board.'

Someone shouted: 'I can smell smoke.'

And so could I. The school's fire alarm went off. Its noise hurt my ears.

It was an explosion inside the school that started the stampede.

Monica screamed: 'Everyone out!'

Looking through a window and down into the yard, an explosion from the solvent factory showed me two men, pushing and shoving each other. When one of them fell over the other one jumped on top of him.

Then, Thomas passed me clutching the hands of a 'ladybird' and a 'badger'.

'Thomas,' I told him, 'down the stairs and into the yard.'

'I know, Miss. I'm not daft, Miss.'

I spotted, Joe.

'Joe, follow, Thomas. Thomas, look after, Joe.'

'I divent need looking after, I'm a bear. Roar! Roar!'

'Boys,' I shouted, 'down the stairs… now!'

The hall was filling with smoke.

I'm a witch. I fear fire. Too many of my ancestors have been burnt at the stake.

Parents of children taking part in the show wanted to come backstage to collect their children. I told them the children were being escorted to safety down the stairs at the front of the school.

Some parents would not listen; they pushed me out of the way. They screamed their children's names.

I could see the flashing light on the tip of Howard's conductor's baton.

'Follow the lighthouse… follow the lighthouse…' he was chanting.

He was leading the choir and musicians to safety down the stairs at the other end of the hall.

The hall was not so full of smoke that it stopped me seeing Mary and Monica. They were holding handkerchiefs over their mouths. Monica wanted to know if Belinda was safe. I assured her that she was.

'I saw her going down the stairs with the mice.'

'That's good.'

Only when we were as certain as we could be that the hall was empty did we make our way down smoke-filled stairs and into the yard.

In the yard there was a fire engine, an ambulance and a police car. Sirens… flashing blue lights… the yard was a fairground.

A fireman was climbing a turntable ladder. Every few seconds, an explosion from the burning solvent factory lit up the yard.

In the safety of a nearby street, I heard the appalling news… a policeman had been stabbed… that the policeman was dead.

'I thought he was the caretaker,' a parent told me.

'He was in disguise… wasn't he?' another parent said. 'Plain clothes… undercover.'

I remembered the two men I'd seen fighting in the yard. A 'ladybird' grabbed my hand. She was in my class. She was shivering. She was not wearing shoes.

A story began circulating that a child had died in the fire.

Parents, desperate to find their children, were pushing and shoving through the crowd.

'Jane!'

'Dylan!'

'Have yuh seen George?'

'Divent worry… he's safe. He's in the street ower there.'

It was dangerous to be too close to the school. Its roof was ablaze. Debris was falling off its roof. The police moved us to a street out of the range of flying debris.

The residents of the 'safe' street were at their front doors.

At one front door, an old lady told her husband: 'Ern, don't stand there deeing nowt… put the kettle on.'

'Bring the bairns in here,' shouted another resident. 'It might be Christmas but there's room at this inn. You can't let bairns stand outside on a night like this… the poor mites will freeze to death. It's not a fairy costume you should be wearing, pet–' this to a child dressed as a fairy– 'it's a fur coat. Howay inside and warm yourself.'

It was through this mayhem that I spotted Gwen and Una. Gwen was pushing a double buggy. The twins?

'Where's Joe?' said Gwen.

'Where's my Thomas?' said Una.

'He's safe in number forty-nine,' I said.

'I've lost Michael… if I lost Joe, I'd gan mental.'

'Mam!' shouted Joe, running towards us from the doorway of a house.

'Joe, you alright?'

'Course I'm alright.'

'What you eating?'

'Crisps… the wife in there, she gave them to me.'

'At least you've got Joe, Gwen; what I want to know is, where is my Thomas?'

'He's…' said Joe, pausing to put a potato crisp in his mouth, 'he's in number forty-nine having a shit.'

'Good night, Miss,' said a fairy riding piggy-back on her father's shoulders.

'Night, Michelle.'

'Thank goodness she's safe,' said her mother. 'Is it true a policeman's been murdered?'

'I don't know,' I said. 'I've heard rumours.'

Mary came up to me with a cup of tea.

'Thanks,' I said.

I smelt brandy.

'A toddy,' I said, 'just what I needed. Have you seen Howard?'

Mary shook her head. No matter where we looked, we could see no sign of him. Had he gone AWOL? He'd left me alone with Michael's dead body in the yard, had he now left me and the other teachers to look after the children stranded in the street?

I spotted Monica and Belinda sitting on a wall. They looked exhausted. I know this is an awful thing to say but... they looked like gargoyles.

Residents, with folded arms, stood gossiping at their front doors. Over and over again I heard it mentioned that a policeman had been murdered.

After flickering for a second the streetlights came back on.

A policewoman was pushing her way through the crowd towards me.

'Hello, Mrs Thayne.'

'Hello, Tracey.'

Tracey looked the worse for wear. She was hatless. Her hair was dishevelled. Her face was smudged with soot.

'Mrs Thayne,' she said, 'I'm looking for witnesses. What can you tell me about tonight?'

'There's been a murder, hasn't there?' said Mary.

'How'd you know about that?'

'Everyone is talking about it.'

'Has the detective I met in the hall... the one disguised as a school caretaker, been murdered?' I asked.

'Yes, he has. What do you know about it?'

'I saw two men fighting in the yard.'

'Anyone you know?'

'Too far away for me to tell.'

'The word on the street,' said Mary, 'is that Ma Mason's grandson, Stanley… him from the pie shop, was in the yard fighting with someone.'

'I've heard that as well,' said Tracey.

'He lives with his grandmother,' I said, 'above the pie shop… you know, Ma Mason's pie shop in Fenwick Street.'

'The pie shop, Mrs Thayne, is a crime scene.'

'What's happened? I know the shop was closed.'

'You know, Ma Mason?'

'I was a customer in her shop. She tried to convert me to naturism.'

'I loved her mince and onion patties,' said Mary.

'Tasty, were they?' said Tracey.

'Very moreish… not good for the figure though.'

'That's interesting…'

'We all loved Ma Mason's pies,' I said. 'They were moreish. Are you not fond of a mince and onion, Tracey?'

'I am when I know where the meat came from.'

'What do you mean by that? Dear me, was Ma putting horse meat in her pies?'

'I'm not here to spread gossip, Mrs Thayne… there's enough of that already. What I know is sub judice… though I've no doubt it will find its way into the newspapers. There's money in selling information to the press and… believe me, the tabloids will love this. ASAP someone will contact you to make a statement about the two men you saw fighting in the yard.'

It was Monica who dismissed us, told us to go home. To the best of her knowledge all the children were safe.

Mary and I had parked our cars far enough away from the school for them not to have been damaged. Before we went our separate ways we hugged. We discussed the 'Howard problem'. Where had he gone? Where was he? Why had he disappeared? What would happen tomorrow? It was clear the school would not be open to pupils. The start of the Christmas holiday was only a day away. Would the children be given an extra day's holiday?

Entering my home I shouted 'Tilly'! I hadn't forgotten she was dead. My hollering for her was by way of trying to bring her back to life. I knew it wouldn't. I was playing a game... a silly game. Without her the house was cold and empty. The thermostat disagreed.

I am an English witch and, ipso facto, a great believer in the restorative powers of a cuppa.

I was on the point of removing a teabag from my mug when my front doorbell rang. It rang in code. The code told me it was Mary. What did she want? We'd only just parted company.

'Muriel,' she blurted out, when I opened the front door to let her in, 'the Arse Hole's wanted by the police... he's on the run. He's scarpered. The police have a warrant to search my home. They are all over the house. Without a by-your-leave they've taken his computer. Where's the bugger diddled off to? That's what I want to know. Can I stop the night? I keep ringing his mobile but there's no answer.'

That night, Mary and I, dressed as witches, held a vigil in front of Tilly's grave.

We were meditating... trying to find answers to the questions: Where was Howard? Where had he disappeared to when the school had been burning? Had Stanley murdered the detective? And, where was the Arse Hole? And, for that matter, where was Ted? Was he on bread and water in a cell or, was he too, on the run?

Every so often we heard a miaow. What was Tilly trying to tell us?

# I MEET HOWARD IN A POLICE STATION

**M**ary and I ended our vigil at six in the morning. It was while we were tucking into tea and toast that Monica sent us an e-mail on group chat. We read:

School is closed. Today, you work from home. My headteacher's room is toast. The cause of the explosion, therein, was the overturning of my Calor gas heater, by the hooligan who murdered the detective. The children have been informed re the closure. Their Christmas holiday starts from today. Should any child not have received our e-mail, Belinda and I will be in our cars outside the school to put them right. Some good news. Juniper will be back off the sick after Christmas.

Snowflakes and hugs.

'I have a hair appointment at five,' said Mary; 'now that I know I'm on holiday, I wonder if I can bring it forward... on the other hand... now that the Arse Hole's on the run, I don't have to look glamorous.'

'You can look like a mature witch...'

'With bags of poison under my eyes...'

'Cackle!'

'Cackle!'

In private, witches succumb to fits of cackling the way non-witches succumb to fits of the giggles.

It was in between cackles that my phone rang. It was Tracey, the policewoman.

'The police,' I told Mary, 'want me to make a statement.'

'About the men you saw fighting in the yard?'

'Yes.'

At the police station – Mary drove me – Tracey made us mugs of tea. Mary's mug was decorated with a repeat pattern of tiny handcuffs; mine, with crossed truncheons. It wasn't like having afternoon tea at Harrods and the tea wasn't Darjeeling, but it was nice. I signed my statement.

It was on our way out that we spotted Howard. He was sitting on a wooden bench. The old woman sitting next to him was clutching a posy of flowers. I'd a pretty good idea where the posy had come from.

What the hell was he doing here? Why was he dressed in camouflage fatigues? Why did he look like a piece of washing which, having been hung out to dry in cold weather, had frozen on the washing line?

'This is Elsie,' said Howard, introducing his companion, 'she's lost her purse.'

'It was stolen off me,' said Elsie, 'by a bloke with a bald heed… and he was wearing an earring. He was a bad'n, not like Howard, here,' patting Howard's hand. 'I've had my share of bad blokes. I knars a good man when I sees him. Last time a bloke gave me flowers–' sniffing the posy– 'I married him.'

'Howard…' I began.

'He's here to identify a deed body,' said Elsie, 'that's what he told me and I'm here for a cup of tea... with two sugars... I likes sugar... speak of the devil, here comes Jimmy now... Jimmy, where's my cup of tea? I always gets a cup of tea when me purse is stolen.'

'Not, now, Elsie, if you don't mind. This is a police station, not a coffee shop... you ready, sir?'

Howard nodded that he was 'ready'. When he stood, he swayed. I thought he might be going to faint.

'Howard...'

'I'm OK... I'm OK... meet me in the Dyer's Hand... I'll be there as soon as I have done... as soon as I have done what has to be done... they do an excellent lasagne.'

'You alright, sir?'

'Where's my cup of tea?' said Elsie. 'I always gets a cup of tea when my purse has been stolen.'

# HOWARD TELLS US SOMETHING WE FIND HARD TO BELIEVE

---

**M**ary and I waited for Howard in one of the Dyer's Hand's snugs. We were as much on edge as if we were at a Whitby coven meeting. When you were at Whitby you had to be on your toes. Some of the witches were lawyers.

When Howard slid in beside us, I offered to buy him a drink.

'That's very kind,' he said. 'I will accept anon. After what I am going to tell you… you may not feel like imbibing.'

'Do you know,' said Mary, 'that my husband is on the run from the police?'

'Mary, forget about the Arse Hole…'

'If only I could…'

'Howard,' I said, 'cut to the quick.'

'If you have eaten Ma Mason's pies you are a cannibal. You may have eaten my wife. Stanley bulked up the meat he used in his pies with human flesh. He is a grave robber.

The body the police asked me to identify was the head and shoulders of my late wife.'

'The rest of her…'

'Went into Ma's pies…'

'How do you know all this?'

'For weeks I have been working with the police. I was there last night when they broke into Ma's pie shop.'

'Mary and I were wondering where you'd disappeared to.'

'No doubt you thought I'd gone AWOL.'

'Your name was mud.'

'My apologies.'

'Carry on…'

'Stanley kept the bodies in the pie shop's freezer. The police refused to let me peek. They thought I might faint.'

'Can wizards faint?' said Mary.

'It varies from wizard to wizard.'

'And your good self?'

'When they told me they'd found body parts in the freezer I came close to fainting. In the mortuary this morning the missing parts of my wife's body were bags of ice under a white sheet. She looked like an ice maiden… but it was her, alright. I have recovered from the shock.'

'I was going to order the Dyer's steak and ale pie,' said Mary, 'but not now.'

'I know what you mean,' I said.

'I apologise, ladies. I fear what I have told you has killed your appetite.'

I looked at the bowl of assorted nibbles that had come with our drinks.

I picked up a stuffed olive.

'What's it stuffed with?' I asked Mary.

'Pimento.'

'That's what it looks like, but after what Howard's just told us... well, we could be eating anything; that black pepper on the crisps could be dust from an urn containing the mortal remains of a loved one.'

I found it hard to take on board what Howard had told me. On the other hand, all you needed to open a grave was a strong stomach and a spade. No witchcraft or wizardry was involved.

'When the tabloids got hold of the story,' said Mary, 'our town will attract ghouls the way a turd attracts flies.'

'So,' I said, 'not to beat about the besom, Stanley dug up your wife's body and put her flesh into Ma's meat pies.'

'Yes,' said Howard, 'that's exactly what he did. There were parts of two other bodies in the freezer; plus a spare leg. I had come to like Ma's meat and potato pies. I would like to think Pamela's flesh had only been used to bulk up the mince and onion. If I knew that, I'd be a much relieved wizard. If my fellow wizards get to know I've eaten my wife, I'll be a laughing stock.'

'I wonder,' I said, 'if cannibalism is addictive. You know, once you get the taste, you want more.' Looking round the lounge of the Dyer's Hand: 'Anyone you fancy?'

'How very English,' said Howard, 'to make light of the serious. Muriel, eating people is wrong. What Stanley has done will not go unpunished. I will be avenged. Stanley is more than what you English call a "nasty piece of work". He is evil, incarnate.'

'Howard,' I said, 'surely your fellow wizards would not give you a yellow card for eating a pie? You did not know what you were eating. You were an innocent muncher. I once had an affair with a Hindu. A very sexy man if ever there was one. He couldn't resist my Sunday roast. He used to tell me: "Please do not tell me I am eating the roast beef". He loved my Sunday roast more than he loved his religion… a lovely man.'

'I'm thinking,' said Mary, 'that once, after eating one of Ma's pies, I felt randy… could that have been because I'd eaten a cannibal pie?'

'Mary,' I said, 'did the Arse Hole like Ma's pies?'

'He found them moreish.'

'Would that explain his sex drive?'

'The Arse Hole?' said Howard.

'My husband,' said Mary.

'The Arse Hole,' mused Howard, 'not, I'm thinking, a term of endearment. By the way, I know where he is. Since I came to work at the Jubilee, I have built up a network of informers. Ma Mason was one of them. Do you know she is dead?'

'Ma Mason… dead,' I said.

'Stanley, so the police believe, cut her throat. Stanley is on the run with your husband, Mary, and so is the school's caretaker. Stanley pushed Michael off the roof. When I was on duty in the yard, I caught a glimpse… just a glimpse, of him on the roof. So did some of the children. He is the ghost they keep going on about. They have been bribed with pencil cases not to blab. My wife, Pamela, was murdered because she was close to finding out that Stanley was exhuming bodies… that he was bulking up the meat he put in his pies with human flesh… that he was selling cannibal pies. My wife's body was exhumed and eaten in the belief that when she'd been eaten… everything she knew would be destroyed.'

I reminded him: 'On the Wagon Way you humiliated Stanley in front of his pals.'

'My finding my wife's wedding ring on Michael's finger was his revenge. Stanley gave my wife's wedding ring to Michael… more than likely Stanley slid it on Michael's finger himself… when the poor kid was out of his mind… high on drugs. Ted told Stanley I was on yard duty. I was meant to find the ring. Stanley was sending me a message. He was putting me in my place for showing him up in front of his pals. It was his way of telling me that he had power over me. Muriel… Mary, I need your help. I know from reading your private histories…'

'You have read the files Whitby keep on us?'

'Yes. I know of your expertise in the subtle art of "facilitation". Mary, your first husband drowned in a fishing accident…'

'His waders filled with water. He was trying to catch a salmon.'

'Come, come… you drew his attention to the fish. You knew he was competitive. You encouraged him to take a risk. And you, Muriel, the "banana skin facilitator". How many skins did you drop in front of Reg? And "windy" Albert who wanted to get into the Guinness Book of Records by farting "God Save the King" while jumping off a bridge.'

'He was a show off… Albert only came to life when he was showing off.'

'Why are you letting us know, you know our secrets?' said Mary.

'So, he can blackmail us into doing anything he tells us to do,' I said.

'Blackmail us and we'll tell your fraternity you ate your wife,' said Mary.

'When we want to be, Mary and I can be ruthless,' I said. 'Last year we let down the tyres of an OFSTED inspector's car.'

'He didn't like us and we didn't like him.'

'I did the deed while Mary kept watch.'

'Tut! Tut!' said Howard. 'You let the tyres down, manually... you didn't use a spell? When I want to deflate a tyre, I look at it... concentrate... give it the "wizard's glare" and down it goes. Hiss! Hiss! Hiss!'

I do not like being 'tutted' at. To put him in his place I launched a spell at him.

'I do believe I felt a tickle,' he said. 'Muriel, do behave.'

Spells and bullets have this in common... they ricochet. When my spell bounced off Howard it removed a soup spoon out of the hand of a nearby diner.

'Shooting pain in my hand...' said the diner, 'strange... never happened before.'

'Muriel,' said Howard, 'do behave. You know the rules: a witch does not put a spell on a wizard and vice versa. Will you never learn?'

I shook my head.

'Give me your hands... look into my left eye.'

For as long as I can levitate, I will not forget what happened next. The handles of the beer pumps, I could see, standing proud above the bar counter turned into fire-breathing dragons. The mirror behind the counter instead of reflecting bottles and glasses, turned into a cinema screen showing mesas and buttes. I was no longer in the Dyer's Hand. I was in the Wild West. Mustangs were galloping through chicanes of cacti. The stallion in charge of the herd, the alpha male, was Howard.

'I've got the message,' I told him, blinking and screwing up my eyes, as if, for too long, I'd been staring at the sun. 'What do you want me to do?'

'Have another drink. I'll get them.'

When he was at the bar, Mary wanted to know what the hell was going on.

'For goodness' sake, Muriel, pull yourself together. The last time I saw you look like that was when you looked into Albert's Building Society account and saw how much you'd inherited.'

'I've ordered champagne,' said Howard, returning from the bar. 'The work we are about to do requires fizz.'

'Howard,' I said, 'were you the stallion in the mirror?'

'What… you on about?' said Mary.

'It worked, did it?' said Howard, looking pleased with himself. 'The old left eye trick… never known to fail.'

The "old left eye trick"?' said Mary.

'Howard was showing off,' I said, 'he made me see things in the mirror behind the bar that weren't there.'

I was impressed by Howard's wizardry. It made me look at him the way a Kalahari bushman, who only knows how to make fire by rubbing two sticks together, looks at a white man who strikes a match to light a cigarette.

'I wish to propose…' he said.

'To me …?'

'Muriel, you flatter me… I wish to propose that we join forces to send Stanley to hell. He murdered Tilly. He ate my wife. He murdered his grandmother. He made Michael think he could fly.'

'Stanley is the devil, isn't he?'

'A junior member of that species. He thinks he is above retribution. He is, of course, wrong. My spies tell me, Mary, that your erstwhile husband and his pal, Ambrose, are big time fences. They sell what they have stolen through a network called the "Knockers". I'm afraid, that when they became involved with Stanley, they did not know with whom they were dealing. They thought they could keep Stanley on a leash. They were wrong. If it is any consolation, Mary, I do not think your husband or Ambrose, knew about the cannibal pies. Your husband, Mary, is not evil but he is greedy.'

'And sex mad.'

'And not at all keen to make a will,' I added.

The arrival of a waiter with the champagne made us stop talking. Howard told the waiter that he would pour.

While Howard poured, I said: 'It can't have been easy for Stanley, having a grandmother who was a naturist. Ma was an eccentric. I will miss her. I wonder if she knew what was in the pies.'

'Cheers!' said Howard, raising his glass of fizz. 'Here's to revenge.'

We sipped our fizz and licked our lips.

'Nice,' said, Mary, 'I love champagne.'

'I am not trying to make excuses for Stanley,' I said, 'I am trying to understand him. I am trying to put yourself in his shoes.'

'If you don't mind,' said Howard, 'I'd rather not put myself in Stanley's shoes. He ate my wife. I want revenge.'

'Young people are sensitive,' I said. 'I once had a boy in my class who blushed every time I mentioned wooden legs. His mother had one. It embarrassed him that his mother was missing a limb.'

'Muriel,' said Howard, 'how often does the subject of prosthetic limbs crop up when you are teaching nine year olds?'

'Treasure Island… Long John Silver had a wooden leg.'

'Ah…'

'I'm thinking,' said Mary, 'how many of Ma's customers might have found their cannibal pies, moreish. I mean without knowing what they were eating.'

'It has been known,' said Howard, 'for sailors, cast adrift in a rowing boat, after their ship has sunk, to eat the cabin boy. It is called, I believe, the "law of the sea".'

'Howard,' I said, 'to stay alive, would you eat me?'

'Assuming you were dead, yes.'

'For a wizard, you are very down to earth… very practical.'

'I am a wizard who knows how to peel a potato. On a survival course in Wyoming, I skinned a rattlesnake. I know how to use modern technology. It is through technology that I know the whereabouts of Stanley. I stuck a tracking device on the van he drives. I've had him under surveillance for weeks.'

'Howard!' I exclaimed. 'You went manual. You are a hypocrite. You chastised me and Mary for letting the OFSTED inspector's car's tyres down manually. You said you would have used a spell.'

'I use technology to conserve my supernatural powers. Mary, tell me about your husband. The more I know about him, the easier it will be for me to facilitate his exit. I believe you would be happy for that to happen?'

'I do not want him to go to hell until he has made a will leaving all his worldly goods to me.'

'Wills can be forged.'

'His signature?'

'My forgery will be so real, it will not be a forgery. Ladies... Muriel... Mary... will you help me?'

'Yes, we will,' I said. 'We will be like the three musketeers... all for one and one for all.'

'What I find disturbing,' said Mary, 'is how moreish Ma's pies were. I can't stop wondering if the one's I found most tasty were the cannibal ones. We'll never know, will we? It would be unethical to set up a blind tasting... wouldn't it?'

'Worse still,' I chipped in, 'if we found we liked the cannibal pies best.'

'I liked them best when they were hot, straight out of Ma's oven.'

'Yummy!'

'Very...'

'Ladies,' said Howard, 'I am sorry to end your eulogy on the tastiness of Ma's pies but... we must to horse. Before we ride off to exact revenge, some ground rules. As a wizard of some standing in Cincinnati, I do not wish it to become common knowledge that I may have eaten my own wife.'

'You'd lose Brownie points,' I said.

'Your street cred would be zilch,' said Mary.

'How well you put my problem. Until I right this wrong, I am a vulnerable wizard… never mind… nil desperandum… pack an overnight bag.'

'Oh Howard,' I exclaimed, 'are we off on a dirty weekend?'

'No, we are not. When you pack your bag, Muriel, leave your libido in the safe in which you keep your besoms. We are going to Adder Palace, a stately home in the Highlands of Scotland.'

'It will be freezing up there.'

'Pack plenty of woollies.'

'How are we getting there?' said Mary.

'Easy-peezy,' I said, 'Howard will wave his wizard's wand and, hey-presto, we'll find ourselves sitting on cushions of purple heather looking up a highlander's kilt to see if he's wearing underpants.'

'You flatter me, Muriel. You credit me with supernatural powers I do not possess. We will be going to the Highlands by car. Ladies, I give you a toast… to our mission… to justice and revenge.'

We clinked glasses.

'Do we smash our glasses?' said Mary. 'Like I've seen them do in the movies?'

'Certainly not,' said Howard, 'we don't want to draw attention to ourselves, do we?'

# THE MISSION

**T**wo hours later my doorbell rang. It was Howard. He opened my front door… naughty man… with a spell. In the supernatural world it is well known that a wizard on a mission has carte blanche to break the rules of etiquette.

Before we set off to the land of heather, kilts and bagpipes, I asked him, by way of blessing our mission, if he would do an incantation over Tilly's grave.

I think he was flattered that a witch – not just any old witch but yours truly – was asking him to perform a duty traditionally the prerogative of the head of a coven.

I will refrain from describing the incantation, not because I don't want to but because if I did I would be breaking my coven's official secrets' act… a document signed, by yours truly, with a thumb print smeared in bat's blood.

He insisted – bless his gentlemanly ways – on carrying my bag.

As we were approached his car, its boot popped open.

'In you get,' he said.

'In the boot?'

'Your bag goes in the boot. You go in the front seat.'

'Silly me… nice car.'

'It's a customised Bentley.'

On our way to pick up Mary, he did not once touch the car's steering wheel.

'Howard,' I said, 'is this a self-drive car?'

'Sure is,' he said. 'I love it. You are forgetting, Muriel, I am an American wizard. American wizards love technology. I can override its computer with telepathy… do stop clutching the dashboard… trust me. I'm a wizard.'

'I wish you wouldn't keep saying that. I have too much experience of men telling me to trust them.'

'But, I'm not a man… I'm a wizard.'

'A wizard is a man writ large.'

'And a witch is a woman writ large.'

The journey to Mary's house took only minutes.

The car self-reversed into a space I judged to be too small. Howard, supremely confident in the car's AI programme, folded his arms and closed his eyes.

'It's going to be a long night,' he said, 'I need to get as much rest as I can.'

I was not in the least surprised when Mary kept us waiting. It was her modus operandi. Howard did not let the wait get to him. Instead of drumming his fingers and screaming 'where the hell is she?', he closed his eyes and went into a trance.

Mary kept us waiting for two minutes. It seemed longer. When she did appear, Howard, ever the gent, snapping out of his trance, placed her overnight bag in the car's boot.

'What a lovely car,' she said, as she strapped herself in.

Mary is a car snob. I am not.

'Mary,' I told her, 'you are sitting in an upmarket tin box on wheels… Howard… where are we going?'

'I'm picking up Gwen Rowe. Stanley pushed Michael off the roof. She wants revenge. I am happy to oblige. I know how she feels.

The folk who lived in Gwen's street were not gardeners. In their front gardens they grew fridges, cookers and tricycles with twisted wheels.

This afternoon the street was a fairground. A roundabout blared out music; jugglers, juggled; clowns did handstands. An ice cream van was handing out free ice creams. Tightrope walkers walked across an ad hoc tightrope. A clown, standing next to a barbecue, was handing out free hot dogs.

A stilt walker knocked on the Bentley's roof. A dwarf did a handstand on its bonnet. When Howard let down the car's window, a dwarf popping up from nowhere, polished his face with a stars and stripes bandana.

The headless Red Knight, this time riding a hobby horse, instead of a real horse, speaking through the mesh that covered his head and made him look headless, said, looking through the car's open window: 'Mrs Rowe is waiting for you in a teacup on the roundabout, Aurora.'

Aurora? Only wizards of the highest order were named after the Northern Lights.

'Muriel,' said Howard, 'would you mind letting Mrs Rowe, know we are here. She is in a teacup on the roundabout.'

As he'd asked ever so politely, I obeyed; also, love makes you jump through hoops which, before you fell in love, you'd never have jumped through. I know a Sunderland witch, who, when she fell in love with a Geordie, bought a black and white football shirt!!

Gwen was in the teacup with Joe and the twins. The twin's lips were white with ice cream; Joe's were red with tomato sauce.

'Hi, Gwen,' I said. 'I understand you are coming with us. Are you ready?'

'Me bag is packed, Mrs Thayne. Joe, take your mam's bag to the big posh motor car. Eddy! I'm ganin now. When I'm off,' she explained to me, 'Eddy's promised to look after the twins. Yee two be good for your uncle Eddy when your mam's away... duh yuh hear? Give's a kiss...'

On our way to the Bentley, Gwen told me: 'Poor Eddy, he's putting on a brave face. I call him "Eddy the Ostrich". He doesn't want to nar that his missus... me cousin, Una... has done a runner with Dick Hedgerow. Such a nice man, as well... Eddy, a mean, not Hedgerow... do anyone a good turn. When she married him, Una didn't nar she'd struck gold... not that he was perfect – what man is – Una used to tell me he never flushed the toilet. Una had a thing about hygiene. When she went with anyone she always insisted they used a condom.'

'Hi!' said Howard. 'Welcome aboard. Your bag's in the boot. Joe put it in for you.'

'Where is the little bugger?' said Gwen, looking around.

'If I know him, he'll be at the barbecue,' I said.

'It would have been nice if he'd stayed to wave me off... never mind. Hello, Mrs Hedgerow. Where are we going?'

'North,' said Howard.

'For revenge?'

'Yes.'

'I like the sound of that.'

Every time we approached a set of traffic lights they turned green.

'No red lights for us,' I said. 'Would that be your doing, Howard?'

'No point being a wizard if you can't enjoy the perks; just think, if you were president of the United States of America and only clerical staff could use Air Force One Air… who would want the job?'

'What's ganin on?' said Gwen, from the back seat. 'What's aal this talk about wizards? Mr Star, would yuh mind keeping your hands on the steering wheel.'

'It's a driverless car,' explained Mary.

'You taking the piss, Mrs Hedgerow? A car needs a driver like a man needs a woman… he's doing it again… nodding off at the wheel. Mr Star, if you divent wake up and put your hands back on that steering wheel, I'm out of here.'

'Trust me,' said Howard.

'I've never trusted a man in me life. When are we having a comfort stop?'

'You need to urinate?'

'I want a piss… pull in somewhere off the road where there's bushes.'

This was easier said than done. We were driving over Otterburn Moor; a wild and desolate place; a place where few trees and bushes grow.

'Pull in,' shouted Gwen, 'anywhere…'

Howard obliged. It was turning dark. All I could see ahead of us was a twisting ribbon of moonlit road. It was going to be a long night.

For the next three hours no one spoke. We got used to the fact that Howard was asleep at the wheel. So far we hadn't had a crash. We begin to trust the AI that was driving the car.

It was the car's lack of motion that woke me.

'Where are we?' I asked Howard.

'Scotland,' he said, 'and by gum, lad, it's cold up north.'

'Howard, that's a Yorkshire accent.'

'Where are we?' said Gwen.

Scotland,' said Mary, 'Howard said we were in Scotland.'

By the light of a full moon I read on a lopsided board… the sort of board you see outside a parish church naming the saint after whom the church is named… ADDER PALACE PRIVATE PROPERTY TRESSPASSERS BEWARE MAN TRAPS

My nose began to drip. If ever you see a witch with a dripping nose do not assume its cause is a head cold; it might be, but, more than likely, she is scared. It is well documented that if you show a witch a ducking stool her nose will start to drip.

'My nose is dripping,' said Mary.

'So is mine,' I said.

'What you two on about?' said Gwen.

'Everybody out!' said Howard.

'Everybody out' indeed… we weren't schoolchildren. We were adults.

'I don't like it here,' said Gwen. 'This place gives me the willies.'

'My antennae is picking up bad vibes,' said Mary.

Looking at Mary, I said: 'One, two, three...' whereupon we cackled a cackled a cackle so loud it was like an explosion whose soundwaves are powerful enough to start an avalanche.

'How'd you do that?' said Gwen. 'You sounded like witches. You've made me piss my knickers.'

'Mrs Rowe,' said Howard, 'before we begin our mission to avenge the deaths of my wife Pamela and your son, Michael...'

'And Tilly,' I said. 'Don't forget Tilly.'

'And Tilly,' said Howard. 'Mrs Rowe, before we begin our mission, I have something to tell you that you may find difficult to believe. Not to beat about the besom...'

'The, what?'

'The bush... not to beat about the bush... I hereby inform you that I am a wizard and, furthermore, that Muriel and Mary are witches.'

'Get on with yuh... pull the other one. You're bonkers, you are. This place gives me the willies.'

'I am trying to enlighten you. Muriel... Mary... another cackle, if you don't mind.'

Mary and I let rip. We liked nothing better than a good cackle. An owl hooted.

'You telling me, Mrs Thayne and Mrs Hedgerow is witches?'

'Yes.'

'On your bike; you're trying to scare me 'cos we're in the country and if the moon wasn't out, shining... and there's nee streetlights, we would think we were doon a coal mine without a Davy lamp. Just 'cos we're in a scary place and it's the middle of the neet, doesn't mean 'am ganna start believing in witches. Pull the other one. We duh yuh think yuh are?'

'I am Aurora, an American wizard.'

'And I'm the Queen of Sheba.'

'Trust me; take my word.'

'Why should I?'

'Because, Mrs Rowe, I am a wizard.'

'For fuck sake, will yuh stop ganin on about witches and wizards... this place gives me the willies... and stop calling me "Mrs Rowe"... call me Gwen... and why can't I call you Howard?'

'Wizards don't like mortals getting familiar with them,' said Mary, 'isn't that right, Howard?'

'Ladies...' said Howard.

'Ladies!' said Gwen, looking around at the frozen vegetation. 'I wish to god there was a Ladies. I'm bursting for a piss. Christ! I'd do anything for a ciggy... I don't suppose...'

We shook our heads.

'Ladies,' said Howard, 'may I remind you why we are here. We are not on a picnic, we are here to avenge the murder of loved ones taken from us by the forces of evil. Mrs Rowe, raise your right hand.'

'Why, what's your game? What you up to?'

'I'm going to deputise you.'

'You mean like I've seen them do in cowboy movies when the good guys gan hunting the bad guys?'

'Just so, Mrs Rowe.'

'I wish you'd call me Gwen.'

'All in good time, Mrs Rowe, all in good time. Look into my left eye.'

'Can I not look into both of them? You have bedroom eyes, Mr Star... Howard. What if a bear attacks me when I'm ogling?'

'My left eye, Mrs Rowe, my left eye... trust me.'

'I wish you wouldn't keep saying that...'

'Raise your right hand and say, "I swear".'

When Gwen said, 'I swear', her voice echoed the way footsteps echo in a film noir when the heroine is running down a moonlit cobbled alley.

'Mrs Rowe,' said Howard, fluttering his fingers in front of her face, 'you now have the powers of a junior witch.'

'Get on with yuh,' said Gwen. 'What can I do now, that a couldn't dee before?'

'Hear that owl?'

'It sounds loud.'

'That, Mrs Rowe, is because you now have the enhanced hearing of a junior witch.'

'What's that banging? Bloody hell! I'm hearing voices.'

'One thing at a time, Mrs Rowe... one thing at a time. There is an owl watching us.'

'Is there?'

'I command you to command it to sit on my head.'

'Gan on with yuh. I can't tell an owl what to do.'

'The owl, Mrs Rowe... the owl. Close your eyes and command it to land on my head.'

Gwen, as if under a spell, which, of course, she was, closed her eyes. When she opened them and saw an owl perched on top of Howard's head, she exclaimed: 'Bloody hell! I did that?'

Mary and I rolled our eyes. We were not impressed; furthermore, if I was any judge of character, from now on, Gwen would be hell to live with. She would have illusions of grandeur. She would be like all converts... over-zealous. When she thought no one was looking she'd be trying to turn a frog into a prince... a prince who had eyes only for her.

'All your own work,' said Howard.

'Hoy!' said Gwen, as the owl flew off. 'The bugger's shit on me.'

'I'll bet it's a male owl,' said Mary, 'it has to be, doing that to a woman.'

'OMG!' screamed Gwen. 'I'm seeing wizards and witches.'

'Dear Mrs Rowe,' said Howard, 'you are now seeing myself, Mrs Thayne and Mrs Hedgerow through the eyes of a deputised junior witch. You are seeing your companions in their true colours.'

'I need a ciggy. This place gives me the willies. Witches... wizards... I don't believe what I'm seeing... and I'm hearing voices. I'm hearing banging. What you lot done to me? I can hear Joe. What tricks are you devils playing on me now?'

'Gwen,' I said, 'it *is* Joe. He's in the Bentley's boot. He's been shouting he wants out since we stopped.'

'Has he? First time I've heard him and I'm his mother.'

'Now you are a deputised witch, you have amplified hearing.'

'I thought that owl sounded loud.'

'I think we should let Joe out of the boot… Howard.'

Howard opened the boot by looking at it.

Joe came out of the boot the way a chicken hatches out of an egg; that is to say, with a lot of jerky movements; his legs didn't want to take his weight.

'Joe, me pet,' exclaimed Gwen.

'Mam,' said Joe.

'Just look at you… where duh yuh think you've been?'

'In the boot of a car.'

'Joe,' said Howard, 'raise your right hand. Now that you are here we must make you part of the team.'

'You're not deputising my Joe,' said Gwen. 'He's too young; there's laws against child labour. I'll not have him used the way in the bad times kids were pushed up flues to clean them. I won't allow it.'

'Mrs Rowe, if we are to work as a team, it is important we all have the same equipment. Deputising him is all about standardising our communication systems, don't you see? Joe, raise your right hand… look into my right eye.'

'Just you hang on a second, Mr Star. I had to look into your left eye. Why the difference?'

'Joe is male. You are female. Joe is young. You are old.'

'Cheeky bugger. Divent you gan calling me old. I could teach you a thing or two if you'd let me.'

'My right eye, if you please, Joe. Concentrate. Think about something nice. Joe, I'm surprised at you… thinking things like that at your age.'

'How'd you know what he's thinking?'

'I'm a wizard.'

'What's he thinking? Why's he smiling? If he's owt like his dad he'll be thinking about the nudist magazines he used to look at in Ma's shop. Dirty little bugger... men.'

'Mrs Rowe, your son loves you dearly.'

'Do yuh love me, Joe? Do you love me? Give's a kiss.'

Seeing that Joe was not at all keen to oblige, Howard said: 'Joe, just think about kissing your mother... close your eyes and think you are kissing her.'

Joe closed his eyes. For a second a crater appeared in one of Gwen's cheeks.

'By gum, Joe, you've fair melted your old Ma's heart. You've warmed me up better than a double brandy.'

'Excuse me,' said Howard, disappearing behind a bush.

'Where's he off to?' said Gwen. 'What's happening now?'

'I think Howard needs a wee-wee,' said Mary.

'I don't like it here... mist and damp. This place gives me the willies... bloody owls... hooting. What's that I can hear?'

'Nothing to worry about,' I said, 'it's a spider spinning a web.'

'How can I hear that?'

'You are a deputy witch... you have enhanced hearing.'

'Do I?'

'Yes, you do... enjoy.'

'This place gives me the willies...'

'Mary and I feel at home here... don't we, Mary?'

'I love mist and owls,' said Mary.

'One, two, three,' I said.

On cue we cackled. In truth, our cackling had more in common with what non-witches call nervous laughter. Mary and I were more apprehensive than we cared to admit. I was also of the opinion that the habit Howard had developed of repeating phrases was a sign that he too was on edge.

'Ladies, please,' said Howard, emerging, like an apparition, from out of a bush, 'think of the foraging badger... the hibernating adder.'

He was brandishing a six-foot wooden staff. When he banged the lay-by's frozen tarmac with it, the pearl berries of the mistletoe sprouting out of its tip flashed on and off.

'My direction finder,' he said.

'I've read about devices like that,' said Mary.

'Me too,' I said.

'Those things wriggling on the end of the pole, Mr Star,' said Gwen, 'they're not snakes, are they?'

'They are flexible antennae, Mrs Rowe... flexible antennae... trust me.'

'I wish you wouldn't keep saying that, Mr Star.'

'We go where the mistletoe points.'

'The mistletoe, thingy, will take us to Stanley?' said Mary.

'It will take us to the van in which he drove here... and please do not call my direction finder a "thingy". It is a PED... a parasite evil detector.'

'I know what PED stands for,' said Mary. 'Whitby has books about them. They were first used in the crusades.'

'You are very well read, Mary... but, have you ever seen one?'

'I might have...'

'That means you haven't.'

'Why should I lie?'

'Status, Mary… status. You do not like admitting that I, Aurora, know more about the supernatural than your good self.'

'Mam,' said Joe, 'I want a shit.'

'Go behind a tree,' I told him.

'What if something bites me bum?'

'It won't… trust me.'

'Now, you're saying it, Mrs Thayne,' said Gwen. 'Joe, you listen to your mother… never trust anyone who tells you to trust them… this place gives me the willies. When I look at them wagging trees, I see graves opening.'

'I want a shit,' repeated Joe.

'Joe,' I told him, 'trust me. You didn't want to be a bear but you trusted me… I was right, wasn't I?'

'The audience was clapping for me.'

'That's right, Joe, they were clapping for you; they loved your bear.'

'Miss, a liked them clapping for me.'

'Off you go… hide behind a tree.'

'Hurry up,' said Gwen, 'you either want a shit or you divent.'

'Don't anyone watch,' said Joe, 'a won't be able to gan if a think you are watching me.'

It was while he was emptying his bowels, hidden behind a tree that he shouted, 'Ok, Mr Star, I'll dee that.'

'What have you told him to do, Mr Star?' said Gwen.

'I have told him to use bracken as toilet paper and also, when we move out, to stay behind and guard the Bentley.'

'I never heard you tell him anything… how'd he know?'

'Telepathy, Mrs Rowe, telepathy. I have also told him there is a bar of chocolate in the car's glove compartment.'

'Not dark chocolate, I hope, Mr Star; Joe's not fond of dark chocolate.'

'Milk chocolate, Mrs Rowe, milk chocolate.'

'You think of everything, don't you?'

'I try to, Mrs Rowe; I try to. This way, everyone, and watch out for man traps.'

We set off in single file. The last we heard of Joe was a fart. We followed a dry-stone wall. The mistletoe berries on the PED alternately glowed and dimmed.

Sometimes I saw Howard dressed as a wizard; sometime as a hunter dressed in camouflage fatigues.

'Yo!' said Howard after we'd been following the wall for ten minutes.

'You mean "stop",' I said.

'Muriel, this is not the time...'

'Or the place...' I added.

'Muriel, this is not the time or place for quibbling. I am stopping to allow Mary and Mrs Rowe to catch us up. It is important that we stick together.'

'Howard,' I said, while we waited for them to catch us up, 'the mistletoe on the PED is pointing over the wall. Should we not be flying over the wall... you know, wizard and witch style?'

'Mrs Rowe... Gwen...'

'What about her?'

'Deputised witches do not have the power to fly over walls. You should know that.'

'Sorry, I forgot, I'm under a lot of stress. I am missing Tilly. A witch without a cat is like a car that has run out of petrol.'

'What about me? I have lost my wife… a wife whose flesh and blood was put into a pie. Don't talk to me about stress.'

His exclamation was so full of supernatural energy that for a second I saw him in the full regalia of a high ranking wizard.

Ignoring these signs that were telling me I was in a hole and should stop digging, I said: 'Can't Mary and I and your good self, air-lift Gwen over the wall the way I've seen a Chinook helicopter lift a tank? Once on holiday in Switzerland I saw a helicopter lift a cow.'

'I do not think Mrs Rowe would thank you for comparing her to a tank or a cow.'

'Just trying to help.'

'Mrs Rowe is overweight. She is not a sylph. To fly her over that wall we'd need three Chinooks.'

'If she heard you say that, she'd kill you.'

'I know… mum's the word.'

When the slow coaches caught us up, puffing and panting and full of moans, Gwen said (apropos of Joe), 'I hope he's not eating too much chocolate. He'll not stop eating until its aal gone and he's made himself sick… and where's that sod Stanley? That's what I want to know. I hope I'm not doing this bloody hike for nowt. It'll be a miracle if I divent break a leg… I know it will. I divent like it here. I keeps standing on things… slithery things what move… I'd murder for an oily rag.'

'Howard,' I said, 'when I breathe out in the frosty air, my breath makes a cloud… Yours doesn't. Why is that?'

'What an observant witch you are. If I suddenly have to disappear, I do not wish to leave a vapour trail.'

'You sure no one's got an oily rag?' said Gwen.

'I stopped years ago,' I said.

'Me too,' said Mary.

'Mr Star, I don't suppose…'

'No.'

'It's alright for some…'

'A smoker's cough can ruin an incantation,' said Mary; 'remember, Muriel, when we tried to conjure up a storm to ruin that woman's garden party?'

'We didn't like her, did we?'

'Horrible woman… and you coughed, Muriel, just before you'd incanted the last two words…'

'Instead of making it rain we brought on a heatwave.'

'Ladies,' said Howard, 'I implore you, cease the reminiscing… and keep your voices down. On the other side of that wall there may well be hidden microphones. I suggest we communicate, henceforth, using telepathy.'

'Hoy!' said Gwen. 'I'm hearing voices inside me heed. What yuh telling me to do on television?'

'Telepathy, Mrs Rowe… telepathy.'

'Hoy… I'm not deeing that… no way.'

'Not doing what?' said Mary.

'Mr Star… he wants me to expose myself… dirty old bugger.'

'Howard,' I said, 'shame on you.'

'I wouldn't mind if it wasn't so bloody cold,' said Gwen.

'Ladies,' said Howard, 'I was not asking Mrs Rowe to become a stripper. I was asking her if she'd be prepared to expose herself to the enemy the way a fisherman puts bait on a hook. In days of old, when knights were bold and my great-great-great-grandfather was an alchemist turning mercury into silver, and brass into gold, a maiden tied to a stake outside a castle was a Trojan Horse.'

'You should have made that clear to Gwen,' I said.

'Telepathy is like texting,' said Mary. 'Ok to tell people to put the kettle on but not for life and death, complicated stuff. Anyway, Howard, why can't you be tied to a stake?'

'I am too important.'

'Hark to him,' said Gwen. 'I'm the doughnut, am I, and you're the cream?'

'Muriel, hold my staff.'

'Say, please...'

'Please...'

While he punched numbers into his mobile, I examined the staff. What I found out about it, I *would pass on to* Whitby. It was important that Whitby kept its files on the gadgets used by wizards up to date.

Hitherto, the taxonomy of Howard's staff had been, to me, as mysterious as an exoplanet.

'Howard,' I exclaimed, 'it's plastic. It was made in China.'

'My staff, please.'

'Sort of thing you'd pay two quid for in a toy shop.'

'Who were you ringing?' said Gwen. 'It would be nice if you were ringing a greasy-spoon, to bring us the full English. I'd kill for an oily rag.'

'I was ringing my helpers, Mrs Rowe, to let them know I am close to the main entrance to Adder Palace. To defeat the evil we are on the cusp of encountering, we'll need help.' Then, looking at me: 'Muriel, you are quite right, my staff is plastic; and it was made in China. Its Pound Shop provenance is camouflage. In Australia a fish looks like a stone. A leaf in a jungle is an insect. In public you are a primary school teacher. In private you are a witch. Behind his red lipped smile the clown is sad. Nothing is what it seems.'

I watched, in awe, as out of a hidden pouch on the staff, he materialised, a black dodecahedron the size of a golf ball.

'May I introduce you... Mrs Rowe, do pay attention. The snakes you are seeing are imaginary. Thank you... may I introduce you all, to Mildred... my... our secret weapon. Muriel, Mary, you will not find any reference to Mildred in Whitby's archives. Mildred is top secret. She is cutting edge wizard technology. Watch...'

So that we could all see, he placed the black dodecahedron, the size of a golf ball, on the palm of an outstretched hand.

'Watch...'

At first, nothing happened. Pride before a fall, I was thinking. Howard loved showing off. After what seemed an eternity but wasn't, the dodecahedron began to change shape... began to melt.

'Watch... Watch...'

As a butterfly emerges from a chrysalis, a black spider began to emerge from the dodecahedron.

'Ugh!' said Gwen. 'I wouldn't want to find that in me knickers. What the hell is it?'

'It's a drone, Mrs Rowe... a drone.'

'I heard yuh the first time... stop repeating yourself, will yuh. I'm not deaf and I'm not daft. I'd kill for an oily rag.'

'It's a drone, Mrs Rowe… a drone… Mildred is our eyes in the sky.'

'Looks more like a toy to me.'

Mildred's rotors were smaller than matchsticks. They began to turn… slowly at first, then… faster and faster. They became a blur.

She flew from Howard's palm and hovered above our heads without making a sound.

'Look,' said Howard, 'look.'

On the palm Howard held out for us to look at we saw the dark shapes and white faces of our good selves.

'Hi!' exclaimed Gwen, 'that's us. I'm on the telly.'

She was thrilled when she waved at the image on Howard's palm and saw herself wave back.

Howard touched a finger. The drone soared upwards. On Howard's palm I saw trees and moorland.

'Your fingers control the drone?' I said.

He nodded.

I saw the moonlit silhouette of a rowan tree… patches of snow… a herd of deer.

'Hi!' exclaimed Gwen. 'There's a castle… divent like the look of that place.'

'That, Mrs Rowe, is Adder Palace.'

'Mr Star, how'd you turn the palm of your hand into a telly?'

'Wizardry, Mrs Rowe, wizardry.'

I would describe the architectural style of Adder Palace as Witchy-Gothic. It had turrets and barley sugar chimney pots.

By touching his little finger, Howard flew Mildred over a courtyard.

On his palm I saw a dumper truck, a bulldozer and a mobile crane that looked like a giraffe on wheels.

'Stolen goods,' said Howard, 'stolen from Roger and Heather.'

'But,' said Mary, 'Roger and Heather are Dick's friends. They often came to my house for a meal. I have made them my signature dish... prawn linguine. I don't do that for any old Tom, Dick or Harry.'

'Mary... your husband and his pal, Ambrose... they'd steal from anyone.'

'The Arse Hole once took a tin of beans from a food bank,' I said.

'Men!' exclaimed Gwen. 'Why should I be surprised? What do you expect? Years ago one of my boyfriends... he was sea going ... told me he had to have sex to stop him feeling sea sick... men! Why should I be surprised? They'll say owt to get what they want.'

Howard now hovered Mildred in front of a window. The room's lights were on; its shutters... open. What I saw... what we all saw on Howard's outstretched palm... grabbed our interest the way a public beheading in times of yore helped peasants forget they were hungry.

'Tut! Tut!' I said. 'Such goings on.'

'Well, well, well,' said Mary.

'Men!' exclaimed Gwen. 'I'm glad Joe's not here. I'd be embarrassed him seeing ganin-ons like that.'

The room was a nursery. The Arse Hole and Ambrose were wearing nappies. Una was breastfeeding the Arse Hole. Ambrose was in a playpen... sucking a dummy.

'The dirty old buggers,' said Gwen. 'Men!'

'I wonder,' said Mary, 'if I'd put the sod in a nappy… would he have signed a will leaving all his worldly goods to me.'

'Enough… a surfeit,' said Howard, hovering Mildred in front of a different window.

On Howard's palm I saw Ted sitting on a swivel chair behind a very large desk.

'What's he writing?' I said. 'Howard, can you zoom in.'

Howard touched a finger. The image on his palm zoomed into the room. We were now looking into the room as if we were looking into it through binoculars.

In between doing little swivels on his chair, I watched Ted dip a quill pen into a pot of ink.

'Closer, Howard, please… more zoom.'

Ted was practising writing his signature… Sir Ted… Lord Ted… King Ted the tenth.

Living in Adder Palace had clearly gone to Ted's head.

'I'd murder for an oily rag,' said Gwen.

'From what Mildred has shown me,' said Howard, closing his fist to stop Mildred transmitting, 'I am of the opinion that the enemy have no inkling we are here. We have the advantage of surprise. Ladies, your attention, please…'

He paused. When he was certain Gwen was looking at him and not thinking about her need for nicotine, he said: 'Mildred is on reconnaissance. Beyond the palace's gates there is a long drive. My plan is to march my men down that drive in full view of the enemy.'

'Your "men"?' I said.

'Wait and see…'

'At least you didn't say "trust me", Mr Star,' said Gwen. 'I'd kill for an oily rag.'

'Have a Fisherman's Friend,' said Mary.

'I thought you said you hadn't any left...'

'Onward, ladies... follow the wall. Walls lead to gates. Do be careful where you are putting your feet, the ground is uneven. We don't want anyone breaking an ankle, do we?'

'Mr Star,' said Gwen, 'it would help me not to break an ankle if I had a walking stick. Can I borrow your staff?'

'Of course you can. Press that switch and a light will show you where it is safe to put your feet.'

Then, the mist came down. The genius loci had dropped a fire blanket over us. I couldn't see a thing. The lack of visibility stopped me in my tracks; coming up behind me, Mary and Gwen bumped into me. Where the hell was Howard?

'Howard,' I hissed into the mist, 'where are you? Gwen, press the light on the staff, the one Howard told you about.'

'What you think I'm trying to do... it's bust. Bloody Chinese rubbish. It's like that plastic car I bought for Joe off the Knockers... never worked... not proper it didn't.'

'Don't be alarmed, ladies,' said Howard, appearing out of the mist like the iceberg that sank the Titanic, 'follow my halo.'

From the top of his wizard's cone hat there glowed an LED halo.

'Follow me,' he said, 'I am the light.'

We followed the halo down into dips. We followed it up steep banks. We followed it the way a ship entering port is guided by the flashing light of a lighthouse.

'Yo!' exclaimed Howard, sounding like a US cavalry officer in a western movie when he has spotted smoke signals coming from the top of a mesa.

Out of the mist there emerged a flexible tube.

'Bloody hell,' screamed Gwen. 'A snake... Oh my god... it's lifting me up. Help! Put me down.'

'Demetrius, where are you?'

'Here, Aurora.'

'I've wet myself,' said Gwen. 'Help, put me down.'

'That is not snake, Mrs Rowe; that is an elephant's trunk. Rajah is giving you a cuddle.'

'No, it isn't, it's one of them anacondas and it's squeezing me to death.'

There now emerged out of the mist an elephant. Its mahout, sitting cross legged on top of its head, wrapped in a padded jacket, was a dwarf.

'Demetrius,' said Howard, 'do tell Rajah to put Mrs Rowe down.'

'It is the cold, Aurora, Rajah is using the memsahib as a hot water bottle. She is woman of very big size. She give off a lot of heat.'

'You calling me fat?' said Gwen. 'Put me doon.'

Back on terra firma, she said, 'I'd kill for an oily rag.'

'Have a Fishermen's Friend,' said Mary.

'I thought you said you hadn't any left.'

Howard said, 'Yo!' Once again we were on the move. We were walking through mist, so thick it was like walking through interminable rows of net curtains.

Having an elephant on my side gave me confidence. When Hannibal crossed the Alps he must have slept like a baby. What's a Roman legion when you have, at your command, a herd of elephants?

Also, it is not easy to get lost in mist, even in the thickest of peasoupers, when you are following a farting elephant... you follow the smell.

After fifteen minutes of following Rajah, the elephant who couldn't stop farting, and Howard's halo, all the time making sure the branches of trees pushed aside, by Rajah, as he lumbered forward, did not knock any of us out, when they snapped back, Howard hollered, 'Yo!'.

Through the swirling mist I made out the iron railings of a gate. The pillars supporting the gate were three metres high. A sign, tied to the bars of the gate, told me I was at Adder Palace's main entrance and that trespassers would have their heads chopped off.

On the top of the two stone pillars, supporting the gates, there came and disappeared through the mist the shapes of two stone lions; their tails were sticking out of their backsides like Nazi salutes.

'What's those turnips on the gate's spikes?' said Gwen.

'They, Mrs Rowe,' said Howard, 'are human heads.'

'Urgh!' said Gwen.

'Trust me, Mrs Rowe, they are not real... someone with a macabre sense of humour has been to a joke shop.'

To get a better look at the heads – they kept disappearing in the mist – Gwen went up close to the gates.

'That one, Mr Star,' she said, 'looks like you.'

'It's a passable likeness,' said Howard. 'The work of a young Michelangelo.'

'And that one is you, Mrs Thayne.'

'And that one is me,' said Mary.

'You sure they're not real?' said Gwen.

'Mrs Rowe,' said Howard, 'look at us. Has Mrs Thayne lost her head? Has Mrs Hedgerow lost her head? Have I lost my head? No, of course we haven't.'

'I can see that,' said Gwen, 'I've got eyes in me head. I also know you are all off your heads… you are all barmy.'

'They are totems,' said Howard, 'see them in daylight and you wouldn't give them a second glance. They have been put there to scare us. It tells me, ladies… Ambrose, Stanley and your husband, Mary, know about our mission. It tells me, ladies… they are in fear of their lives. We are the sword of Damocles. If they did not fear us they would not have gone to the bother of sculpting our images… but, we don't scare easily, do we, ladies?'

'Speak for yourself,' said Gwen. 'Anyways, why have we stopped in front of the gates? How we going to open them? If Stanley's on the other side of them, somewhere in Adder Palace, drinking wine instead of IPA… how we going to get to him? When I get me hands on him I'm ganna drown the bugger in a chamber pot full of piss.'

'Rajah will open the gates for us,' I said. 'A few pushes from him and the gates will be flat on their backs.'

To show he disapproved of my suggestion, Rajah cocked a leg, the way a dog cocks a leg against a wall… and I was the wall… and let rip a jumbo fart.

'Rajah,' said Howard, rubbing the elephant's trunk with his halo, 'you will not be used as a battering ram. Have a banana…'

From somewhere – I've not a clue where it came from – Howard gave Rajah a banana.

'Rajah will not have to head butt the gates open. I know how to open them.'

'Is there anything you don't know?' said Gwen.

'There is very little I don't know about you, Mrs Rowe.'

'Blackmailer…'

'I am a wizard, not a blackmailer. My powers make blackmail unnecessary.'

'Lucky you.'

'Howard,' I said, 'how do we open the gates? Do you have a key?'

'Do you see the lion atop the left stone pillar? Pull its tail down and the gates will open. I have done due diligence on Adder Palace. It was built in 1580 for a wizard, who, like my good self, had a penchant for gadgets… excuse me, Mildred is transmitting.'

On Howard's palm, I saw the Bentley; parked next to it was an ice-cream van. The lights on the ice-cream van's roof were flashing on and off. The ice-cream van looked to me, very like the one I'd seen in Gwen's street; the one giving out free ice-creams.

'There's my Joe,' said Gwen.

'He's eating an ice-cream,' I said.

'Let me see.'

The enthusiasm with which she grabbed Howard's hand stopped Mildred transmitting.

'Now look what you've done,' said Howard.

To get the picture back, Howard touched his line of longevity. At once, the moving images on his palm glowed back to life; touching a finger-tip he flew Mildred to another location.

'Let me show you my helpers.'

After a few blurry seconds of flying fast at treetop level, I, Mary and Gwen saw a removal van; coming out of it – coming out of it the way soldiers pile out of a Chinook helicopter when they have landed in enemy territory and are going into battle – I saw monkeys, gorillas and bears. They were doing backward somersaults, press ups and handstands.

'My helpers,' said Howard.

'What are the two gorillas carrying?' I said.

'That, Muriel, is a catapult.'

'Looks like an ironing board, to me,' said Gwen.

We watched the plasma television screen on Howard's palm, as if we were in a cinema watching the latest James Bond movie.

On Howard's palm we watched a gorilla place the 'ironing board' on a piece of sawn-off log.

'They are making a see-saw,' explained Howard.

A bear, wearing a sword belt and with a knife clamped between his teeth, stood on one end of the 'ironing board'. A gorilla with a chimpanzee standing on his shoulders stood at its upturned end.

When the bear put out his arms, the chimpanzee jumped off the gorilla's shoulders. When he landed on the 'ironing board's' upturned end, he catapulted the bear into the grounds of Adder Palace.

'Acrobats!' exclaimed Howard. 'Wonderful... quite wonderful. The SAS of the circus world. You wouldn't believe this but the gorilla letting the chimpanzee stand on his shoulders has a hernia. You wouldn't think it, would you? Sometime next week he's booked in for an operation... key-hole surgery. He's an American. He thinks our NHS is wonderful... and so do I.'

We ignored Howard's non sequitur; our focus was on the gorillas, chimpanzees and bears being catapulted over Adder Palace's boundary wall.

Then, Howard flew Mildred over the wall. To scare the living daylights out of the inhabitants of Adder Palace – the way the Scots go into battle playing the bagpipes – gorillas were thumping their chests... chimpanzees were doing cartwheels... bears were making clubs out of branches.

I saw a man wearing a kilt, take a swing at a gorilla with a golf club. To avoid being hit the gorilla did a backward somersault. While the golf club was buried in soft earth, instead of in the gorilla's skull, the gorilla punched the man in the face. When the kilt wearer fell over, his kilt flew up.

'That's another myth down the drain,' I said, 'he's wearing underpants.'

'My advance guard are doing well,' said Howard.

'When do we gan ower the top?' said Gwen. 'I'm itching to get me hands on Stanley... itching... I'd kill for an oily rag.'

'We go "ower the top", Mrs Rowe, when my reinforcements arrive–' looking at his palm– 'they are on their way.'

We heard the ice cream van before we saw it. Its chimes were playing something rousing from, I think, Wagner; then, its headlights lit up the swirling mist.

Monkeys sat cross-legged on its roof; bears clung to its running boards; two gorillas were sitting on its bonnet; clowns were squeezed inside the van as tightly as if they were sardines in one of those tins you open by pulling on a ring.

The van was like one of those trains in India, where passengers sit on the train's roof and cling to its sides the way climbers cling to the north wall of the Eiger.

Before the van stopped, those clinging to its sides began jumping off.

'Howard,' I said, 'some of those monkeys look very real.'

'That, Muriel, is because some of them are real… not all, of course; most are dwarves in costume.'

'And the bears?'

'No real bears… too dangerous.'

'Look at the arse on that one,' said Gwen, 'that's disgusting, that is.'

'Hi, Mrs Rowe,' said a panda, 'I'm Amanda the Panda. You fancy an oily rag?'

'Aye, I do… but, how'd yuh know me name?'

'I told her,' said a bear in a cub bear costume.

'Eh?'

'It's me, Mam,' said Joe, removing his bear mask.

'Joe, thank god you're alreet… give your ma a hug and you… Amanda the Panda, or whatever it is you call yourself… give's an oily rag.'

'I'm afraid, Mrs Rowe, I can't do that.'

'Why'd you ask me if I wanted one then? You're like the Grand Old Duke of York, you are… you've led me up to the top of the hill and now, you're telling me to piss off.'

'Mrs Rowe, trust me…'

'OMG… not another one…'

'I am the circuses' health and safety officer. Joe told me of your addiction to nicotine. Mrs Rowe, Joe loves you dearly…'

'I should think so, too, I'm his mother.'

'Joe wishes you, for the good of your health, to give up smoking… try one of these.'

'Chewing gum! I've got false teeth.'

'Don't chew… suck… trust me.'

'Trust me! If I hear that one more time I'll dee to mesell what that Japanese, Harry-Kerry, did to himself with a bread knife.'

'Mrs Rowe,' said Howard, 'Amanda the Panda means well. He is trying to help you.'

'Funny way of showing it… and why's he called Amanda when he's a bloke?'

'Mrs Rowe, do not ask the reason why…'

'Don't you dare say "trust me"… if you do I'll stick chewing gum up your nostrils.'

'And that would gum up the works… and we don't want that, do we?' Then, looking around at the admixture of humans, real chimpanzees and humans in gorilla, bear, panda and chimp costumes, he said, sounding like Henry V addressing his troops on the eve of Agincourt: 'While many of your compatriots lie abed in big tops in America and elephants and chimps languish in zoos or romp through savannahs, as the good lord meant them to do… you are here… on active service. When you are old and grey you will remember this day… trust me…'

'Where's me chewing gum?' said Gwen. 'Mr Star, bonny lad, cut to the chase, will yuh?'

'Just so, Mrs Rowe… you have a way with words… now that we are all here, Joe will open the gates.'

'Eh?' said Joe. 'How am I ganin to dee that?'

'You see that lion up there?'

'I thought it was a dog.'

'Well, it's not, it's a lion…pull its tail down and the gates will open.'

'How am I ganin to get up there?'

'Rajah will lift you up in his trunk. Rajah, payment for this job is two bananas… a deal?'

Rajah agreed the deal. I know this because, without any further discussion, he lifted Joe, ever so gently, up on to the pedestal.

'Pull the tail down,' shouted Howard.

'A divent like it up here,' said Joe.

'Yes, you do.'

'No, a divent.'

'Aurora,' said Amanda the Panda, 'sometimes you expect too much… with your permission.'

Amanda the Panda climbed the pillar the way a real panda climbs a eucalyptus tree; his feet were hands and his hands were feet.

I observed all of this, you must remember, somewhat fuzzily, through a net curtain of mist.

'Pull down the lion's tail,' shouted Howard.

Amanda and Joe were sitting on the lion's back. They were facing its tail.

Amanda was doing his best to push the tail down.

'Aurora, the tail will not move.'

'Leverage,' shouted Howard, 'use leverage... put Joe on your back and shuffle down it... your combined weight is sure to budge it.'

'What if the tail moves and we slide off?'

'Rajah will catch you... Rajah... three bananas?'

To show that he and Howard had cut a deal, Rajah swayed towards the gatepost. He sniffed the air under the lion's tail with his trunk. If anyone fell, he'd catch them.

Amanda, with Joe clinging to his back, began shuffling towards the end of the lion's tail.

'I can't watch,' said Gwen. 'What if Joe falls and breaks his neck? I've lost one child, I can't lose another.'

The tail, upon which Amanda and Joe were shuffling along, was over a metre long.

'Keep going,' ordered Howard, 'keep shuffling. Rajah, stand by to catch them. Demetrius, is Rajah ready?'

'He is ready, Aurora.'

'You will get maximum leverage when you are at the end of the tail... that tail may not have moved for two hundred years.'

'I hope, Mr Star, you knows what you are doing... don't you go getting my Joe hurt.'

'Trust me, Mrs Rowe.'

'I was hoping you wouldn't say that... but, old habits die hard, don't they?'

It was through bandages of swirling mist that I made out that Amanda, with Joe like a rucksack on his back, was sitting on the tuft of hair at the very end of the lion's tail.

'Howard,' I asked, 'why aren't the gates opening?'

'They are not opening because the tail appears to be stuck. Amanda—' cupping his hands over his mouth to make a megaphone— 'swing from the end of the tail… your weight and Joe's will budge it… I know it will. Rajah is on standby… Rajah…'

'You can't ask Amanda to do that, Howard,' I said. 'It is too dangerous.'

'Muriel, Amanda is not a kindergarden teacher, he is an acrobat. He is a high wire walker. He can do a hundred back flips one after the other.'

'Hoy!' said Gwen. 'This bloke Amanda might be able to do aal the things yuh said he can do, but, my Joe's not a high wire walker. Joe's never walked on anything higher than a backyard wall.'

'Amanda,' shouted Howard, 'show the limeys what you can do.'

'Hang on, Joe,' shouted Amanda.

'Joe… you hang on tight,' shouted Gwen. 'Oh my god, they're falling off.'

In an attempt to budge the lion's tail, Amanda, with Joe clinging to his back, began doing pull-ups on the tail, as if the tail was a parallel bar… up and down he went… up and down.

'Howard,' I said, 'are you sure the tail opens the gates?'

'It's the frost,' he said, 'I know it is. The frost has jammed the mechanism.'

Amanda had grit, I'll give him that. Up and down… up and down, he went, as regular as a Victorian beam engine. OMG! Joe was sliding down… down off Amanda's back. Every time, Amanda pulled himself up on the lion's tail, Joe slid a little further down… shoulders… waist… legs… Joe was now swinging from Amanda the Panda's ankles.

In case Joe fell, Rajah had his trunk around Joe's ankles.

There were now three forces pulling on the lion's tail... Amanda's pull-ups, Joe's weight and Rajah's tugging.

A sound, as if the dead were pushing open coffins with rusty hinges, alerted me to the fact that machinery, hidden somewhere underground, was starting up.

What happened next, happened, fast... suddenly the tail dropped down and then, just as suddenly, the way a gun recoils when it has been fired, it shot upwards.

The unexpectedness of the tail's upward movement, like when you are flung forward in a car when it suddenly brakes, flung Amanda and Joe so high into the air that for a second they disappeared into the mist. It was Rajah's quick thinking stopped them having a hard landing. He slowed their fall by using his trunk to blow air under them; then he used it as a crane to plonk them on his back next to Demetrius.

The lion, now with a vertical tail, was shooting flames out of its mouth. Did it think it was a dragon? Then, I remembered Howard had told our group that the palace had been made for a wizard with a fondness for gadgets. The fire coming out of the dragon's mouth was a typical wizard's trick. Wizards were men and men love showing off. For me, it was OTT, like a witch wearing too much green eyeshadow. But, never mind my carping, the gates were swinging open.

'There you are,' said Howard, 'I was right... pull the lion's tail and... hey-presto, the gates open. It was the frost slowed things up.'

'I think you were worried they might not open,' I said.

'Rubbish… never had a moment's doubt… Mildred is transmitting.'

On Howard's palm, I, and as many of our group as could get close to the palm to see, saw a close-up picture of Adder Palace. It looked like a ship, sinking in a sea of mist. Every light in every room seemed to have been switched on; fireworks were exploding in its forecourt; people were jumping out of windows… as if they were sailors, abandoning ship.

'Howard, how far away is the palace?' I said.

'Half a mile… cobbles all the way; follow the cobbles and we will be there… also, no one will get hurt; in the grass, on either side of the cobbles, there are man-traps. We follow the ice-cream van and Rajah, the way infantry follow tanks.'

It worried Gwen that Joe was on Rajah's back. She was forever shouting up to him: 'Joe, you alreet up there?'

Once, when he didn't answer, Amanda said: 'You'll have to wait until the gobstopper he's sucking, melts.'

'What if he swallows it? I thought you was "Health and Safety"?'

When a man, wearing a cook's white hat, threatened our progress with a wooden spoon, a gorilla, thumping his chest to show he meant the business, chased him into a copse. I do not know what happened in the copse; all I know is, the gorilla reappeared and the cook didn't.

We stopped when a headless horseman came, trotting towards us, spectral, out of the mist.

'Where's your head?' said Howard.

'Saddle bag…'

'You look more scary when you carry it under your arm.'

'I've run out of batteries to make its eyes flash.'

'Careless… what's happening at the palace?'

'Chaos… mayhem.'

'Any sign of Stanley? He's the one I want.'

'Me too,' I said.

'And I want my husband… dead or alive,' said Mary.

'Divent forget me,' said Gwen, 'I wants Stanley, not dead or alive, I wants him dead.'

'No sign of them, Aurora; the palace is full of secret passages… excuse, me, I think someone needs my help.'

In the mist a palace flunkey was getting the better of a chimpanzee. When the headless horseman charged them, the flunkey ran off the cobbles and onto grass. A second later there was an explosion.

'Booby trap,' said Howard, 'stay on the cobbles… never forget we are dealing with thieves, murderers and cannibals.'

'Aurora,' shouted Demetrius, 'Rajah is feeling the cold… he is finding it difficult to keep up with the ice-cream van.'

'Yo!' exclaimed Howard. 'Comfort stop.'

'A comfort stop at a time like this?' I said.

'Rajah is cold. The batteries in his electric coat need to be recharged.'

'You alreet up there, Joe?' said Gwen. 'It's a piss stop.'

'I'm coming doon, Mam,' said Joe, 'and so is me pal, Amanda… aren't we, Amanda?'

'We… ee!' exclaimed Joe as he and Amanda slid down Rajah's trunk.

'If it's a comfort stop,' said Gwen, 'I wants an oily rag. When I did that bus trip to Llandudno, I had a fag every time we stopped… they were the days, sex and an oily rag.'

'Have some gum,' said Amanda.

'I've told you… false teeth… chewing gum and false teeth fight like what cats and dogs dee.'

'Suck,' suggested Amanda, 'try not to chew… suck. When you are concentrating on sucking, instead of chewing, you won't have time to think of wanting a cigarette.'

'Will I not, now?'

'No, you won't.'

'Get away…'

'Amanda,' said Joe, 'can a have an ice cream? Yuh divent chew an ice cream, yuh suck it… everybody nars that.'

'Of course you can,' said Amanda.

'Mam, yuh want an ice cream?'

'I wants an oily rag.'

A dwarf served them.

'Two ninety-nines,' said Joe, 'with double flakes.'

'Say, please,' said Amanda.

'Please,' said Joe.

'I'd kill for a fag,' said Gwen.

'I'd kill for a fur coat,' said Mary, 'I'm freezing… and what's all this talk about us having to stop to recharge batteries for Rajah's electric blanket? I've never heard of anything so ridiculous since that left wing witch proposed admitting wizards to our coven.'

'Ladies,' said Howard, 'who can do a mushroom light?'

'I can,' I said.

'Thank you, Muriel. Demetrius, move Rajah closer to the ice-cream van.'

To alert everyone he was preparing to reverse, a light on the end of Rajah's tail flashed on and off.

'The jump leads, Aurora,' said a dwarf.

'Thank you, Martin.'

'Snow White and I are sorry to hear you have eaten your wife.'

'How'd you know that?'

'Dwarf gossip, Aurora… everyone knows.'

'If everyone knows, my street cred is zilch. A wizard who has been duped into eating his wife is a wizard in the gutter.'

'Revenge, Aurora, will put you back on a pedestal; I know it will.'

'You are very knowing for a dwarf.'

'I am an optimist. I no longer want to be tall. When I wanted to be tall, I was a pessimist; revenge will put you on a pedestal, I know it will. Hail, Aurora!'

'And all hail to you too, Martin.'

'Well, yuh bugger,' said Gwen, 'if yee scratch my back, I'll scratch yours.'

'Martin,' said Howard, 'the leads are connected to the van's battery?'

'Yes, Aurora.'

'Muriel, I see you have a mushroom light.'

Indeed, I had; while he'd been blathering and wittering, I'd been foraging. I know a lot about fungi. I know an eater from a poisoner.

'Here is your light,' I told him, holding up a fly agaric. The spell I had cast on its red top made it glow like a night light in a submarine.

'You will be my light,' said Howard. 'Follow, me.'

'Where to?' I said.

'When I fix the jump leads to the battery in Rajah's electric blanket, I will need to see what I am doing.'

'Where is the battery?'

'Under Rajah's tummy… follow me.'

If Whitby ever got wind of my subservience – being a torch bearer for a wizard – I'd become a cauldron anecdote; the witch's equivalent of a campfire song.

Under Rajah's tummy I was able to rub shoulders with Howard. I had a legitimate reason to be kiss-close to him.

When he asked for more light, I lay on top of him as if he was a mattress and I was a duvet. Our intimacy was that of commuters on the London Underground at rush hour.

'More light,' he said, 'I mean in wattage, not in intimacy.'

To make the mushroom grow brighter, I breathed on it.

'Thank you, Muriel, that's better… more to the left, I need to see which terminal is which.'

It took Howard only seconds to attach the jump leads; our intimacy ended when he announced: 'Job done.'

I will say this for him, he did help me to crawl out.

'It will take a good fifteen minutes for the ice-cream van's battery to recharge Rajah's battery. While we are waiting, may I suggest we have a coffee. Muriel, Mary, Mrs Rowe, Amanda… coffee? Martin, four coffees, please.'

'Aurora,' said Demetrius, from way up high on Rajah's back, 'you forget, I too, like the coffee.'

'Five coffees, Martin.'

'What about our advance on the Palace?' I said. 'Shouldn't we be getting a move on?'

'Mildred has informed me, we have time. The enemy know we are here. They will be wondering why we have stopped. They will be worried. Besides, when we reach the palace's front door I want Rajah to be warm and happy. Our stopping is not a comfort stop, it is a stop of necessity; isn't that right, Rajah?'

To show that he knew what was going on and by way of telling Howard that he appreciated him recharging his electric blanket, Rajah blew Howard a kiss with his trunk.

'The coffee tastes wonderful,' said Mary.

'It would taste better,' said Gwen, 'if I had an oily rag to gan with it.'

'When the battery is recharged,' said Howard, all the time glancing at Mildred, 'a green light will flash on Rajah's battery.'

'What a load of shite,' said Gwen, 'I divent believe this… an elephant with an electric blanket… and you two—' meaning myself and Howard— 'if yuh have to gan back under Rajah, just remember you're not in a bedroom with a double bed, you're under an elephant's belly.'

'Mrs Rowe,' said Howard, 'you have a way with words; have you ever thought of writing poetry?'

'You taking the piss?'

'Muriel, the light is flashing green. It is time to unplug. Once more, may I ask you to lead the way?'

Going under Rajah's belly was like going into a cave full of hairy stalactites. When you bumped into one it didn't scratch you but it did tickle.

'You do a ten out of ten mushroom light,' said Howard, 'I'll give you that.'

'I'd rather be flattered with a kiss than with words.'

'You know as well as I do, Muriel, that when a witch and a wizard become an item, thunderstorms and tsunamis become as common as drizzle and ebb tides. I have unplugged. You go first. I will follow you out.'

We squeezed out from under Rajah's tummy not unlike the way toothpaste is squeezed out of a tube.

Martin was waiting for us.

'Stow the jump leads, Martin,' said Howard, 'there's a good fellow.'

'Yes, Aurora.'

'And, Martin…'

'Yes, Aurora?'

'That rumour… the one about me having eaten my wife…'

'It is not true, Aurora?'

'It might be and it might not be.'

'You wish me to take my foot off the gossip pedal?'

'I do.'

'A kiss and a cuddle and your word is my command.'

'Martin, dear thing, I'm a heterosexual wizard.'

'More's the pity, darling.'

The mist was thick. The shapes of trees and bushes were phantoms… owls were hooting.

'I've heard of the dawn chorus,' I said, 'but, a dawn chorus of owls is a new one on me.'

'Them's not owls, Mrs Thayne,' said Gwen, 'that's Joe and Amanda blowing across the tops of bottles... Hi! Rajah, what you doing? You're a dirty minded elephant, you are... putting your trunk up me skirt... get out of it.'

'He means no harm,' said Howard.

'That's what all men say.'

'Mrs Rowe, Rajah is trying to warm you up. He is trying to warm you up the way the electric blanket is warming him up. He is sharing his hot air with you.'

'I stink of grass... you've got bad breath, you have, Rajah.'

'Yo!' exclaimed Howard. 'Move out. Martin, turn up the jingles... lots of noise. I want the bad guys to know the good guys are coming to get them.'

As moonlight shines through a gauze of clouds I saw the lights of Adder Palace shining through the mist. A few seconds later I saw the building itself.

At its front door, a gorilla, face mask up, was smoking a pipe; two monkeys, face masks up, sitting on a crate, were swigging beer from bottles.

'Yo!' sang out Howard.

We stopped.

'Where's "Health and Safety"?' said Gwen. 'Joe, you tell your pal Amanda, he's not doing his job... there's a gorilla ower there, smoking a pipe... that's disgusting, that is... tell him to give him some chewing gum.'

I ignored Gwen's rabbiting. My attention – and so was Mary's – was on the two figures a dwarf was prodding towards us with part of a drain pipe. One was the Arse Hole; the other was Una. They were arguing.

Dick was wearing a nappy; Una was wearing the sort of underwear that suggests more than it covers. The heat of their argument seemed to have made them oblivious to the cold.

'Mam,' said Joe, 'what's that man got under his nappy? The twins' nappies divent look like that.'

'Gan and play with Amanda,' said Gwen.

'It's not my fault,' Una was telling the Arse Hole, 'you told me to give you them.'

'Not a fucking overdose,' shouted back the Arse Hole. 'I told you to read the instructions... when's it going to go down? That's what I want to know... I don't feel well.'

'If you hadn't gone aal floppy on me... yuh wouldn't have needed pills.'

'The wart on your tit put me off.'

'Cheeky bugger, what about that tattoo of Margaret Thatcher on your bum?'

'Bloody hell... fuck... I'm seeing things.'

'If only you could...' said Una.

'Mr Hedgerow,' said Howard, 'where is Stanley?'

'And who might you be? Why are you dressed like a...'

'Like a wizard?' said Howard.

'Yes... like a wizard.'

'That, Mr Hedgerow, is because I am a wizard.'

'You don't happen to know a spell that will deflate an erect penis, do you?'

'I do not have a spell to mitigate the effects of an overdose of Viagra.'

'Mary... it's you, is it? Fuck... why are you dressed as a witch? Help me... take me to a doctor... when's it going to go down, that's what I want to know.'

'Where's Stanley?' repeated Howard.

'If I tell you, will you take me to a hospital?'

'Trust me,' said Howard.

'He's hiding in the dungeons... there, I've told you... now take me to a hospital... I don't feel well.'

'Joe,' said Gwen, 'go and get Mr Hedgerow an ice-cream.'

'I don't want a fucking ice-cream, I want a doctor. I don't feel well.'

'Mr Hedgerow,' said Gwen, 'the ice-cream is not for you to eat; it's a cold poultice for your willy. When Joe had a bump on his heed the size of a satsuma, I took the swelling down with three ice cubes wrapped in a hanky.'

'I don't feel well,' said Dick.

'How many Viagra tablets did you give my husband?' Mary asked Una.

'Three,' said Una, 'I only gave him three because the first one didn't work. If the first one had worked, he wouldn't have needed boosters... would he? Mr Hedgerow... what you doing lying on the ground? First you can't get it up and now you can't get up... Mr Hedgerow... Dicky... get up.'

'The Arse Hole,' said Mary, after she had bent over her husband and closed his eyes, 'is dead.'

'The Arse Hole...' said Una. 'You shouldn't speak ill of the dead, Mrs Hedgerow. I don't think that's nice.'

At Howard's command a trio of dwarves picked up Dick's corpse. I have no idea what they did with it... nor did I care

'Good riddance,' said Mary.

'We should be praying for him,' said Una.

'Bullshit!' said Mary. 'Who's in charge of the chimes on the ice-cream van?'

'I am,' said Amanda the Panda.

'And me,' said Joe.

'Play me something to help me forget the bastard died intestate.'

I don't know whose choice it was to play the Blue Danube, but that was the tune that now blared from the ice-cream van's speakers.

Joe and Amanda the Panda led the dancing.

'A never thought I'd see my Joe dancing a waltz,' said Gwen.

A bear gave Una a gorilla costume.

'To keep you warm, pet.'

'Ta, very much, that's very kind, I'm sure. What's your name?'

'Henry.'

'That's a nice name.'

'I'm from Texas.'

'Are you rich?'

'Sure, I'm rich... I'm an American. You wanna dance?'

A chimpanzee asked Mary to dance. I ended up dancing, as you do, with a gorilla.

The gorilla was a good dancer. It was when he spun me through Adder Palace's open front door that, before I passed out, I had an inkling I was in trouble.

# I AM ROASTED ALIVE

came-to, hanging in a net like a Parma ham, from a hook, some ten feet off the ground. Where in the name of all the white witches who had ever lived, was I?

'She's coming round, Stan,' said Ted.

'Welcome to Hell, Mrs Thayne,' said Stanley.

Looking down I saw Stanley and Ted. Perhaps it was my distressed state but I could see horns... embryonic horns... growing on Stanley's temples. My looking at them seemed to be making them grow... as if I was looking at time lapse footage of a bud breaking into a flower.

'I always knew you was a witch,' said Ted. 'The aches and pains you gave me... not to mention the itches. You wanted me to be your slave, didn't yuh? I'm a free man, I am.'

'What are you going to do to me?' I asked. 'My friends will be looking for me. Do you know... have you any idea who Mr Star is? When he gets his hands on you, you will be dead meat. You made a big mistake, Stanley, when you put the flesh of Howard's wife, into your grandmother's pies. You are going to learn the hard way, Stanley... that cannibalism doesn't pay.'

'Eating human flesh, Muriel – you don't like me calling you that, do you? Too familiar, am I? Tucking into a human rib chop is an addiction, more powerful than cocaine. And I'm addicted. What you think, Ted–' prodding me through the net with a poker– 'nice bit of how's your father on that arse.'

'Prime cut, Stan, prime cut.'

'Not to mention breast.'

'I likes a slice of breast cooked in bacon fat.'

'Know what this is?' said Stanley, bringing an iron pole with a white-hot corkscrew tip close to my face.

The heat coming off the corkscrew made me twitch... made me flinch... made me squirm. In my agitation I made the net swing.

'You going to brand her, Stan?' said Ted.

'All witches should be branded... you pissing your knickers, Mrs Thayne... Muriel?'

'You going to burn her, Stan?'

'I'm going to roast her first. I like a roast... help me drag the brazier under her bum.'

I could not see the brazier but I could feel its heat. The air around me began to shimmer. My bum began to feel hot.

'A slow roast,' said Ted, 'I likes a slow roast.'

'When you going to scream, Muriel... when are you going to beg for mercy?'

I did not reply. Damn it... Stanley was a junior devil. I was a senior witch. If I kept calm I should be able to put a spell on him.

'What big eyes you have,' said Ted.

'That's fear, that is,' said Stanley. 'Fear opens your eyes the way a tin opener opens tins. She may not be screaming, but, she's scared… you scared, Mrs Thayne?'

'Show her the torture box, Stan… show her the torture box.'

Stanley drew my attention to the 'torture box' by banging it with his corkscrew-tipped pole. Twisting, to look down, I saw an Egyptian sarcophagus. Its lid was open. The inside of its lid was spiked. When the lid closed on the person inside – me? – I did not like to think what the spikes would do. It was a coffin designed to turn a flesh and blood body, into a colander. I was looking at the open jaws of a T-Rex coffin.

I came close to fainting. I came close to voiding my bladder. The heat coming off the brazier was becoming hard to bear.

'Lower the bitch another two inches, Ted,' said Stanley.

Ted untied a rope wrapped round a cleat.

'Steady,' warned Stanley, 'I don't like eating burnt meat.'

Somewhere, above my head, in a net curtain of cobwebs, a pulley squeaked. I inched closer to the brazier. To stop myself crying out I bit my lips. I bit them so hard I tasted blood. But, no matter how hard I tried, I could not stop squirming. My agitation was making the net swing as if I was in a hammock in a ship in a storm.

'She's feeling the heat, Stan,' said Ted.

'She's squiggling like a worm in sunshine… feeling the heat, are you, Mrs Thayne? You're squiggling more than that bloody sharp-clawed cat of yours squiggled before I spatchcocked her… sent her to pull a chariot in Hell.'

His reference to Tilly touched a nerve. It made me react the way you do when someone tickles your toes. In the net, I twitched this way and that.

'Love your perfume,' said Stanley, 'you are starting to smell like a Sunday roast.'

'I loves a Sunday roast,' said Ted. 'You going to finish the cow off, the way you did your gran?' said Ted.

A shadow on a wall showed me a hand, holding a knife.

Something pricked my thigh. In a futile attempt to escape the point of the probing blade I thrashed like a fish caught in a net. Fish don't like it one bit… being caught in a net… and nor did I. I wanted to live. I did not have a death wish. I did not want to die.

I did not hear Rajah knock the dungeon's door off its hinges. Fear had made me deaf, the same way as grief stops you hearing the music played at the funeral of someone you love; all of which explains why it took me a few seconds to take on board that I was at the beginning of the end of my ordeal. You will believe me, when I tell you, I have never been so pleased to see an elephant in all of my life.

Howard, Gwen and Demetrius were on Rajah's back.

To show he meant business and knew what he was about, Rajah kicked over the brazier. The relief at not feeling its heat on my bum, was like jumping into a river on a hot summer's day.

I breathed slowly and deeply. If I could regain my self-control, I might… just might… be able to cast a spell. I closed my eyes and concentrated.

The pain I gave Ted doubled him up.

Putting a spell on Stanley, a junior devil, with powerful backers in Hell, would be much more difficult. I would need help.

Telepathy takes a lot of power; it is like spending a month's wages on something you can do without... like a personal trainer. But... and it is a big 'but'... there are times when it is wise to count the pennies... times when it is wise to lash out and spend; this was a time when it was wise to lash out and spend. I closed my eyes. I concentrated.

Tout suite I was having a telepathic group chat with Rajah, Mary, Gwen, Howard and Demetrius. It was a unanimous verdict ... Stanley was going in the sarcophagus.

'And when he's in the box,' said Howard, 'we sit on the lid.'

I twisted until I could see Stanley. Did he know his fate? Was he able to eavesdrop on telepathic communications? How minor a devil was he?

When I caught his eye, I gave him the finger. My gesture made him lunge at me with the pole with the corkscrew tip the way an infantryman uses a bayonet. It was Rajah who saved my bacon. He picked Stanley up, the way you may have seen elephants pick up a tree trunk; then, he... squeezed.

Imagine the world's strongest man hand-squeezing the juice out of a lemon... Rajah being the world's strongest man and Stanley, the lemon. Stanley did not scream... How could he? All the air in his lungs had been squeezed out. I heard the sound you hear when folk with nothing better to do crack their knuckles.

Stanley was not a bespoke fit for the sarcophagus. To get him in, Rajah had to squeeze, nudge and blow.

The embryonic devil's horns on Stanley's temples were smoking. Had someone in Hell, a senior devil, pulled the plug on him; given him up as a bad job?

When he struggled to climb out, Rajah blew him back in.

'I'll close the lid on the bastard,' said Gwen. 'Michael would want me to... I knows he would.'

To help her off his back, Rajah made his trunk into a slide.

'Oh my arse,' she said, as she hit the dungeon's cobbles.

Two chimpanzees helped her up.

The lid was hinged.

'Help,' said Gwen. 'I needs help to close the lid... revenge has made me strong but it hasn't given me muscles like I've seen on male strippers at the club.'

'One, two, three,' said one of the chimpanzees.

The hinges were like old people who didn't want to get out of bed... they weren't at all keen on moving.

'Eins, zwei, drei,' said a chimpanzee.

The hinges groaned and creaked.

When the lid was vertical and poised to fall – dear me... its awful spikes began flashing, on and off. Howard's doing? As, I have mentioned, more than once, wizards love showing off.

'Eins, zwei, drei...'

The lid closed in a series of jerks; the sort of jerks you see a learner driver make a car do when he has yet to learn how to raise the car's clutch and press its accelerator, all at the same time.

In a futile attempt to save himself, Stanley, more dead than alive, raised an arm.

'It won't bloody shut,' shouted Gwen. 'It won't bloody shut.'

And why should we be surprised it would not shut? It takes a lot of force to puncture a flesh and blood body with hundreds of spikes.

When Rajah sat on it blood oozed out of the sarcophagus's busted dovetails.

Everyone in the dungeon was staring at the sarcophagus the way gravediggers rest on their shovels when they have finished filling-in. Stanley's departure to hell had made everyone forget that yours truly was swinging in a net like a Parma ham in a Venetian deli.

'Hoy!' I hollered.

It was Ted of all people who lowered me to the ground and helped me out of the net. I stumbled and fell out of it the way spacemen, who have been in space for months and have lost the use of their legs, exit their space capsule.

'I wouldn't have let Stan burn you, Mrs Thayne… you do know that, don't you? You and me… we always got on, didn't we? I always said you could take a joke, you know, a bit of rough and tumble.'

'Take him away,' said Howard, to a gorilla, 'you know what to do with him.'

'Hi, what yuh gannin to dee with me?'

'Cut out your tongue, for a start, if you don't shut up,' said the gorilla.

It was then that I fainted. It was Mary who told me Howard carried me to the great hall. She told me: 'He carried you, over his shoulder, the way a farmer carries a sack of potatoes.'

# THE WINNERS
# CELEBRATE

I was sitting at a long table in a hall that made me think of tabors and tabards? A place where, a long time ago, a rich lord might have boasted how he'd ordered a witch to be burnt.

Creosote torches stuck in iron mangers were the hall's only source of light. The slabs on its floor were uneven. Were they covering a prehistoric burial ground? Were the souls of the long-departed pushing them up? If this hall hadn't witnessed rape and pillage, I'd eat my besom.

As I pulled myself together it dawned on me that I was 'top table'. My companions were Mary, Gwen, Joe and, of course, Howard, on a throne, wearing the ceremonial dress uniform of a high ranking wizard.

Since he'd breezed into my life I had watched him, as if through a kaleidoscope. He was pieces of moving coloured glass. In his time, he'd been Howard the surfer... Howard the piano player... Howard the composer... Howard the writer of pantomime scripts... Howard the conjuror... Howard the wizard; now, he was... Caesar at the Battle of Alesia... Leonidas at Thermopylae.

I was an honoured guest; close, as they say, to the salt. On the rows of seats below me, pandas, chimps, polar bears, brown bears, rats and mice, were quaffing, eating and throwing bones to dogs.

The Headless Knight was there and so too was the stilt walker I'd last seen in Gwen's street.

'Hail, Aurora! Hail, Aurora!' exclaimed the Headless Knight.

'All hail, Aurora,' shouted the stilt walker.

A fire eater breathed out fire.

'Careful, mate,' said a gorilla, 'you're singeing my costume.'

'Aurora! Aurora!'

Howard acknowledged his worshippers with posies of flowers; as usual, where they came from was a mystery. His gold-coloured soutane was embroidered with red poppies and blue forget-me-nots. He looked magnificent.

'The toast,' said Howard, raising a champagne flute, 'to the victors the spoils.'

'To the victors the spoils,' shouted back the menagerie.

It was between a bout of toasting and mutual back slapping that he asked if I was alright.

'How are you? In the dungeon I was worried about you.'

'Were you really?'

I'm a sucker for flattery. His concern for my well-being was a blow lamp to an ice cube. I melted. My god! Mon dieu! Was he going to propose? Of course he didn't, but the mere thought of it being a possibility made me think I was eating at Harrods; that the monkeys and gorillas I could see belching and eating ham off the bone without using a knife and fork, were waiters, wearing tailed coats.

'My storm troopers are letting their hair down,' said Howard. 'If they become too boisterous, blame Ambrose – he keeps an excellent cellar.'

'To the victorious the spoils,' I said. 'The winner takes everything.'

'Has it not always been the case? You are a witch, I am a wizard. Our histories provide us with different examples of battles won and lost. The common factor in all battles is that the winner is the cat who gets to lick the cream.'

'Are we drinking champagne?'

'Surely a witch of your calibre can tell the difference between prosecco and champagne? It is from the cellar of our unwilling host, Ambrose.'

'Where is the groper?'

'At this moment–' looking at his palm– 'he is attempting to escape… look.'

'Mildred is transmitting?'

'Yes.'

On Howard's palm I saw Ambrose… a near-naked Ambrose… he was wearing only a baby's nappy… abseiling down an ivy-clad wall on a rope made out of a bed sheet.

'You are letting him escape? He has a lot to answer for. He is a co-conspirator.'

'I have plans for Ambrose… trust me.'

It was then I spotted Una and Ted pulling a barrow, over-loaded with logs. On top of the logs, like a stagecoach driver aloft in his box, there sat a dwarf with a whip. Every so often, to encourage Una and Ted to keep pulling, he cracked it over their heads.

'Howard,' I said, 'what a benevolent wizard you are. You have not had them executed.'

'Ignore them, they are servants... barrow pullers... more champagne?'

I held out my glass. While he poured, I ogled him. He pretended he didn't know I was ogling, but I knew he knew I was ogling.

'This is excellent champagne. Ambrose keeps an excellent cellar... don't sip, Muriel, swig... this is not a wake, it is the celebration of a victory. It is our VE day... don't sip... swig.'

'It is very good,' I said, sipping; no wizard was going to tell me how to drink champagne; anyway, to me it tasted like prosecco. It would be typical of a wheeler and dealer like Ambrose to have stuck champagne labels on bottles of prosecco. Wine snobs are easy to fool; whatever I was drinking, it was going to my head. My ordeal in the dungeon was becoming a distant memory.

I was impressed by everyone's good behaviour. When a tipsy brown bear dropped a fork, a gorilla retrieved it for him.

'Don't use it, Paddy,' the gorilla told the bear, 'germs... you can get VD off a flagged floor.'

When one of the flaming brands lighting the hall showed signs of dying, the fire eater gave it the kiss of life.

A knife thrower – a palisade of impaled knives around a plate of sausages – was feeding tit-bits of sausage to a real chimpanzee.

The trouble began when a dwarf in a chimp costume insisted on singing 'Danny Boy'.

'Sit down,' his mates told him, 'you know you can't sing... you always want to sing Danny Boy when you've had a drink.'

'You've no head for the booze, Tiger.'

'Sit down.'

'Howard,' I said, 'why is he called Tiger?'

'He helps the lion tamer.'

'Microphone... microphone,' shouted Tiger. 'Where's my microphone... can't sing without a microphone.'

'Here you are, Tiger,' said a gorilla, handing Tiger a banana.

'Hoy! I was going to eat that,' said a brown bear.

'Testing! Testing!' said Tiger, tapping the top of the banana, as if it was a real microphone; then, shouting 'Dive! Dive! Dive!' he disappeared under a table.

When he reappeared he was carrying a stilt walker's stilt.

'One... two... hiccup... three... four...' said Tiger, counting the strides he was taking from the table.

'Eight, nine, ten,' shouted a gorilla.

'Eh? That's not right... start again.'

'Don't do it, Tiger,' shouted a bear.

'What's Tiger going to do?' I asked Howard.

'Pole vault onto the table. It's his party trick.'

'Stand-by to repel boarders,' shouted a polar bear sitting at the table on which Tiger was going to vault.

'Watch your beer,' shouted a gorilla.

'Go for it, Tiger, you can do it.'

Wolf whistles... clapping... cheers...

Tiger landed on a bunch of grapes. The juice his landing squeezed out of them, slid him down the table like a Dutch speed skater on a frozen canal; chicken legs, flutes, goblets, beer mugs, cheeses, flans, pies, a whole salmon… he sent them all flying. He was a wrecking ball.

'Bloody dwarves,' said a gorilla.

'It happens all the time,' said a badger.

'Dwarves and booze don't mix.'

'Where's my microphone?' said Tiger, standing, arms on hips, in the middle of the carnage he'd wrought.

'Have a banana,' said a bear.

'Tank you wery much,' said Tiger. 'A one… a one, two, three…'

To help him find the right tempo Tiger tapped a foot in a pool of beer.

'Watch it, mate,' said a rat, 'you're splashing me. This costume is hired; it will cost if it has to be dry cleaned. I'm wardrobe, I know about such things. It's my area of expertise.'

'Oh, Danny boy…' sang Tiger.

'Can't hear you!' shouted a mouse. 'Your banana isn't working; try plugging it into a pineapple… Ha! Ha! Squeak! Squeak!'

'Try an orange,' boomed a gorilla, 'everyone knows an orange makes a better microphone than a banana.'

'Who says so?' said the rat.

'Oh, Danny boy…'

'It is play time,' said Howard. 'Demetrius… Rajah.'

Rajah was in the hall with us; for an elephant, he was very well behaved. He'd a bail of straw and a tin bath full of water.

The tin bath was one of those you'd have found hanging from a hook on a back yard wall in a worker's humble dwelling anywhere in England circa 1930.

'Oh, Danny boy…the pipes are…'

'Watch,' said Howard.

I heard a sucking noise. Surely, I thought, he wouldn't… but, he did. Rajah sprayed the tables with water. He sprayed the revellers as if his trunk was a water cannon… the sort used to disperse rioters.

The curious thing was that neither Howard, nor myself, got wet. Water, water, everywhere, but not a drop had touched us.

'Where's my umbrella?' said a chimpanzee.

'That water smells of elephant,' said a polar bear. 'I don't like that.'

'Oh, Danny boy… the pipes are calling…'

Rajah returned to the tin bath.

'Is Rajah reloading?' I asked Howard.

'Watch,' said Howard.

The force of the sluice Rajah now let rip from his trunk swept Tiger off his feet; it swept he-who-was-hell-bent-on-singing-Danny-Boy down the table the way a fast flowing river carries a leaf. The rocks over which it swept Tiger were cruets and fruit bowls.

The unceremonious sluicing of Tiger down the table was the signal for the start of a free-for-all. It was as if a bell had been rung to start one of those ancient games where two teams scramble in a cobbled street to fight for possession of a pig's bladder.

Bottles of champagne were shaken to make spray guns. A fillet of salmon became a cudgel. A chicken leg became a dagger; apples were thrown the way a fielder in a cricket match throws a cricket ball at stumps. A mouthful of masticated nuts, when spat into someone's face, was shrapnel. The 'World's Strongest Man' (that's what it said on his tracksuit) was pouring a pint glass of beer over a panda's head. Spoons were being used to flick dollops of mayonnaise into faces. Cucumbers were truncheons. A rat and a mouse were having a sword fight with corn cobs.

What I found interesting was that none of the missiles came close to hitting Howard or me. The free-for-all had rules. Howard and those close to him were a no-go zone. Howard and I were off-limits. I know this sounds silly, but this made me feel important.

I don't think Mary had been hit, but Gwen and Joe had. Gwen had an ice cream cone sliding off her head; Joe had a dollop of mushy peas hanging off the end of his nose like, yes, you've guessed… like, snot.

'Mam,' said Joe, 'can a not throw something back?'

'We're top table, darling,' said Gwen. 'Top table folk are supposed to set a good example… just keep ducking and diving.'

It was only when Howard stood that the mayhem stopped; by standing he had sent out a signal.

At once a gorilla dropped a hard-boiled egg he'd been about to throw at a mouse. A chimpanzee aborted throwing an orange. A badger, instead of squirting champagne out of his mouth at a bear, grinned and swallowed the fizz. Two rats shook hands and apologised for the blobs of mayonnaise they'd thrown at each other.

'Sorry about that, Bert.'

'That's alright, Gilbert.

A bear rubbed ice-cream off another bear's nose.

'Sorry, mate.'

'Turn around, you've a banana stuck up your arse.'

'Bloody hell!'

The headless horseman let everyone know he'd a bump on his head.

'Let's have a look,' said a chimpanzee.

To enable him to see down into the collar hiding the headless horseman's head, the chimp stood on a chair.

'That's a whopper. Where's the medic? Medic! Medic!'

In the middle of the hall there was a double door high enough for a man on horseback to pass through. A man on stilts, dressed as Uncle Sam, was drawing its top bolts. A gorilla was lifting its bottom bolts.

'Keep three steps behind me,' said Howard, 'etiquette is everything in the circus world.'

'Joe,' said Gwen, 'I think it would be nice if, in the procession, you held my hand.'

'Do a have to?'

'Yes… we're top table.'

A guard of honour was forming in front of the double doors.

Every so often on our way to the door, Howard stopped to do a high five with a well-wisher.

A gorilla played 'Hail the Chief' on bagpipes; someone shouted, 'All hail, Aurora… hail, Aurora!' I was in ancient Rome. I was part of the victory parade of a victorious Roman general.

When the doors creaked open a blast of cold air ruffled my hair. I saw the Aurora Borealis. The night sky was swirling with an energy I had never seen before.

Gwen and Joe were enjoying themselves. Gwen was waving to Howard's fan club the way royalty waves to crowds from Buckingham Palace's balcony. Joe's bows made a mouse shout, 'Hail, Joe!'

The hall's double doors were a triumphal arch; outside, Adder Palace's courtyard, lit by flaming torches, seemed to be on fire. It was by the light of these fiery beacons that I made out four white horses hitched to a Roman chariot of the sort you'd have seen in the Circus Maximus during the reign of the Emperor Augustus.

Ghostly shapes crowded the courtyard's battlements. Some were Tudor peasants; some were wearing top hats.

'Howard,' I said, tapping him hard on the shoulder – it takes a lot to get a wizard's attention when he is basking in adulation – 'your fan club seems to have grown, I mean, where have they all come from? One is wearing a top hat…'

'Adder Palace has a long history, Muriel. My fan club is the ghosts of all those who have tried to do good, while living at Adder Palace; they are here to bid me adieu… if you'd care to step into the chariot.'

'Where are we going?'

'Back to the Bentley.'

'What about the rest of our party? Gwen and Joe and Mary…'

'Yes,' said Mary, 'there's not room in the chariot for all of us, and, Howard, I hope you haven't forgotten about the promise you made about forging Dick's will in which he leaves everything to me… your gift of signature you called it.'

'Trust me…'

'There he gans again,' said Gwen.

'With your permission, Muriel,' said Howard, gesturing towards the chariot, 'I will take you for a ride.'

'You can trust him do dee that,' said Gwen.

'Muriel, I am offering you a ride in a vehicle of the sort in which Cleopatra and Antony rode.'

'We are an item?'

'Not quite… and here comes transport for Mary, Mrs Rowe and Joe.'

The jalopy, banging and wheezing towards us, looked to me like the one I'd seen in the big-top. Its driver had two heads; no matter how hard I looked I could not be certain which of the two heads was flesh and blood and which was wax.

'Mary, Mrs Rowe, Joe—' gesturing at the jalopy— 'your bespoke transport to the Bentley. I pride myself on thinking of everything. You will have noticed that your driver has two heads, yes? On the old adage that two heads are better than one, I think you will agree, I have placed you in safe hands.'

'I want to go in the chariot,' said Joe, 'why can't I go in the chariot?'

'Because, Joe,' said Gwen, 'your mother needs you. I've never been in a car before with a man with two heads… been in cars with men with more hands than an octopus has tentacles, but never with a bloke with two heads.'

'Hail, Aurora! Hail, Aurora!'

The chant of Howard's fans was uplifting. I was a player at St James' Park and had just scored a hat-trick.

The chariot encouraged intimacy. It was a single bed with two people sleeping in it. When I placed an arm round Howard's waist, to stop myself being tumbled out, he did not object.

'Howard,' I said, as we cantered off and the noise of his farewell 'hails' was fading, 'what is going to happen to Una and Ted?'

'Hang on, this corner is tight... Una is washing the World's Strongest Man's leotard. She finds his muscles irresistible.'

'Poor Eddy; he's a good man. I wonder how he will manage without her... and Ted?'

'He is in the tender care of the Amazons... the circus's female sword swallowers... big girls... benders of iron bars... bang six-inch nails into railway sleepers with their foreheads. Once saw them eat a twenty-piece dinner service, gravy boat, tureens, the lot... wonderful act... leaves the audience gobsmacked. They've taken a fancy to the rogue. No accounting for taste. He's going to be their skivvy... wash their thongs, that sort of thing. They know his history. The moment he steps out of line they'll put red hot tongs on his nose pustules. Hang on...'

On the open road Howard gave the horses their heads.

If you think going over a pothole in a car is bad, try going over one in a chariot.

Was he showing off? As I have mentioned more than once, wizards love showing off; it's an itch they can't resist scratching. Was he trying to see if he could scare me? If so, I wasn't having any of that.

'Can we not go faster?' I said, egging him on the way schoolboys egg on their friends in a fight.

'We can if you want to.'

And we did.

When the jalopy carrying Mary, Gwen and Joe – doing its best to keep up with us – backfired, the horses, to get away from the noise, galloped faster.

'There's Ambrose,' said Howard.

Mildred was transmitting. On Howard's palm, I saw Ambrose, naked but for a nappy, riding a quad bike.

'I'll text Roger and Heather to let them know where he is.'

'Roger and Heather?'

'You know them... the guy who buys his wife a chainsaw for her birthday.'

'I know who they are, I just didn't know they were, you know, in the area. How do you know them?'

'Spies.'

He began to text.

You may be wondering how he managed to do this while in charge of four galloping horses. I will tell you; whether or not you will believe me is another matter. If AI can drive a Bentley, why not a chariot?

While he was texting, the reins floated in the air in front of him.

Going round a corner on one wheel, he told me, 'Trust me.'

At the Bentley, he helped me down from the chariot the way, in days of old, a footman would have helped a lady out of her coach.

I had lost all sense of time. It was only when I saw the sky turning light, that I realised a new day was dawning. The sky was changing to the colour of a bruise and so, I suspected, was my left thigh; bones had not been broken in the ride, but, if I'd been a parcel delivered by Fedex, my packaging would have been ripped.

If I was the worse for wear, so were the horses. The steam coming off their backs, out of their nostrils, made them look like equine steam engines.

I looked at the lopsided sign warning the literate of the dangers they faced if they trespassed into the grounds of Adder Palace.

In the dark, in the mist, it had looked scary. In daylight, on a fine crisp winter morning, its warnings looked like something bored schoolboys scribble on paper aeroplanes and fly to each other when they think teacher isn't looking.

From a small green tent pitched alongside the Bentley, there now appeared a dwarf, dressed as a jester. He ran towards us, carrying a bunch of carrots and a bucket of water.

'Hail, Aurora!' he exclaimed.

'Thank you, Oswald,' said Howard. 'That's Oswald, the ostler. He'll feed and water the horses.'

Two loud bangs announced the arrival of the jalopy. Mary, Gwen and Joe climbed out of the open top the way children, especially boys, leapfrog over walls, instead of opening gates.

'I was shit scared,' said Gwen.

'It was horrendous,' said Mary.

'It was lush... geet lush,' said Joe.

We hugged and kissed. I knew Joe had been overawed by the journey in the jalopy when he allowed me to peck him on the cheek.

'Ladies,' said Howard, bowing, 'and Joe... mission accomplished... excuse me.'

'Is he going for a piss?' said Gwen, when Howard disappeared behind a holly bush. 'If he's bursting for a piss, I'm dying for a fag.'

'I wouldn't be surprised if he disappeared,' said Mary, 'and left us to drive ourselves home. He's a wizard. You can't trust wizards. He hasn't kept his promise to forge the Arse Hole's will. Men! "Trust me, I'm a wizard"… typical.'

The holly bush hid all of Howard except for the tip of his wizard's cone-hat. The flash of light that came from the holly bush made me blink the way you do when, in the middle of the night, you switch on your bedroom light.

Howard had not disappeared in a puff of smoke. He had used the holly bush as a changing room. He reappeared, not dressed as a top-ranking wizard in cloth of gold, but as a hunter or bird watcher, in camouflage fatigues.

'Bloody hell!' exclaimed Gwen.

'Voila!' he exclaimed. 'I am no longer Aurora. Once again, I am Mr Star.'

'How'd you do that, sir?' said Joe.

'Wizardry, Joe… wizardry. Mary and Muriel, if you'd like to disappear behind the holly bush on the other side of the road; that is, the ladies changing room… off you go.'

And we did.

The flash of light made by our metamorphosis from witch dress to mufti was not as bright as Howard's. When I thought about it, I would have expected nothing less.

'What's ganin on?' said Gwen. 'I divent like this… Joe, you stay close to your mam.'

It was while Gwen was holding Joe as close to her as a person who is feeling the cold hugs a hot water bottle that

Howard indicated he wished to talk to Mary and myself in private.

'It is time,' he said, 'to deal with Mrs Rowe and Joe. They cannot be allowed to remember, to blab to their friends, that I am a wizard and that you, Muriel and Mary, are witches. Do you agree?'

We nodded that we did.

'Extermination or amnesia?' said Mary.

'Mary,' I said, 'you know as well as I do, it has to be amnesia.'

'What you lot whispering about?' Gwen shouted at us... 'two days without a fag... can't believe it. Joe, you keep away from them horses... they're devils, they are.'

Howard, Mary and I held hands. We formed a circle.

'You lot going to dance?' said Gwen.

In the circle we put our heads together as if we were rugby players bonding before the start of a match.

When a wizard of Howard's rank – in the pecking order of English royalty, at least a duke – and two witches – at least dames in the House of Lords – combine to cast a spell, snow falls in August and rain pours down from a cloudless sky.

The spell we incanted was ecumenical.

When we broke our congregation, Gwen and Joe were fast asleep. They were babes in the wood. They were curled up, side by side, on tufts of grass white with frost.

'Will they have a headache when they wake up?' said Mary.

'I hope they don't get frostbite,' I said. 'A spell as powerful as the one they are now under might affect their circulation.'

'They will wake up as refreshed as if they had had a good night's sleep; trust me, I'm a wizard,' said Howard.

'The will... when...' said Mary.

'Not now... not now... anon; trust me, I'm a wizard.'

Mary sighed. She was cold, tired and weary. And so was I. I am not at all sure how it is with a wizard, but casting a spell takes a lot out of a witch; it makes you feel a bit like the way a marathon runner feels at the end of a marathon... knackered.

And now we had to get Gwen and Joe into the Bentley.

'Can Oswald help us get them into the Bentley?' I asked Howard.

'Negative,' he said, 'circus rules... Oswald is an ostler not a lifter... demarcation. You have rules in your coven about who can and cannot cast certain spells.'

We struggled to get the 'sleepers' into the Bentley. Gwen was snoring; Joe kept smiling as if he was dreaming about a Knickerbocker Glory.

Mary and I took Joe's feet, Howard took his shoulders.

'Gently into the Bentley,' said Howard. 'Joe is not a sack of potatoes, he is a human being; he is flesh and blood; he is mortal.'

I found Howard's chuntering irritating. Mary and I exchanged knowing glances. As I said before, casting a spell takes a lot out of a witch. Mary and I were knackered, and a knackered witch is no different to your everyday, run of the mill mortal; she is prone to snapping, to opening her mouth without thinking.

Getting Gwen into the car was the problem. She was big and heavy.

'She weighs a ton,' said Mary.

'We need a crane,' I said.

'It is a good job Mrs Rowe is comatose,' said Howard. 'If she was awake and heard such comments, I fear I might be looking at two witches with two black eyes... altogether... one, two, three, lift.'

I had the suspicion that the spell, while having sent Gwen to sleep, had not knocked out her libido. When Howard picked her up by her shoulders – Mary and I had her feet – she draped herself over him like a shawl. When he pushed her, ever so gently, onto the Bentley's back seat, she dragged him into the car with her. It took the combined strength of Mary and myself to free him. Howard was mine and I wanted him all to myself.

'They will remember nothing,' said Howard, emerging backwards from the car. He was out of breath. In fairness to him, I supposed sending Gwen and Joe to sleep had also taken a lot out of him. I concluded that witches and wizards had more in common than the PhD theses I'd read in the coven's archives suggested.

'When they wake, they will have none of the supernatural powers I gave them when I made them deputies.'

'Howard...' said Mary.

'I know... I know, the will... trust me, I'm a wizard.'

'When you say that you sound like all the men who have told me I was the love of their life... bullshit.'

'Mary, as King Canute failed to turn back the tide, I know I will never change your view of men...nor will I try to. Muriel, may I give you the keys to the Bentley.'

'You are not driving?'

'I am not coming with you.'

'What?'

'Don't sound so surprised. Why should I? I have avenged the death of my wife. I have sent a minor devil to Hell. My troops need me and so do the good people of Aberdeen. A billionaire American is upsetting the locals. He wants to demolish a row of fishermen's cottages to extend the golf club he owns. I dislike bullies. One of my heroes is your English Robin Hood. What a guy! He could use a longbow the way I use a spell. Ladies–' bowing– 'it has been a pleasure making your acquaintance. Muriel–' kissing me on both cheeks– 'adieu!'

He jumped into the jalopy whose driver had two heads the way in cowboy movies the good guy jumps onto his and rides off into the sunset.

For as long as I live, I will never forget watching the jalopy… a bespoke, circus joke car, driven by a driver with two heads… speed away from me. My mission to ensnare Howard had failed. I was the poacher who had failed to poach. Howard was the big fish I had failed to hook. Would I ever see him again? I don't know why but I thought I would.

I had shown more interest in him, than he had in me. He was a wizard off on another mission to right a wrong. It would have been impossible, indeed, foolhardy, for me to have tried to have stopped him.

'We've been jilted,' I said.

'The bridegroom has scarpered,' said Mary. 'No bloody will, either. Men! Trust me! I'm a wizard Ha! Ha! I feel sick. I'll never trust a man again… never.'

'Mary,' I said, 'when did we ever trust men? Give me a hug.'

We cut a deal that we'd take turns driving back to Whitley Bay. I drove first. The car belonged to Howard; what we'd do with it when we got back home, I hadn't a clue; nor did I care.

The road was quiet and empty. I put my foot down. In the back seat Gwen and Jo were sound asleep. Lucky them, they were out of it.

'It will take us longer to get home than it did coming,' I said to Mary.

'It was amazing how, when Howard was driving, we never once had to stop for a red light,' said Mary.

'Or, when he was tired the car drove itself; good job there are two of us... share the strain.'

'I'll bet we never see him again; so much for his promise to forge Dick's will... Men! Trust me, I'm a wizard. You know, I don't even have the combination to the safe the Arse Hole had built into a wall in his den. Where money was concerned, the Arse Hole trusted nobody.'

'What will happen to the Arse Hole's mortal remains?'

'His body?'

'Yes.'

'Couldn't care less.'

The satnav told me I was approaching a crossroads. I slowed down. In the distance I saw flashing blue lights. Had there been an accident? Why were an ambulance, a fire engine and a police car blocking the road?

A policeman held up his hand to tell me to stop.

'Accident?' I asked.

'Wine gum?' he said. 'And take one for your friend,' then, seeing Gwen and Joe fast asleep, he said, 'good job those two are fast asleep. If they'd been awake I'd have had to open another packet. Fret yee not, ladies, you'll soon be on your way… another ten minutes and the rescue truck, with its wee crane, will have pulled the wreckage out of your way… going far?'

'Newcastle,' I told him.

'That's a long way. I'll bet the cops down there don't give out wine gums.'

'They give out parking tickets,' I said. 'What's happened?'

'Funny business… I've been in traffic, aye, nigh on thirty years; thought I'd seen it all. But, not for the first time and not for the last, I'm thinking, I was wrong. Have you ever seen a collision between a quad bike and a dumper trunk?'

'Anyone hurt?'

'A gentleman wearing naught but a nappy, a bairn's nappy, has a muckle bump on his head. If he'd behaved himself and not called me "Haggis Head", I'd have given him a blanket. He has a lot to say for himself; fancies himself like those gentlemen who come up for the shooting. Aye, and he's a name dropper, as well… he's a river in spate going over a weir; he's no, a listener. He wasn't interested when I told him I've had a wee dram with Richard Burton and Elizabeth Taylor… years ago but it did happen … aye, they were up in the glens making, what the Americans, call a movie. Lovely couple. The Englishman wearing naught but a bairn's nappy made a mistake when he tried to bribe me… aye, he did… he made an error of judgement. I ask you, tell me the truth and I'll give you another wine gum, do I look the sort of copper who'd take a bribe? Look at my profile—' twisting his head sideways so Mary and I could see what he was talking about– 'you could put that on a Scottish five pound note.'

'Indeed you could,' I said. 'But what happened?'

'Have I not told you? A collision between a quad bike and a dumper trunk. You're like all folk from south of the border, you do not listen; you're like the laird who was no listening to the crofter when the crofter told him he was starving. The posh fella wearing the nappy says he owns Adder Palace. And I'm Rabbie Burns, I told him. He was riding the quad bike.'

'Who was driving the dumper truck?' I asked.

'A man and his missus. They told me they'd driven the dumper all the way from Newcastle. Who drives a dumper truck that far? Mind you, I will say this, they were dressed for it; there's no a cab on a dumper truck. They were dressed, like, for that race between London and Brighton... vintage cars... cloth caps, ulsters and goggles; that sort of thing. I'm thinking, you know, you saying you're from Newcastle, you wouldn't be knowing them, would you?'

'Newcastle is a big city, constable.'

'Aye, that's true.'

'Where are the reprobates?'

'They are cooling their heels the way my gran cooled broth by putting it on a doorstep... there they are, over there, handcuffed to the hoarding advertising Oscar Wilde Tractors... and that's a funny thing, that hoarding, it wasn't there yesterday. Who put it up, that's what I want to know... and who in the name of the McGregor tartan are Oscar Wilde Tractors?'

'I've no idea,' I said. 'I'm not local… I'm from Newcastle.'

'Aye! Aye! So you said. Off you go then. No more than five miles an hour when you drive past the dumper truck and quad bike. I'll be watching. I loves fruit gums but–' putting a finger in his mouth– 'they plays havoc with my fillings.'

I drove off slowly. When I saw Ambrose, Heather and Roger handcuffed to the hoarding advertising Oscar Wilde tractors, I did not slow down. Their predicament had nothing to do with me.

'I think Howard had that sign put up,' I said. 'Do you remember, at your house party, when Marcus groped me, I made a joke about Oscar Wilde Tractors.'

'But Howard wasn't at the party,' said Mary.

'You are forgetting, Mary, Howard, he of distant memory, he who has buggered off…'

'Without forging a will…'

'You are forgetting, Mary, Howard had spies everywhere.'

'Maybe Mildred was hiding under a gravy tureen.'

Gwen and Joe woke up at Otterburn. Mary was driving. I was half asleep. I knew they'd woken because they were farting. What a smell. One of the side effects of the spell Howard, Mary and I had put on them was that it made its recipients fart. Spells, like all medicines, have side effects.

I was amused that they were both blaming each other for the smell.

'What you been eating, Joe?' said Gwen.

'That's not me... that's you, 'replied Joe. 'Who smelt it, dealt it.'

'Where am I?' said Gwen. 'Hello, Mrs Thayne.'

I turned around. 'Hi, Gwen, you'll be home in a couple of hours.'

'Will I?'

'Yes, you will.'

'I'm hungry,' said Joe.

'My mouth's like a sewer,' said Gwen. 'Joe, for Christ's sake will you stop farting.'

'Can't help... not my fault.'

For the next twenty minutes Gwen and Joe went back to sleep; the sort of sleep from which, every few minutes, you wake up, before nodding off again.

Moorland rolled and tumbled away from us in every direction. The road was narrow and twisty. It was while we were going slow round a hairpin bend that I spotted a sandwich board advertising that three hundred yards down the road, refreshments were on sale. I told Mary to get ready to pull in.

In the layby in which we parked there was a mobile greasy spoon. Its awning was decorated with stars, planets and moons.

'Gimme four full English, please,' I told the young man behind the counter.

'You American?'

'No, why should I be?'

'What's with the "gimme" then?'

'Oh, that... I was thinking of an American friend I have just left.'

'Boyfriend?'

'Sort of.'

'Eggy bread?'

'What's eggy bread?' said Joe.

I explained.

'Don't like that.'

'Have you ever tried it?'

'Don't like it.'

'You sell fags?' said Gwen.

'Against the law, pet... health and safety. I'll sell you a star atlas.'

'A what?'

'A star atlas...when I'm not frying, I'm star gazing. I make a mean Aurora burger. Last night... wow! The Aurora Borealis.'

Was it by chance he'd mentioned Howard's wizard's name? Was he telling me, in a roundabout way, he knew our secret? That he knew Howard? Was I being paranoid? I didn't know. I didn't care. I was knackered.

Despite the freezing cold we ate the FE al fresco. The table at which we sat, wobbled. The plastic chairs on which we sat, wobbled. My vibes were telling me, Howard was sending us a message.

To find out if our spell had worked, that Gwen and Joe had no recollection of all that had happened at Adder Hall; that the spell had erased from their conscious memories that Gwen and I were witches and that Howard Star was a wizard, I asked, Gwen if she was pleased Stanley was dead.

'We got him, did we?'

'Don't you remember?'

'It's all a bit vague. Joe, you want my beans?'

'I love beans,' said Joe.

'Joe,' said Mary, 'all things considered, I don't think you should have any more beans.'

'Mam says I can have her beans. I like beans.'

'They exacerbate your ability to make smells.'

'Mam, Mrs Hedgerow says beans make me fart.'

'You have a bad dose of flatulence, Joe,' I said.

'Have I?'

'Yes, you have.'

'Miss... Mr Star, he's gone away, hasn't he?'

'What makes you think that?'

'Divent nar, just sort of think he has. Mam says I'm getting a new dad for Christmas.'

'I've been texting Eddy,' said Gwen, 'him and me are going to become an item.'

'Will I have to call him "Uncle Eddy", Mam, like a did "Uncle George", "Uncle Ted" and "Uncle Jimmy"? I've got lots of uncles, Miss.'

'Lucky you,' I said.

An hour later I was parking the Bentley outside Gwen's front door. The fairground had gone. The street was Cinderella after she had fled the ball.

'Mam,' said Joe, 'if Eddy's going to be my new dad, will I have to share a bedroom with Thoma?'

'I don't know,' said Gwen. 'I hadn't thought about that.'

'Thoma sleeps with Percy. I don't want to sleep with a snake. I don't like snakes.'

'Oh, look, Eddy's seen us... give him a wave. He's a good man, Eddy. Such a pity the gooduns don't turn me on the way the naughty ones do... never mind. Bye, bye, Mrs Thayne and you, Mrs Hedgerow. Ta, very much, for the ride. I don't know why but I feel as if I've been to

Heaven and seen my Michael eating toast and honey on a blow up bed in a heated swimming pool in Spain. Michael loved toast and honey. It's a comfort to me he's alreet. Out you get, Joe.'

'Where to?' I asked Mary. 'Your place or mine?'

'Mine,' said Mary, 'I want that safe opened, the one the Arse Hole had built into the bedroom wall. There must be someone at Whitby who can help us work out its combination. I'd rather open it with brains than with a sledgehammer.'

'I'm wondering,' I said, 'what do we do with the Bentley. I mean, who does it belong to?'

'I'll have it in lieu of Howard not keeping his promise to forge the Arse Hole's Will… trust me, I'm a wizard … bullshit!'

I was driving. When my mobile rang, to answer it, I pulled into the side of the road.

'That was our chair of governors,' I told Mary.

'Marilyn, the hedgehog lover?'

'Yes, she wants to see us.'

'When?'

'Now.'

Marilyn was waiting for us on her doorstep. She was wearing an evening gown, and on her head, a pair of felt reindeer antlers.

'My husband and I,' said Marilyn, 'are going to the Mayor's Christmas carol concert. Our taxi is late. If it doesn't come soon, Stockdale will bag our seats… I know he will.'

It was while she was looking up and down the street to see if she could see the taxi that she handed my good self a foolscap envelope.

'You made quite an impression on Howard,' she said. 'Marilyn,' I said, 'who was he?'

'He was my niece's husband. Not a blood relation, thank god. Where is that taxi? He was like all men; he didn't lift the toilet seat when he went for a pee. He did not make his own bed... not once. Edward, darling... Edward, where are you? The taxi is here. You've not met my husband, have you? Edward, Mrs Thayne and Mrs Hedgerow... Muriel and Mary... they are schoolteachers at the Jubilee Primary School.'

'Pleased to meet you, ladies. Did you see the Aurora Borealis last night? If I had mistletoe, I'd ask for a kiss.'

'Edward, have you been drinking?'

'Yes.'

'Stop flirting, get in the taxi.'

'Hail, Aurora,' said Edward as he climbed into the taxi.

Mary and I watched them drive off the way guests at a wedding watch the bride and bridegroom drive off to their honeymoon.

'Did you see he winked at us, when he said... "Hail Aurora",' said Mary.

'Yes,' I said, 'I wonder if Edward is also a wizard. How much does he know of all that's going on? I think the way he lets Marilyn boss him around is a cover.'

We opened the envelope in the Bentley.

'It's the Arse Hole's will,' screamed Mary, grabbing that document off me. 'I know it is... Muriel, the Arse Hole has left everything to me. Howard, I could kiss you. I'm rich. The house is worth a million... and... look at the signature... amazing... so like the real thing... and look who witnessed it... Marilyn and Edward... both JPs.'

In a separate letter I read:

*'Dear witches,*

*I wish to give you advice, which I know you will hate: MARRY FOR LOVE; not for investment.*

*Find a nice man, love him and look after him; warm his slippers by the fire; iron his shirts. In return he will do things for you like digging a well so you do not have to go to a supermarket to buy bottles of water.*

*Muriel, you will be looking to replace Tilly. A witch needs a cat. Look up Rescuecat.dot.com. Ask for a cat called Howard. He's a ginger tom, he likes to have his tummy tickled.*

*Thank you for helping me to avenge my wife's murder. Dear me, what naughty witches you are.*

*One more piece of advice: beware cheap meat pies.*

*Yours, Supernaturally, Aurora.*

*PS Howard is not my real name.*

*PPS The mug you sent to your coven laboratories in the hope of finding my identity through my fingerprints will not be successful.*

*PPPS Leave the Bentley in your drive, Muriel. Leave keys in the car. Perfectly safe. Car will be collected, as and when.'*

I watched the car all night. I suppose I must have nodded off. In the morning it wasn't there... don't ask me how?

Rescuecat.co. did have a ginger tom called Howard. I had him neutered.

www.ingramcontent.com/pod-product-compliance
Lightning Source LLC
Chambersburg PA
CBHW070630260626
47161CB00007B/2646